Dear Readers,

Many years ago, when I was a kid, my father said to me, "Bill, it doesn't really matter what you do in life. What's important is to be the *best* William Johnstone you can be."

I've never forgotten those words. And now, many years and almost two hundred books later, I like to think that I am still trying to be the best William Johnstone I can be. Whether it's Ben Raines in the Ashes series, or Frank Morgan, the last gunfighter, or Smoke Jensen, our intrepid mountain man, or John Barrone and his hardworking crew keeping America safe from terrorist lowlifes in the Code Name series, I want to make each new book better than the last and deliver powerful storytelling.

Equally important, I try to create the kinds of believable characters that we can all identify with, real people who face tough challenges. When one of my creations blasts an enemy into the middle of next week, you can be damn sure he had a good reason.

As a storyteller, my job is to entertain you, my readers, and to make sure that you get plenty of enjoyment from my books for your hard-earned money. This is not a job I take lightly. And I greatly appreciate your feedback—you are my gold, and your opinions *do* count. So please keep the letters and e-mails coming.

Respectfully yours,

William W. Johnstone

WILLIAM W. JOHNSTONE

BLOOD
OF
EAGLES

PINNACLE BOOKS
Kensington Publishing Corp.
http://www.kensingtonbooks.com

PINNACLE BOOKS are published by

Kensington Publishing Corp.
119 West 40th Street
New York, NY 10018

All Kensington titles, imprints, and distributed lines are available at special quantity discounts for bulk purchases for sales promotions, premiums, fund-raising, educational, or institutional use. Special book excerpts or customized printings can also be created to fit specific needs. For details, write or phone the office of the Kensington special sales manager: Kensington Publishing Corp., 119 West 40th Street, New York, NY 10018, attn: Special Sales Department; phone: 1-800-221-2647.

PINNACLE BOOKS and the Pinnacle logo Reg. U.S. Pat. & TM Off.
The WWJ steer head logo is a trademark of Kensington Publishing Corp.

ISBN-13: 978-0-7860-2841-2
ISBN-10: 0-7860-2841-6

First printing: May 2000
Tenth printing: February 2012

18   17   16   15   14   13   12   11   10

Printed in the United States of America

*What I must do is all that concerns me,
not what the people think.*

—*Ralph Waldo Emerson*

PROLOGUE

Grief is a white-hot molten anguish that shatters a man's heart, then sinks into his gut and solidifies there—a knot of heavy lonely agony that will not go away. Time can encase it in scar tissue, and the day-to-day business of living can dull the pain. But it does not heal. Grief is a loss of which cannot be regained, and even the satisfaction of vengeance will not banish it.

There was not even vengeance for Falcon MacCallister when he lost his beloved Marie Gentle Breeze to renegade Cheyennes. She was already dead by the time he learned of it, and the cut-fingers who took her from him were dealt with by others, at another time and in another place.

In the seasons following, Falcon rarely returned to his home ground in Colorado—in the valley settled by his father. Too many painful memories lived there. Instead he drifted, as though by being constantly on the move he might somehow shake off the ghosts that rode with him.

Some said, as those years passed, that Falcon Mac-Callister was a cold-blooded killer. Some claimed he was an outlaw, though those who knew him knew that the dodgers once circulated on him had been rescinded. He himself rarely spoke of such things. People would think what they chose to think.

Sensational stories circulated in his wake, and some of them were true. They called him a gunfighter, a gambler, and a bad man to crowd, and he was all of these. They said he was a skilled tracker, a solitary hunter, and a formidable foe, and there was ample proof that he was.

Some said he was a desperado, though, and that was a lie, like the stories that he was a highwayman and a mercenary assassin. That he was a solitary drifter and went his own way was obvious, but if the trail he rode was the owlhoot trail it was by no design of his.

There were many who sought him out—some to hire him, and some to test themselves against him—and as the seasons passed the stories grew. Of those who sought to kill Falcon MacCallister, the lucky ones were those who never found him. It was a big country, and a man on the move could be elusive even if he didn't try to hide.

Falcon MacCallister was the spitting image of his father Jamie in more ways than one. At six-foot three, moon-blond and heavily muscled, Falcon was a man not easily forgotten. Like his father, he was a deadly shot, a skilled fighter, and a hunter who some said could track a buzzard's shadow. And, like his father, he literally did not know his own strength.

Yet wherever he went he was a haunted man, and even his bloody season in the Apache campaigns, as scout for Captain Buford in the Arizona Mountains, did little to dull the ache of his grief.

By the time he headed northward from Tombstone, after bidding farewell to his friend "Doc" Holiday, Falcon had accepted that nothing but unseen providence could ever make him whole again . . . providence, and the mounting need to somehow atone, to make up for not being there when Marie needed him, for never having found the means to avenge her death.

From Tombstone he headed north, astride the big black horse he called Diablo. He wasn't going anywhere especially, just drifting, although he thought of spending a little time at Valley visiting with kin. Thinking of Valley gave him a direction, and he followed it, through lands that held other memories, other visions to distract him.

Up through New Mexico he rode in those early months of 1881, keeping to the east slopes of the high ranges still white-flanked with winter's snow, and into an unseasonably early spring. He followed the old trails across the lava beds, skirted around Mount Capulin's cone, and saw the mining settlements below Raton. And when the peaks to the west of him showed signs of melt, he set his course for Denver.

Eastward the land fell away into that wilderness of breaks and canyons that some called Purgatory and others called the Cimarron breaks. From a high ridge on a clear day he could see a hundred miles, all the way to that vague flat-topped monolith known as Black Mesa.

Beyond, he knew, was No Man's Land, and the drifter's curiosity in him pulled his eyes that way. But there were folks in Valley who cared about him, and he went that way. He was weary of fighting, weary of seeking the diversions that never seemed to dull the hard bite of his loss.

Ahead, to the north, the long slopes flowed outward like a lady's skirts, and up there, just coming out of winter's shrouds, lay the high Rockies and the melancholy trail home.

ONE

Fourteen miles west of the sorry little dugout settlement called Hungry, Owen Blanchard hauled his tired team to a halt and rubbed his eyes. For the past two hours the cold glare of spring sunlight had been in his face, and he felt half-blind.

He set his overland's brake, tied off his reins, and slumped forward, resting his face on crossed forearms on the high toeboard while he rolled his shoulders slowly, easing the cramps from his back. When he straightened up again, he could see a little better, and he gazed around bleakly.

Ahead, the sun was down now, hiding behind the toothed blue-white peaks in the distance—peaks like a giant erratic saw blade that sliced upward out of the horizon and seemed no closer than they had this morning. All around, as far as he could see in the muted rays of early evening, the plains rolled away endlessly—surging upward toward the west, toward the seemingly near yet far-off mountains. In all other directions they just went on and on until they simply disappeared into the deepening sky.

"I guess we're lost," he admitted. "They said back there that we'd come to a town of some kind after we crossed Horse Creek, but that was way back yonder and I don't see any town out here. I don't see *anything.*"

Beside him, Ruth pulled her skirts around her against the chill of evening wind. "I haven't seen anything since we left that place this morning," she admitted. "Those people said stay on the road, but I haven't even seen a road."

"Wasn't anything but a few ruts to start with." Owen stood, flexing his tired legs and stretching tall to peer out across the empty plains. "Then they disappeared in that sandy stretch." He peered to his left and pointed. "I see some treetops or something . . . I think. Off to the left there, just a little ways. God a'mighty, I can't get used to this, hon. There's a slough there, or a creek, but if it wasn't for those bare limbs sticking up, I'd never know it was there. This damn grass prairie . . . it just goes on and on, and you can't even see where there are holes in it!"

"Maybe that's a river," Ruth said, standing and squinting to see. "There was supposed to be a river, wasn't there?"

Behind them in the covered wagon, Dorothy and Tess pushed forward, curious to see why they had stopped. The girls had a little nest of bedding back there, among the packed furnishings and household goods. During the past few days Ruth had kept them close to the wagon, because of the dangers of walking.

A couple of hundred yards out ahead, young Bob Simms stood on a little rise, looking back at them. He held a forked stick in one hand and a rusty old saber in the other. Bullhide leggings covered his legs from the tops of his shoes to his knees. Ever since the scare two days ago, when the wagon had rolled out of a sage stand into a nest of rattlesnakes, Bob had made it his business to clear the trail of snakes. These first few days of spring sunshine had brought them out of their holes in droves, and they were everywhere.

The people at Hungry hadn't helped matters, either, with their talk of snakes. "That mound ye passed by, back a ways," an old man had said, giggling, "that were Rattlesnake Rock. Call it that cause the buzzers winter there. Stick aroun' a while, we'll fry some up for you. Tastes a mite like chicken."

They had left Hungry in a hurry. Now Owen wondered whether they had made a mistake. Two or three days more, maybe a week, and there would have been a supply train coming up from Raton to meet the rail at Big Sandy. They could have traveled with the supply wagons, then gone on to Denver, but Owen had scoffed at waiting. At the next real town, there would be a road. How difficult could that be, just to push on to the next town? He wondered now whether his logic was sound. With all the charts and maps he had studied before setting out from Meade's, and with the biggest of landmarks—the high Rockies up ahead—still, he was lost.

"They said we'd come down to a river," Ruth reminded her husband. "Maybe that's it."

"That's no river." Owen shrugged. "I don't see any river. Just a whole lot of . . . well, of nothing. Whatever's over there, it's no more than a little creek. Damn these high plains!" He lowered himself onto the high seat, grunting as his aching legs and back protested the movement. "I guess we'd better take a look. At least maybe there's a place we can make camp, and some wood for a fire."

"Maybe we'll see lights after dark," Ruth said. "I thought a while ago that I saw some riders up ahead.

Maybe we'll see their campfire. There's bound to be somebody around, to give us directions."

Bob Simms came walking back, and he had the same idea. "I saw them, too," he said. "Hour or so ago. Several riders, coming from maybe north. They'll be stopping, too." He grinned reassuringly. "Maybe we'll see them."

"You're just like your sister, Bob," Owen growled. "How can you always be so cheerful? Remember what they told us at Newton?"

"Oh, sure." Bob shrugged, still grinning. "Outlaws and Indians, they said. Well, we haven't seen either one, and I don't believe we will. Those sure weren't Indians I saw on that ridge out there. Just some men on horseback. And as for outlaws—well, brother-in-law, I don't see what they'd want from us. We aren't carrying any gold or anything."

Owen felt uneasy, but what Bob said made sense. They were just harmless movers, heading west. What would anybody bother them for? The Blanchards were of eastern stock, of modest roots and gentle background. It would never have occurred to any of them that a fully provisioned ten-span overland wagon, the kind often called a prairie schooner, might be valued in these wild lands.

"Can we stop for the night, Daddy?" Dorothy urged. "I'd sure like to heat some water and get cleaned up. I feel as if my hair is full of sand."

Ruth glanced around at her daughters. "You both need some washing and combing," she decided.

The treetops led them to a sharp little gully that opened out into a wide ravine. Scrubby cottonwoods, still with their winter limbs, lined a foot-deep creek where clear cold water flowed from a spring. There was plenty of firewood, and winter grass stood pale and thick downstream. When the stars came out, Owen climbed to a high swale and looked all around. He had hoped to see firelight, where there might be friendly strangers, but he saw nothing anywhere.

In the ravine, limestone walls blocked the chill wind and reflected back the heat of a good fire. While Bob Simms tended the stock, Ruth and her daughters bathed themselves, put on fresh dresses, and combed out their hair. *Three of one stamp,* Owen thought, coming back. The girls, now fourteen and twelve, were becoming young ladies, and would be as pretty as ever their mother had been.

He would find and stake the land he had bought, and they would begin the building of cabins. His brothers would be along soon, with their families, to prove up their own claims.

Maybe when the cabins were in they could all go up to Denver. They could enjoy town life for a while, and he could talk with men there about his plans to breed highland stock. The summer would be time enough to begin settling in.

Asa Parker knew, as he watched the last railroad man fall, that it was time to leave Colorado for a while. He watched for a time to make sure none of them were moving. Then he got to his feet and came down from the water tower, carrying his rifle. As Asa stepped from the ladder Tuck Kelly joined him, and he saw the others coming—from the old corral, the broken-down barn, and the cabin.

"Slick as a whistle, Asa," Tuck purred. "They never knowed what hit 'em."

A few steps back, Billy Challis laughed. "Wonder what them rail spur promoters will think when they show up tomorrow for their land meetin'! Sorry, boys, but the buyers turned up dead, and the sale's off?"

"Shut up," Asa rumbled. "Just get over there and make sure they're all dead. You can poke around that cabin, Tuck. Take anything you boys want, but keep it light. We've got travelin' to do. And leave their stock alone! Those are all marked animals. Just take a look around and we'll get out of here."

"You plannin' on sharin' out any of that money, Asa?" Billy Challis demanded. "Looks like there's enough to spread around."

Parker frowned at the cocky little gunman. "The money's for investment, Billy. I told you, we got bigger fish to fry. Now get those horses saddled!"

Aside, Tuck Kelly muttered, "What's the matter, Billy? Don't you trust Asa?"

"Hell, no!" the kid snapped. "Nor any of the rest of you, either. I'll go along, but don't nobody get any notions of shortin' on me!"

Tuck turned away, shaking his head. Billy was about as sociable as a rattlesnake, but that was normal for him.

The three rail agents were as dead as they'd ever be. Two or three bullets apiece, from ambush, had seen to that. Kurt Obermire and Folly Downs went from corpse to corpse, relieving them of their guns, loose change, and pocket watches. The two men looked like hovering vultures in their dark coats, stooping over first one and then another of their victims.

The railroad money—intended to buy rights for a San Juan spur for the Kansas Pacific Railway Company—was fresh stacks of goldbacks in a little wooden chest.

"Nine thousand dollars!" Tuck licked his lips.

"Lordy, I know what I'd do with a share of that. There's a whorehouse up at Denver that—"

"There'll be law crawlin' over each other around here," Asa rumbled. "Besides, we're not goin' to Denver. I told you all, we got a job to do! We're headed for No Man's Land, just as fast as we can pack up!"

It would be a long hard ride on short provisions—down across the Purgatoire and the Cimarron breaks. Casper Wilkerson glanced longingly at the busted buckboard lying askew in a gully. Its team had bolted at the gunfire, and it was a wreck.

"Wish we had that." Casper shrugged. "Be easier travelin' with a wagon."

The six had put a hundred miles behind them when Billy first saw the lone wagon coming westward across the grasslands. A high-bow overland, it rocked along behind its ten-horse team miles from any road or trail. They watched it off and on for an hour or two, then noted where it halted for the night.

Settlers! A wagon like that was a rolling storehouse. With a wagonload of supplies, Asa reasoned, there would be no need to zigzag among the scattered little settlements and trading posts. And the prairie schooner itself was a prize. Where he was going, the big wagon might be very useful.

From a mile away, they watched and waited, letting the little camp settle in for the night. Then, when the fire's glow was low, they went in.

Bob Simms barely felt the razor-edged blade that sliced his throat open. He came out of sound sleep when his blankets were thrown back, and hard fingers in his hair pulled his head back and down. He saw a flash of metal, and then a coldness crossed his throat. He barely felt it, but he heard the sound of it as it sliced across, and he felt the warm torrent of his own blood bathing him.

The pain came then, when he tried to yell and couldn't. The pain slashed at him like fire, but only for a moment. It dimmed, right along with everything else, and Bob Simms sank into a blackness that would never end.

Owen Blanchard went down fighting, screaming and trying to load shells into the double-barrel greener that was the only gun he owned. He managed to swat one of the attackers with the shotgun's butt and kick the feet out from under another one, but then they were all over him. A big revolver was shoved into the pit of his stomach, and three of its slugs had blossomed in him before he hit the ground.

Billy Challis looked down at the writhing gurgling man beside the wagon wheel and grinned happily. He put his iron away and stepped over the body. Folly Downs was at the wagon. Slicing lashes, he pulled the canvas back and Billy peered into the wagon bed. Three pale faces full of terror looked back at him from the shadows—pretty faces above the lace collars of demure sleeping gowns. "Well, well," the gunman crowed. "This here night is our lucky day, fellers! Looky here what we got!"

Stepping up on the rear wheel hub, Billy grabbed a small arm and pulled. Amid screams of terror, he dragged fourteen-year-old Dorothy Blanchard from the wagon and threw her on the hard ground.

Ruth shrieked, and came over the sideboard swinging a skillet. Tuck Kelly intercepted her, swung a hard fist, and sent her rolling.

Beside the wagon, Billy grinned at the terrified girl trying to scramble away. Picking her up by her hair and one leg, he slammed her down again and fell on her. Slapping her hands away, he tore open the front of her gown.

"Come get 'em while they're hot, boys!" He giggled. "This here one's mine first!"

With his knife he slashed away her clothes, ignoring her screams and the blood that welled from a dozen cuts. When she fought at him he punched her in the face, breaking her nose.

Tuck Kelly swore and tugged at Asa's sleeve. "Look what he's doing!" he shouted. "I don't like to see that!"

Asa shook him off and peered into the wagon bed. Behind him the girl's screams died to moans as Billy pinned her arms back and forced her legs apart. Kurt sneered and turned away, not wanting to watch. Even Folly Downs, who would do most anything, turned away in disgust.

"Shouldn't we put a stop to that?" Casper Wilkerson muttered, glancing toward Asa, who was climbing into the wagon. "That crazy son of a bitch makes me sick."

Asa cut him short. "Let him have his fun," he growled. "He isn't hurting you, is he?"

"But, God, that's disgusting!"

"Keeps him happy," Asa said. "Let him alone."

The outlaws took what they wanted that night, and it was a long night. In the dark hours Billy finally slept, sated and content, and the rest stayed clear of him. They all knew Billy was crazy, but he was quick and mean, and no man among them wanted to brace him. The only man Billy feared was Asa Parker, and Asa wanted him happy.

With first light of dawn they hitched up the

wagon, and Casper Wilkerson drove it out of the ravine and headed it southeast. The rest saddled up and rode with him, Asa Parker leading the way. There was no one around to see them go, or to see what they left behind them in the little sheltered ravine.

Buzzards were still circling when a big man on a tall black horse rode up from the south and angled aside to see what was there.

Long hair the color of winter straw whipped in the wind as he removed his hat, gazing down at the mute evidence of a massacre. Eyes like blue steel went hard and cold as he poked around the ravine, studying what he saw, piecing together what he could find—a name in a trampled Bible, a knife, a piece of a map, a scrap of lace, a locket. Together, they told him their story. Travelers from the east. Movers, off to set their roots in a piece of Colorado real estate.

"You poor fools," Falcon muttered, shaking his head. "Poor, innocent, greenhorn fools."

He buried what was left of the family of movers, then stood over the rough grave and bowed his head. "Lord," he whispered, "in case you're paying. any attention now to what you let happen here, these were the Blanchard family, from east of Neosho. I don't know anything to say about them, good or bad, except they didn't deserve this."

They didn't deserve it, his deep grief echoed, *any more than Marie Gentle Breeze deserved what happened to her, back then. But, then, things happen all the time that folks don't deserve.*

In that moment, Falcon MacCallister felt an anger deeper than any he had known in a long time. "I couldn't do anything about you, Marie," he continued, aloud, raising his eyes toward the sky where his beloved wife now dwelt among the spirits. "Lord," he growled, "there's a limit to what any man can tolerate, and I believe I just found it. Help me if you want to, or not if you don't care, but I guess I have to go after those men. Somebody else tracked down those savages who should have been mine, but there's another score here to settle and there's nobody else here right now. Just me. Amen."

TWO

On that clear spring day in those vast empty lands northwest of Black Mesa, nothing seemed very far away, but almost everything was. A dust-plume, rising from a little herd of buffalo grazing its way northward among the scattered bones of the great herds, might seem just past the next rise, and a man could almost count the feathers on an eagle patrolling its range.

But distances were deceptive on the high plains. That eagle might be three miles away, and the buffalo might be twenty.

Nearness was an illusion on the grasslands. What seemed close was usually far away, while the remote might lurk just over the next rise. A campfire or a flash of color might be seen twenty miles away, yet armies could hide where there seemed to be no cover at all. Where horizons stretched past imagination, and the only thing to measure by was the buffalo grass, distance meant nothing.

If it's just yonder, Falcon MacCallister mused, topping out on another rise that was just like all the rises before it and no different from all those ahead, *it's in the next county. And if you don't see it at all, it's probably about to buzz and strike.*

Just at dawn, when the winds had stilled for a moment and the giant land lay hushed, he had seen a tendril of smoke to the east. It rose in the morning sky so clearly that he felt he could almost smell it, but he knew from long experience that it was not as close as it seemed. It might be a mile away, or a day's ride.

He had lost the tracks a day ago, when storm rains and hail swept down from the Sangre de Christos. It had been a cold trail, days old when he picked it up below Hickson's Ford, but for two days he had found sign enough to stay on it.

In that two days he had covered nearly sixty miles, following wheel ruts and tracks.

Five riders, the faint impressions said. *Six men, then,* Falcon thought, *counting the one driving the wagon. Six men, a prairie schooner, seventeen horses—ten in harness, three under saddle, one on a lead behind the wagon, and three more hazed along as extra stock.*

From their trail he learned things about them. They made good time, bearing generally southeast, down through the foothills and onto the high plains of eastern Colorado. The one driving the team knew what he was doing. He was no stranger to teams.

Two of the riders were big men—big boots, deeply imprinted tracks, heavy on their horses. *Big and arrogant,* he thought, judging by the signs they left. Across the bottoms of the Purgatoire, these two had pushed through thickets, shoving aside anything in their way, while the other three riders and the overland wound around the obstacles, letting their mounts find easier paths.

The leader was one of the big ones, and despite his arrogance he was a careful meticulous man. The way he held close to the wagon said he didn't much trust anyone—not even those riding with him.

They weren't concerned about being followed.

The trace they took in the rising grasslands said they didn't expect anyone to be watching them.

Of course, it would be difficult to conceal a Staake Overland traveling across open country behind a five-team splay, but they made no effort to stay off skylines in that wide open country. They rode like men accustomed to having their own way and taking it.

He found where they had camped below a caprock butte, and it was the careless camp of travelers who saw no threat in the land around them. The wagon had been halted atop a little bluff, and they had made their fire just below. The saddle mounts and dray horses had been turned out to graze on spring grass around a seep, and only three of the animals had been hobbled.

While the leader was meticulous, Falcon decided, the rest were lazy. Lazy and lucky. There had been a time—and it was only a few years back, before Sand Creek—when such sloth would surely have cost the bunch their horses, and maybe their scalps, as well.

Still, they had kept a night guard, and at least two of them had climbed to high ground for a long look at their backtrail. Cautions of old habit, Falcon decided. They didn't expect pursuit. They were just taking a look around.

The now cold campsite confirmed what he had already noted. There were six men in the party, two of uncommon size and the others about average. The boots they wore were in fair condition—two of the smaller sets hobnailed in the fashion of mountain dwellers, the rest smooth-heeled and not too run over. The leader's boots were cobbler-new, the boots of a city man.

They had made a meal of slab bacon and biscuit,

with a big pot of coffee. They had finished it off with dried apples and pastries from a tin.

"You fellas aren't wantin' for anything, are you?" Falcon muttered, his eyes as cold as the frigid water pooled in the little grassy draw below where the wagon had rested. "Everything you want is right there in that rollin' store you took."

He saw where they had slept, wrapped in quilted soogans and oiled canvas where the thick grass gave them comfort, and he saw the marks of rifles kept handy—a Henry and a couple of Spencers, and what appeared to be a Colt's cylinder repeater. He saw where the horses had grazed, and he saw their tracks where they had packed up, hitched up, saddled up, and moved on, still heading south.

Then, where the long cap of a distant mesa showed on the horizon ahead, they had turned east. It wasn't as pronounced a feature from the north, but Falcon knew the landmark. That rising monolith out there, still twenty miles away or more, was Black Mesa.

If that was where the men were heading they had picked a hell of a fortress. Whole raiding parties of Kiowa—and sometimes Arapahoe and Comanche war parties—had been known to slip into that wilderness of canyons and gullies that was Black Mesa's north face, and simply disappear. And where the Indians holed up, so did the wildest of white men.

Not everybody called it Black Mesa. Some knew it as Robber's Roost. From the south, they said, where it stood like a sixty-mile-long dark wall above the Cimarron breaks, the mesa was unapproachable. Maybe a man on foot could climb it, given the time and equipment, but no horse could.

If that was where they were going, even Falcon

MacCallister would have his work cut out for him to find them.

But the faint trail he followed turned away from the mesa. Out in the high rolling grasslands the riders had swung eastward. The tracks crossed a couple of draws that would be creeks farther down, then veered due east. And it was there that he lost the trail.

The spring storm swept down from the white peaks westward, and brought hail and wind with it. Hailstones the size of musket balls pelted his back and rattled all around him as he guided Diablo down a cut bank and into the slight cover of an overhung bank. The big black pranced and shied, panicked at the onslaught, but quieted once the punishing hail was blocked.

For nearly an hour, Falcon MacCallister huddled beneath the bank, holding Diablo's head in a powerful gentle arm, stroking the horse's nose and talking to him, soothing him as the pounding ice fell. Then, when it eased off, the sky darkened still more and there was rain. It passed, as such storms do, but by then the sun was behind the snowy silhouette of the mountains and it was too late to go on.

He made his camp right there in that brushy draw, first scouting around to get the lay of the land, then taking his time to attend to Diablo. The big black had come a long way, but with a brisk rubdown he was ready to graze for the night.

By last light, Falcon walked to the top of the highest rise he could find—a long grassy swell a quarter-mile from his camp—and stood there, turning slowly while his eyes, as clear as those of the bird he was named for, catalogued every visible detail of the surrounding miles. Standing better than six feet tall, wide shoulders bulging the buckskin shirt above a slim hard waist, he might have been a statue in the dusk—a flaxen-haired statue that barely moved, slowly and methodically fixing the vastness with his gaze.

When he was satisfied, he returned to the draw and built a hat-size fire right up against the cut bank.

His buckskins and high moccasins were chilling wet, and he stripped out of them and wrapped himself in a blanket. Then he made a supper of jerked meat, bannock bread roasted on a little basketwork of sapling twigs, and strong black coffee.

He knew the trail he was following would be gone, with the hail and the rain. But he knew the direction, and he could reckon the distance. The men with the stolen wagon were a day or more ahead of him, but he would catch up in good time. If they continued eastward, he would overtake them. If they veered off, he would backtrack and find their trail. If they went to ground, he would find them.

It was a big empty land, these high plains tapering down from the frontal ranges of the Rockies. It was a huge region, so broad and seemingly endless that many a man would turn back—as many had—in the face of such enormity.

It was big, but not big enough for men who had Falcon MacCallister on their trail. He had seen what they did back there, and he would find them. For Marie's memory he would find them, and when he was done the wolves and the buzzards could have what was left.

Falcon MacCallister had seen the place where those men had ambushed the family of westers. When he had buried what remained of the victims, the pitiful graves made him remember Marie. He had been on his way to Valley at the time, with the idea of spending a few weeks in the company of kin.

But Valley could wait, now. Those five movers he had buried . . . one had been a woman, and two just young girls!

A limit to tolerance! What the outlaws did to those people reminded him too much of other outrages he had seen—too many, too inhuman, too brutal, to be put aside. He had too many bad dreams already to tolerate any more.

The nearest law, so far as Falcon knew, might be at the little settlement of Pueblo, but more likely was as far away as Castle or Denver. Both were a long way from where he was now, and if there was any law to the east it was even farther—somewhere over in Kansas.

Like most men of his time, Falcon MacCallister respected the law and those who kept it, but recognized its limitations. Law was at its best in cities and settlements—places where people gathered to make their homes. Where there were no clusters of people, the basis of law—the fundamental law of right and wrong—was still the will of any man who drew the line, who decided what he would tolerate and what he would not.

And if that man was known as a gunslick, thought by many to be no better than the outlaws who rode the far places, that made no difference. Public opinion was the stuff of politics, not of fundamental law. That was always, even in the settled places, the function of judgment—the judgment of the individual. Despite the antics of lawyers and politicians, the basis of practical law was still a matter of simple right and wrong.

"If it isn't yours, don't take it," was the stuff from which law was made. "If it isn't true, don't say it." And "If it isn't right, don't do it."

The momentary little tendril of smoke he'd seen

at first light might have been ten miles away, or fifty. But it had been east, in the direction he wanted to go, so he headed that way.

Somewhere ahead of him, six men had a wagon that didn't belong to them, and it was stained with the blood of innocent people who didn't deserve what was done to them.

And that just wasn't right.

THREE

The land office of the Kansas Pacific Railroad occupied two rooms on the second floor of the Waring Building. It offered a bay-window view of Market and Dominion Streets. Beyond were the Opera House, the new Silver Belle, presently under construction, and a panorama of commercial buildings with a sprawling town of fine houses, cabins, avenues, and placer digs in the background and the high mountains beyond.

James Lowell Horner stood in the corner window well, where three sets of double-hung panes overlooked the teeming streets below. To the man behind him, standing beyond a fine maple table that served as Horner's desk, the railroad magnate was a bulky silhouette—a barely contained storm cloud of a man, ready to break loose in lightning and thunder at any moment.

From his posture it was obvious that the Kansas Pacific's project chief had turned away to conceal his anger. For a long moment he stood so, breathing deeply. Then he said, "Say that again, Wylie. I'm not sure I heard you correctly."

Wylie took a deep breath himself, and invited himself into one of Horner's high-backed chairs. "It was a trap," he said. "Brockman and his aides were killed and robbed by the very men they hired . . . *we* hired . . . to protect them. Their bodyguards."

Horner stood silently for another long moment, then turned, his composure recovered. An expressionless mask as perfect as the huge waxed mustache that hid his massive jowls from nose to ears. Only in his hooded eyes were the fires of rage. "You're sure?"

"Very sure, sir." Wylie indicated the open valise on the table. It was filled to the rim with papers, telegraph messages, and various other documents. "It's all there," he said. "The credential and background inquiries we conducted on the Pasco Security Agency, the reference letters from eastern banks, even a note from President Hayes. Sam Brockman was meticulous, sir. The only problem is, the man we interviewed and hired as special guard wasn't Hiram Pasco. He was an impostor. Pasco is probably dead. Our 'Mr. Pasco' and his so-called 'personal security experts' were phonies."

Horner's exasperated sigh was like the cough of a bull elk. "How?" he demanded.

"Apparently the man impersonating the real Pasco was a former employee of his agency, from St. Louis. They may all have been former employees. I don't know. But we're fairly sure of the ringleader. His real name is Asa Parker. He was dismissed by the security company four years ago, and there are warrants out for him in at least seven states, from Missouri to Ohio."

"Nine thousand dollars!" Horner muttered. "And I suppose that explains why Brockman had to conclude the deal on site, instead of here in Denver?"

"Exactly." Wylie nodded. "Pasco . . . or rather, the fake Pasco—Asa Parker—set it all up. As I said, it was a trap from the very beginning."

"This Asa Parker . . . you say he's a wanted man, though he was at one time an employee of a respected armed escort service. What's he wanted for?"

Wylie leaned forward to thumb through some of the files in the open valise. He removed a document and squinted through his glasses. "He was dismissed for misconduct, it says. That could mean anything from petty theft to raping a client's wife. Usually it means embezzlement. Since then, though, he's gone renegade. He's implicated in half a dozen murders, some of them quite brutal. Then there's fraud, forgery . . . Mr. Parker is a busy man. And this wasn't his first impersonation. He's been several different people at various times."

Wylie paused, reading through the list of charges while Horner waited impatiently.

"This is odd." Wylie looked up. "In some of these cases, involving railroads, the investigating officers concluded that Asa Parker and his gang were working with—or for—someone else. An inside man, so to speak, calling the shots. But there isn't a clue who that might have been."

"Get on with it," Horner growled.

Wylie returned to his list. "There are several robberies listed here," he said, "the first with one accomplice, the latest with five. That was in Wyoming, just last year. Another railroad job, where Parker and his thugs robbed a courier for the Union Pacific. Very similar to what happened here. Parker and his gang dropped out of sight just after that."

"Well, we know where they went, don't we?" Horner glared at the valise as though it were full of snakes. "They came here and wound up working for us. You've gone to the authorities with this, I assume."

"Of course I have, sir. Local, state, and federal. They'll do what they can to apprehend the culprits. I've also taken the liberty of sending for a . . . well, a gentleman who might be a lot more effective. He's a known tracker and a highly competent expeditor."

"You've hired a gunman?"

"Not just a gunman, sir. Far more than that. I haven't exactly hired him, but I've sent out messages to various places where he might receive them. I issued a general notice to every Western Union office, marshal's office, and army post in the territories. I expect he'll show up."

"You notified army posts?"

"He was recently employed by the army, as a scout in the Apache campaigns down in Arizona. He's no longer there, but I have word that he might be on his way back to Colorado. He's from here, originally. His home is west of Snow Mountain Pass. Place called Valley."

"Will he take this job for us?"

"I made a good offer, sir. He's a free agent, though. He goes where he pleases. We'll know when we hear from him, I suppose."

"Very well," Horner said. "Keep me posted, Wylie. By the way, who is this man you've sent for? Do I know him?"

"I'm sure you've heard of him, sir. Everyone has, I guess. His father was quite a legend in these parts some years back, and from what I hear the son is everything the father ever was. George Crook told the *Rocky Mountain News* that he'd rather have this jasper at his back than field artillery. His name is MacCallister. Falcon MacCallister."

* * *

Falcon didn't see the smoke again, but late that afternoon he found where it had come from.

For the past hundred miles, the grass plains had rolled out like a flung carpet of mighty swells and ripples, declining from the foothills of the Rockies. Here, though, in the trailing edges of that realm between mountain plains and great plains, the surging swells became more pronounced. The rises were higher, longer to cross, the ever present buffalo grass was mixed with taller bluestem, and a man could see abundant life everywhere he looked.

Little herds of pronghorn antelope flowed on the horizon, swift phantoms racing across the grass. There were jackrabbits, ground squirrels, and great flocks of game fowl, and hardly a mile passed without signs of wolves. Early spring had arrived in full here, and birds of a hundred kinds rose and descended, spiraled and wheeled, while searching hawks and striking falcons darted among them. High above, eagles soared.

Diablo paced the miles nervously, skittish and shying now and then, and MacCallister knew why. The warming winds had brought the rattlers out. Big diamondbacks huddled here and there, almost invisible beneath the clumps of grass. The smell of snake was in the wind, and man and horse could both hear them buzzing.

Somewhere ahead, Falcon mused, there must be a denning region—a place where the rattlers wintered. The snakes were coming out of winter cover now, ravenous, and feasting where they could. Those that had satisfied their winter hunger were beginning to shed their skins. Some of them, the larger ones, would be blind during this process, and that only made them more dangerous. Unable to see, they would strike at anything.

"Watch your step, boy," Falcon muttered as Diablo shied from a clump of sage. "Big diamondback can kill a man, and it could sure lame a horse."

Eyes to the ground, he walked the horse for the next two miles, then swung down and led it on tether, using his rifle as a stick to beat the trail ahead. He saw dozens of snakes, and avoided them.

The sun was quartering in the west when he came to a break. A long, washed-out gully cut across the downward side of a swell, an ugly scar on the endless face of the grasslands. It was an erosion channel, created by countless seasons of runoff from the higher slopes. It ran generally west to east, heading toward some creek or river far away. Its entire south face was a mask of dirty white, the remaining crust of a winter drift not yet melted away by spring temperatures.

Moving carefully, Falcon led the big black into the gully and across it, climbing out through a rime of ice on the far side. A few hundred yards along that bank, and he knew he had made the right choice. There wasn't a rattlesnake to be found.

"Their nest is north of here," he told the horse as he swung into his saddle. "They've just come out, and they don't like crossing that ice."

He put three more miles behind him, then reined in at a low crest. Half a mile ahead, something odd lay on the prairie. Easing back from the skyline he dismounted, got out his telescoping glass and crawled forward. When his view was clear he extended the glass and scanned the distance, slowly.

In the middle of a swath of blackened charred grass, an old two-wheel cart sat broken and burned. It lay aslant on a wheel and a hub, amidst a scattering of what appeared to be buffalo bones. A dead horse and at least two human bodies sprawled around it, singed by grass fire. Two more horses grazed free in the distance beyond, one still wearing a saddle and headstall but no hobbles or tether.

There was no sign of life.

Falcon put his glass away, swung aboard Diablo, and headed for the scene. He was halfway there when he found his lost trail again—those same wagon tracks he had followed, and the imprints of riders escorting it.

The prints led down to the burnt grass, then disappeared there. The wagon had passed before the grass was fired.

He circled halfway around the blackened expanse—the fire hadn't spread far in the recently wet grass—and found the prints again, still rolling eastward.

The old cart had a broken wheel, and the bodies sprawled beside it were Indians—a man and a woman. They were badly burned, and both had been brutalized. The woman's clothing was torn away, and her breasts removed. The man had been hacked randomly with a knife.

Falcon could not identify their tribe, if any, but it was obvious they had been poor scavengers collecting buffalo bones to sell to white traders. Since Sand Creek, and the deprivations that followed the Medicine Lodge treaty, a lot of the scattered plains people had been reduced to such lives.

Squatting beside the bodies, he found what had killed them. The man had been shot, and the woman appeared to have been beaten to death. Then the bodies were mutilated, and they and their broken wagon doused with kerosene and set afire.

He was just turning away, looking for something to dig with, when a bullet whined past his ear, followed a second later by the sharp report of a rifle.

He dived, rolled, and came up behind the burned cart with a handful of Colt .44. Echoes still resounded when a second shot ripped through the cart's timbers, showering him with splinters and ash.

FOUR

Whoever was shooting, he was good. His aim was fair, considering that he had to be at least two hundred yards away, and he knew how to be invisible. Few men could have hidden from Falcon MacCallister in such wide-open country.

Falcon didn't wait for a third shot. In that instant's pause between impact of the second round and the crack of its report, he was up and sprinting, zigzagging across the scorched grass in the direction of the shots.

There was no cover at all—just the bald prairie, scorched and leveled, with grass and a few scrubby stands of sage lining the burnout, and wisps of ash and dust drifting on the fitful wind. Flat prairie, with nothing on it more than a foot tall. Nothing that could hide a man.

Falcon ran as a spooked turkey runs—crouched and spread, dodging and cutting back each two or three steps but covering ground toward the north perimeter where the gunshots had sounded. Fifty yards from the fringe of cover another bullet whisked past him, whining into the distance behind, and now he knew where the shooter was. Where no man could hide, the rifleman was so well hidden that even now Falcon couldn't see him—only the flicker of movement in the grass as the rifle bucked.

He sprinted, straight ahead now toward the place where the shot came from, and the .44 bucked and thundered, a drumroll of fury as he spaced five shots into the grass, spreading them out. He heard a shrill shriek, and the grass seemed to explode. A figure emerged, came bolt upright, then turned to run and stumbled, falling flat. Falcon switched hands and came up with a fresh Colt in his right.

Before the fallen shooter could recover, Falcon was on him, standing over him, twin hammers cocked full back. He froze, a hair from firing, and stared.

A kid! The shooter was just a dirty faced Indian kid, maybe twelve or thirteen years old, gawking up at him with agate eyes the size of dollars.

The boy twisted, tried to bring up his old rifle—a battered Winchester .32-20—and Falcon wrenched it from his grasp. He jacked it open a couple of times, then tossed it aside. It was empty. Those three bullets were all the kid had owned. The boy scurried backward, rolled over, and came up with a rusty, worn-out skinning knife.

With a sigh, MacCallister put away his guns, grabbed the skinny arm that stabbed at him, and plucked the knife away. Then he crouched, hoisted the kid by collar and britches, and carried him—flailing and struggling—out of the grass to where Diablo stood ground-reined at the west edge of the burn.

He stood the kid on the ground there, then kicked his feet out from under him with a swipe of his boot. The boy sat down hard, and Falcon squatted before him. "Who are you?" he demanded.

The boy just stared, and Falcon repeated the question in Spanish, then in French, bastard Apache, and finally Shawnee. None of these got him any response. The boy simply stared at him stubbornly with frightened hooded eyes. He was a scrawny kid, raven-haired and dark-eyed but not brown-skinned like most Indians. His sun-darkened features were copper and apple-red. He was lean and tapered in build, not stocky. His features were angular, and his face and skull more oval than round.

"Maybe you're a Cheyenne," Falcon suggested. He pointed at the kid. "Cheyenne? Sha-he-ena? *Tisi-tsi-ista?*"

The kid stared at him blankly.

"Okay," Falcon nodded. "So you're not a Cheyenne." He tapped himself on the chest. "MacCallister," he said. "I'm MacCallister." He pointed at the boy. "Who are you?"

The boy hesitated, then pointed at himself. "Woha'li," he said thinly.

"Well, we're getting somewhere, I guess." Falcon nodded. "You're Woha'li. That probably means sixteen different things in sixteen Indian tongues. Wonder which kind you are." He stood, and the boy started to edge away. "Stay!" he commanded, and his tone was translation enough.

He unslung his canteen and dug a wrap of pemmican from his saddlebag, and handed them to the kid. Woha'li accepted them suspiciously, took a long pull from the canteen, and sniffed at the pemmican—a mix of shredded jerky, suet, cornmeal and dried fruit. He tasted it, tasted it again, then went to work on it as though famished.

"Half-starved," Falcon muttered. "Prob'ly been hanging around here, saving his bullets in case those killers came back. Guess he thought I was one of them."

While the boy wolfed down pemmican, Falcon scraped away a space, made a little fire, and put on some bacon and coffee. Then, taking his rifle and a US Army Issue short spade, he walked off to complete the task he had set himself. Those people with the cart might have been only Indians, but they deserved a decent burial.

He wasn't concerned about the boy. If he wanted to run away, that was up to him. And as for Diablo—and the supplies in the saddlebags—he wasn't going anywhere. And Lord help anyone but MacCallister who tried to lay a hand on that big mean son of a bitch.

The boy apparently knew what to do with bacon and coffee. While he worked, MacCallister saw him at the fire, helping himself. Then, when the grave was dug and he eased the two tarp-wrapped bodies into it, the boy was there beside him. The kid didn't cry or sniffle, the way a white boy might. He just stood there, watching, and his dark eyes were unreadable.

"These were your folks, weren't they?" Falcon asked gently, spading dark soil over the still forms. "Well, I know it sure hurts, Woha'li. But it's the best I can do."

It was twilight when he finished filling the grave and patted it down. He removed his hat, but didn't bow his head. Instead he looked upward, in the Indian way, so that Man Above could see his face and know that he was sincere. "I never knew these people," he said, "nor what they did in life, good or bad. But I see how poor they were, and how they were treated, and I see this boy's grief that they're gone. Smooth their path to the seventh sky, Lord, and treat them right when they get there."

"Do'da-dagohu'i," the boy whispered beside him. *"Edo'da . . . E'tsi . . . do'di."*

When Falcon turned away, the kid followed. He went to the north grass and picked up the old 32-20 where he had dropped it. He handed it to the boy, then headed for his little fire. It was as good a place as any to camp. The wind was from the west, and would carry away the stench of death.

He built up the coals, put on a pot and a griddle, and left the kid in charge while he rode out and brought in the two strayed horses. The one wearing the saddle was galled and skittish, the other had a bullet welt on its rump, and both of them were shy. It was no wonder Woha'li hadn't been able to round them up.

With Diablo's help he brought them in, then gentled them down and treated their sores with bacon grease and sage. There was an old wallow nearby with snow-melt pooled in the bottom, and plenty of winter grass. Diablo wouldn't stray, and Falcon knew the other horses would stay with the big black.

As stars brightened above they ate some biscuits and drank some stiff coffee. Then Falcon unrolled his soogans and divided up the blankets. It was a mild night, and the kid stank to high heaven. He could share the bedding, but not a bed.

As he rolled in, using his saddle as a pillow, Falcon MacCallister thought about the words Woha'li had said, there at the grave. *"Do'da-dagohu'i."* It was an Indian farewell, and now he knew what kind of Indian the kid was. The word—or phrase—was Cherokee. It meant, simply, good-bye.

Billy Challis wasn't happy. All through supper he kept jumping up and walking to the top of the west rise, to peer beyond it. "There's somebody back there, I tell you!" he repeated, coming in this latest time. "Somebody's picked up our trail, an' they're out there followin' us! I saw a fire back there, sure as hell!"

"You saw that stinkin' cart you and Folly burned," Asa Parker growled. "Damn grass fire's probably flared up again. Now shut up about it and let me think!"

Billy was quiet for a little while, but pretty soon he was up and stomping around the camp again, cursing under his breath.

"You'd better put a rein on it for tonight, Billy," Tuck Kelly warned. "Asa's gettin' mad."

"I don't give a damn!" Billy spat. "I'm tryin' to tell him somebody's out there, on our back trail!" Still, he glanced around, lowering his voice. The gunman might push his luck now and again, but he wasn't quite ready to take on Asa Parker. "I know a campfire when I see one, Tuck," he told the big man seriously. "I don't like it! We didn't leave any witnesses, but there's *somebody* out there. I got a feelin'!"

Tuck stood, squinting. "Damn it, Billy," he muttered. "You'd drive a fencepost crazy."

"What?"

"I said I'll go up and look one more time," Tuck grumbled. "But then I don't want to hear no more about it."

Atop the rise, Tuck scanned the backtrail methodically. The immense distances rolled out and away under a starry sky, but he saw no small spark that might indicate a fire.

"You're imaginin' things, Billy," he said finally. "Asa's right. Maybe that grass burn flared up again. But it's gone now. Wouldn't have been there at all if you an' Folly coulda just left them Injuns alone. Now just settle down. Our trail's been cold for a week. Who'd be followin' us now?"

In their camp, the tall overland wagon stood like a big glowing lamp on the prairie grass, its canvas cover aglow with lantern light. In the covered bed, Asa peered at his maps, muttering to himself. Once or twice he glanced out into the darkness where Tuck and Billy had gone, and frowned.

Sooner or later he would have to get rid of Billy Challis. The little rooster was crazy as a loon, and it was like having a coiled rattlesnake around all the time. Still, he had never found a man better with a gun, and that could come in handy.

Where they were going, he'd need guns around him. He went back to his maps, turning over details in his mind, just as Sypher had laid it out. It was a beautiful plan, but complicated. Still, all he had to do was pull it off and he'd be a rich man.

The nine thousand dollars from the Kansas Pacific courier was only seed money. The real money would show up when they lured one of the big combines— maybe the Atchison Topeka or the Rock Island— into No Man's Land. Despite himself, Asa was impressed by the sheer audacity of Sypher's scheme.

Transcontinental railroading had become a glory dream for the big investors. Ever since the Union Pacific's success, railroad ventures had sprouted like weeds. *Everybody* was building rails, and the competition was fierce. The Animas Spur thing had been small stuff. Railroads paid a few thousand dollars for spur rights-of-way. But for main line routes, they paid millions.

Sypher knew how to set up a route, and Asa Parker knew how to spring a trap. All he had to do was establish himself as a major landholder, right where the railroad wanted to go. Then Sypher could guide the railroad boys toward him, and when the big money came out they'd be there to sweep it in.

Asa looked around him, musing. Folly Downs was over by the fire, hogging the coffee. Kurt Obermier and Casper Wilkerson had already rolled it in for the night. Out on the rise, Tuck Kelly was trying to keep a curb on Billy Challis.

The stolen money was hidden away in the wagon, and Asa wasn't about to turn his back on it. Billy Challis wasn't the only one who wouldn't hesitate to help himself to the loot if he got the chance. They were all of the same stripe. Not a one of them would hesitate to betray or kill for that much money. Only the thought of facing Asa had kept them at bay so far—that, and knowing that whichever one went for it would have the others to deal with.

Rattlesnakes, Asa thought. *Like a damn bunch of rattlers.* But they were all necessary . . . until the job was done.

Then he'd see what he could do about getting rid of them all.

He heard footsteps and pushed back the flap. Tuck Kelly stood just outside, beyond the tailgate. "Billy just can't stand it," he said. "He wants to ride out there and see if there's anybody behind us."

"Then let him go," Asa rumbled. "The wormy little bastard just wants a chance to go down to that tradin' post we passed and raise hell. If that's what it takes, let him go! But you go with him, and for God's sake keep him out of trouble. We don't need a lot of attention right now. Go on, get! Just keep a halter on him, and be at Wolf Creek when I get there!"

"There ain't anybody can keep a halter on Billy," Tuck muttered. "That jasper's crazy as a loon." He ducked his head, then, not wanting to meet Asa's eyes. If there was one man in the world Tuck feared more than Billy Challis, it was Asa Parker.

Tuck turned away, and beyond him Asa could see Billy—out by the horses—picking up a saddle. The varmint just couldn't get enough of hell-raising, and he'd been itching about that Roost place ever since they passed it.

The place was a tiny settlement right at the east end of Black Mesa, where the Cimarron breaks began. They'd have stopped there for provisions if it weren't for the wagon. The overland had enough supplies aboard to last all of them a month, so Asa had just kept on eastward instead of swinging down to the Roost.

Dourly, Asa watched as Billy and Tuck saddled up and rode out under a starry sky. He wasn't especially worried. They would be back, and they'd be around when they were needed.

Tuck was slick enough so that Billy wouldn't brace him if he didn't have to. And nothing this side of hell would keep the sons of bitches away long while Asa held onto the money.

FIVE

Jonathan Boles Stratton arrived at Emporia on the sixth of March—just in time to see the first good thaw of an unusually early spring, had he been inclined to notice such things, which he was not. Porters bowed and lackeys scurried to serve as he stepped from the gold-filigree lavishness of the Rock Island line's best sedan car to the bustling platform before the train depot, followed by his ever present clerk. Crowds parted as a covered carriage pulled up, and a uniformed attendant said, "Right this way, Mr. Stratton, sir. You'll be taken directly to your hotel."

Jonathan Boles Stratton wore importance the way most men wore their britches—casually, carelessly, and always. As an official of the Bureau of Transportation and Railways, he expected the cozenings of politicians and the sumptuous hospitality of boosters. As chief of grants for the high plains region he had become the "man of the hour" in certain circles—the man everyone wanted to know, the man land speculators fawned over and investors scurried to please.

With authority over supplementary federal grants and loans, he had the power to designate public lands as railway grants, and thus to dictate routes for many of the rail lines sprawling ever westward across the continent. Using inducements, he could even dictate where subsidiary spurs might go.

In the national zeal to build new railways, little attention was given to how he served himself in the process. It had become the "American Way" back east—and the custom was spreading westward—to accept that people in positions of public power tended to become proportionately wealthy. It was expected. Old standards of conduct for public servants were eroding before the onslaught of self-seeking. The postwar years had produced a national cynicism that might never be undone, and once meaningful appellations such as "The Honorable" had long since lost any basis in reality.

Stratton had been a small-time politician until the election of Rutherford B. Hayes. In the subsequent realignments, Stratton had schemed his way up in the bureaucracy with ruthless determination—to a position of power with control of the fates of wealthy men, but not so highly placed as to be politically vulnerable.

The new president of the United States had pledged to serve only one term. Stratton's appointment was political, but obscure, and his ambitions were simple. He set out to enjoy the fruits of public trust for as long as the trough flowed, and let others do the work. That four years was ending now, and Stratton was basking in the final glow of glory, but he still held the power of empires.

From the presidential suite at the Hotel Florence, Stratton was escorted to the dining room, where various dignitaries awaited him. Throughout the course of a lavish meal hosted by a combine of land speculators, he was plied with questions. His responses were unfailingly authoritative and hopelessly vague.

Eventually the questioners gave up. They weren't going to learn from The Honorable Mr. Stratton what routes the Santa Fe or the Rock Island would follow westward, or what lands would be involved.

Stratton didn't really know. The only one present who did was a lowly clerk none of the leading citizens even considered acknowledging, much less questioning.

Back in the lavish private suite, Stratton threw off his coat and sprawled out on his bed. "Did you get the names and affiliations of all those gentlemen?" he asked.

The clerk retrieved the great man's coat and hung it up, then strode to a desk by the window and opened a valise. "Yes, sir," he said. "All noted with addresses. Shall I write out the usual thank-you letters to all of them?"

"Yes, of course. Personalize each of them a bit, as usual, and sign my name."

"Yes, sir."

"And I assume you made note of their concerns and suggestions?"

"Yes, sir. The usual things. Most of them are looking for tips on where the Rock Island main line will go. Some are also investors in the Santa Fe, and a few are hoping you'll tell them where to buy land that they can sell to the government at handsome profits. If you like, I'll bring your charts up to date with annotations of who is interested in what." The clerk shuffled papers in his valise and closed it.

"You do that," Stratton said drowsily. "I may want to discuss investments with some of them, privately. You understand."

"Yes indeed, sir. I understand. If you'll excuse me now, sir, I've been given a room just down the hall. I'll get to work on these things for you right away."

"Very good." Stratton yawned. "And please see what arrangements these locals have made for our tour of the operations from here to Division. Ah, where is that, again?"

"A town called Newton, I believe, sir. Seventy or eighty miles west of here. Santa Fe investors and some promoters for the Kansas Pacific. You'll have a private car waiting there. I believe you're scheduled for a tour of the railhead. That will be Dodge City. I'll see to the arrangements." The clerk picked up his valise, along with the bundle of highly secret route charts which Stratton carried with him but rarely glanced at. He started for the door.

"Oh, by the way," Stratton called, "please make some discreet inquiries . . . possibly of the hotel staff. See what sorts of, ah, special entertainments might be available to distinguished guests here."

"Yes, sir. Possibly young ladies, sir?"

"Of course, young ladies!" Stratton chuckled. "See to it for me, if you please. You know my preferences."

"Yes, sir. I'll see to it, sir."

"You're a good man, Sypher. I don't know what I'd do without you."

Sypher spent most of the afternoon in his room, working on the charts. Two main lines presently were expanding through Kansas—one in operation to the Arkansas River at a place called Dodge, the second now laying track westward from Newton. Carefully, Sypher penciled in a corridor running west from this one, fanning it out toward the Cimarron country. He added route notes, and replaced the charts in their leather case.

After checking on Stratton, who was barricaded

in his suite now with a stock of whiskey and three whores, Sypher went to the Western Union office, collected his messages and—for a slight fee— thumbed through the telegrapher's collection of general delivery messages. Sypher was a careful man, and knowing what was on general delivery was always a prudent thing to do.

At first they were of no interest. Then a name jumped out at him. In a coded message—some code he didn't know—was the name Asa Parker. The message was from a Kansas Pacific official in Denver, addressed to a Falcon MacCallister.

Sypher tried to decode the message, and gave up. Instead, he used Stratton's seal to issue a general inquiry to military posts up and down the system, seeking information about someone named Falcon MacCallister.

There was no way to contact Asa Parker directly, but he did learn from the telegraph posters that a railroad courier had been waylaid south of Denver. So he knew that Parker was eastbound now . . . with nine thousand dollars in hand.

It galled him to have to rely on anyone so unsavory as Asa Parker. The man was worse than just a thief and swindler with a talent for complex scams. Parker was a ruthless cold-blooded killer. A dangerous man. Still, there was comfort in knowing how competently Parker had carried out his masquerade as a security expert. It spoke well for the next stage of the plan.

One of the telegrams Sypher sent out was to a settlement called Hardwoodville, near the western terminus of the wire. It was addressed to one Colonel Amos DeWitt—which would be Parker's public name for the duration—and its coded message contained metes and bounds of a fifty-mile square area straddling the southern border of Kansas.

Falcon gave Woha'li's rifle back to him and showed him how to clean it. He had no .32-20 rounds to load in it, but it seemed to brighten the kid's spirit a little just to have the gun in hand.

At dawn, he saddled Diablo and rounded up the two strays. Then he helped the boy saddle the better of them—a long-coupled little dun with a scabbed-over bullet burn—and packed up his camp. They ate the last of the bacon and washed it down with overnight coffee, and Woha'li went to stand once more over the grave of his parents. When Falcon swung aboard the big black and headed out, the Indian boy mounted the dun and followed him, silently.

East of the grass-burn, Falcon studied the tracks again and made a decision. He needed supplies, and he knew there was—or had been—a settlement of some kind to the south, just below Robber's Roost in the Cimarron breaks—a place called Outpost.

The men with the stolen wagon had headed east, and were a day—or maybe two—ahead of him. But with that prairie schooner they wouldn't make more than twelve or fifteen miles a day. Falcon knew Diablo could cover three times that distance without breaking a sweat.

He turned, looking back at the kid. "I'm going to town," he said. He pointed southward, so the boy would understand. "Town," he repeated. "Uh . . . *gadu'h.* A town! *Tsi . . . Tsigi'ah!*"

The boy stared at him blankly, then blinked and shook his head. Something like a half smile tugged at his cheeks. Falcon knew some Cheyenne—or *Tisi-*

tsi-ista, as the Cheyenne people called themselves. He had learned a smattering of Ute, which was similar to Pawnee, and knew a few Shawnee phrases that he had learned from his father. He even knew a few words of bastard Apache. But Cherokee, the language of the *Tsalagi* people, was another tongue, as different from all of those as Mandarin Chinese was from English. The Indian kid gazed at him smugly, and he wondered what he had just said.

"Higi'a?" the boy said, mockingly. *"Galsta-yuhu'sga, yonega. Hawi'ya? Se'lu? Gadu?"*

"All right, cut it out!" Falcon snapped. "You know what I'm talking about!"

The boy lowered his head, turning away, but when he turned back his dark eyes were mischievous. "Better you talk white, *yoneg.* Don' good talk Cherokee."

"I'll be damned!" Falcon rasped. "Why didn't you say you speak English?"

"Who give a damn?" The kid shrugged.

Falcon glared at him, then wheeled Diablo and headed south at an easy lope. When he glanced around, the kid was following along behind him, on the little dun. The third horse, the lame stray, was only a little way behind. Without a load to carry, it was moving all right, and its sprain would heal.

"No town," Woha'li objected after a time. He was squinting, peering at Black Mesa. "No town there. Jus' crazy *yonegs.*"

"What?"

"Yonegs!" the boy repeated, saying it louder so the man might understand. "White men! Tryin' dig holes in river. Crazy!"

"Dig holes . . . in the river? You mean those Black Mesa miners?"

"Sure. They think gold there. *Agido'da,* my father,

he heard it from *Kwahadi* people. Say they be gone soon. That river . . . *unegadihi*. River will kill crazy *yonegs.*"

Falcon set his course for the east end of Black Mesa. A few miles along, the prairie began its gentle slope up toward the great butte, and from a high spot Falcon used his telescope to peruse the prairies to the north and east. The wagon and its captors were not in sight, but far out on the flats—miles away—he saw a speck of movement that might be horsemen. For a moment they were in view. Then they disappeared behind one of those invisible distant swales that made the plainsland so unreadable.

He saw enough, though, to know that they were moving west.

"I guess they're not our concern," he muttered.

Apparently Woha'li had spotted them, too, because the kid shrugged at that. "You see pretty good for white man," he admitted.

"I used to think so," Falcon said. "Tell me something. Back there, where I found you, how did you hide like that? There wasn't cover enough for a sage hen, but I never did see you."

Woha'li gave him one of those taunting patronizing looks. *"Atsalagi tsigi eligwu g'waltadodi ayonega dukana'i,"* he said.

"What?"

"A Cherokee can disappear from white men's eyes."

"Nobody needs a smart aleck," Falcon instructed him. He kneed the black, heading south again.

The kid frowned and fidgeted, but he followed along. He wanted to go east, not south. But after a while he accepted Falcon's lead. As they rode, the boy gave Falcon a description of the men who had killed his parents. Falcon was impressed. The boy was observant. Soon Falcon had a mental picture of each of the six men that was detailed and accurate.

Flocks of pigeons flew above the prairie, and now and then a sleek hawk, swooping among them for a kill. *"Towo'di,"* the kid said, adding, "that means hawk or falcon, *yoneg*. Why are you called Falcon?"

"It's my name," Falcon shrugged. "It's what my pa named me."

A half hour passed, and the kid was looking at the sky again. High overhead, an eagle soared. *"Woha'li* means eagle, he told MacCallister. *"Woha'li* flies higher than *towo'di."*

Three hours of travel, and the south horizon was hidden behind a giant tumble of bluffs and cuts, rising above the plain. Like broken stairsteps, the breaks climbed westward to become the eastern end of Black Mesa: a natural fortress that some called Robber's Roost. And somewhere beyond, where the land dipped toward the upper Cimarron, should be Outpost.

If the place had a proper name, Falcon had never heard it. It was just Outpost. But he had heard stories, mostly from army scouts. It was one of the most isolated, most remote, spots on the western maps, but somebody had settled in there a few years back and built shacks—a couple of old outlaws, some of Colonel Burke's soldiers had told him once, rebels or retired renegades looking for a place to light. In the breaks, no law would come looking for them, because there was no law. They had enough trade to keep a store—mostly for outlaws on the run—and supplied it from pack-mules coming down from Folsom.

Just in the past year, though, he had heard the place had grown. Persistent old rumors of gold—rumors that probably had been around since Spanish explorers first saw Black Mesa rising ahead of them—were circulating again. Most of the footloose men wandering the Cimarron breaks nowadays were running from something. But now, the bluecoats said sardonically, some of them had decided they were miners.

That would be what the kid was talking about. From his own sources, Woha'li's father had heard the same stories.

Outpost—the last refuge of fiddle-footed humanity, Falcon thought as they climbed the rises toward Robber's Roost. *After this place, there's nothing but purgatory one way and No Man's Land the other.*

The bullet that whanged off the limestone bluff to his right as he crested out above Outpost came as no surprise. It came from the vicinity of the nearest cabin, and missed Diablo's nose by at least ten feet.

"Don't come unwound," he cautioned the Indian kid riding close behind him. "That's just to let us know we've been seen, and had better behave ourselves while we're here."

"Yonega!" Woha'li spat, making a curse of the Cherokee word for white men. "Coulda' just put up a sign."

"Some folks can't read signs," Falcon explained. "Everybody understands bullets."

Despite his reassurance, MacCallister eased his guns in their holsters before riding down the steep slope. The little settlement was bigger than he had expected. There were six or seven buildings clustered among the leafless elms, willows, and cottonwoods which lined the bank of a brushy river. A mile or so upstream, right down in the bottoms, was what looked like a second settlement—tents and shacks, lean-tos and lashed wagons.

"So that's the mining camp," Falcon muttered. His eyes took in the panorama and then beyond, to the rising foothills where dark clouds gathered above the crests. "Damn fools," he said. "Don't they look to see where the floodbanks are?"

The largest building in Outpost itself was a low sprawling thing that might have been a barn, hay shed, stable, or storehouse—or all of those combined. And at the hitchrails in front of the second largest, several saddled horses stood waiting.

"Busy day." Falcon shook his head grimly. "Transients and sand miners. Business must be booming at Outpost."

SIX

The warning shot had told everyone at Outpost that a stranger was coming in. As Falcon stepped through the canvas-frame door of the trading post, a dozen sets of eyes were on him. Just inside, he stepped quickly aside, out of the doorway's light, to let his eyes adjust to the gloom. It was an old habit, and one that had kept him alive more than once.

Outside, while he looped Diablo's reins over the rail, he had taken a good look at the horses tied there, and the sign in the muddy street. The mounts were tired. They had been ridden hard, a long way. They had come in from the west, all together.

Some bunch just passing through, he decided. Down from the high breaks of New Mexico and eastbound into No Man's Land. Among other things, the Neutral Strip served as a natural highway from the Territories to the foothills.

As the canvas door opened again, and Woha'li stepped through, Falcon shifted his position once more.

There were an even dozen customers in the big, low, sod-roofed building—four at the plank bar, leaning on their elbows and nursing rotgut whiskey, the rest scattered around at tables and benches. A mixed bunch—travelers and workmen down from the digs upstream. A tough-looking oldster stood behind the bar, and a gimpy swamper was leaning on his mop near the rear.

He felt the eyes of all of them sizing him up, and most turned away after one good look. Standing more than six feet tall, with shoulders that bulged his buckskin shirt and calm hands that rested close to a pair of .44s, Falcon MacCallister was not a man to go unnoticed. But the scrutiny was brief. Only a few of them—a couple of young roosters at the bar and the old man behind it—showed any real interest in the newcomer.

"Lost your way, Mr.?" one of the squirts asked, letting the big gun at his hip be noticed. The kid had carrot-red hair, and the look of trouble trying to happen. "This place ain't on your usual trails."

Falcon ignored him, looking instead at the old man. "I need supplies," he said. "You selling?"

"For a price," the barkeep nodded. "Don't keep nothin' fancy here, though."

"I'll need flour and sugar." Falcon glanced at the dingy shelves and crates around the walls. "Side of that smoke-cured bacon . . . coffee if you have it . . ."

The redhead with the big gun glanced at Woha'li and frowned. "Mose, when did you start lettin' Injuns in this place?"

"I let anybody in that's got the money to buy somethin', Tad," the barkeep growled. "You're here, ain't you?"

"Papoose is totin' a rifle, too," the squirt's partner muttered. "Just like regular folks. I don't much cotton to—"

Falcon cut him off. "Reminds me. I'll want some of those .32-20 cartridges, too. And some soap. I noticed a washtub out back. How about some hot water in it?"

"Cost you a dollar for the bathwater." Mose frowned. "Damn nuisance heatin' up water."

Being ignored didn't set well with the redhead at the bar. His face was flushed, and his eyes glittered as he stepped out clear, his fingers brushing the butt of his low-slung hogleg. "I was talkin' to you, Mr.!"

Over by the east wall, a gent with a dusty dark hat scooted his chair on the gravel floor. "I's you, Tad, I'd watch myself," he said calmly. "Drunk ain't any way to brace a stranger."

The squirt didn't even glance at him. His eyes were fixed on MacCallister, and he went into a slight crouch, like a banty rooster fluffing for a fight. "Knew somethin' was stinkin' in here," he pressed. "I reckon it's that little Injun . . . and maybe the company he keeps."

Falcon shook his head slightly, then stepped forward . . . and again. Before the punk could realize what was happening, a hand like an iron band pinned his wrist and another one closed on his shirt front, wadding the fabric and drawing it tight. With no visible effort, Falcon lifted the young drunk off his feet, held him dangling for a moment, then shook him the way a dog shakes a rat.

Tad's bleary eyes went as wide as dollars, his hat flew off, and his kicking legs swung like pendulums. He tried to cry out, but the choking grip on his shirt collar stifled him.

"I've had all the fuss I'll tolerate from you, boy," Falcon growled. "Now you just settle down!" With a casual flip he dropped the gunny to the floor, off-balance, and brushed his feet out from under him with a businesslike boot. Before Tad hit the floor, Falcon had relieved him of his gun. Calmly he unloaded it, then unscrewed its ejector rod and pried it sideways, jamming the action. He dropped the useless weapon on the floor.

"It's your lucky day, Tad," he said solemnly, standing over the scrabbling gunny. "You're still alive. If you'd touched that gun, you wouldn't be." Without another glance at the young drunk he stepped to the bar. Tad's partner, apparently having second thoughts on the matter, stepped aside obligingly.

"If you can fire up that griddle," Falcon told the storekeeper, "my young friend and I will want a couple of beef steaks off that quarter hanging out front. Burn them good, and throw in some onions and potatoes if you have them. And coffee."

The iron washtub outside was rusty, and the water the swamper hauled out wasn't much warmer than the cool spring air, but Falcon made Woha'li strip down to his longhandles and climb in, then handed him a chunk of yellow lye soap. "Bathe," he ordered. "Get yourself clean. And do it right, or I'll take a wire brush to you."

He cleaned himself up at the rain trough, and shaved. While he was there, Tad and his partner came out carrying bundles. The young gunny didn't look so cocksure any more, but the set of his shoulders hinted at the rage within him. Without so much as a glance at MaCallister, he mounted up and rode out, followed by the other one. They angled down to the river and headed east along the bottoms.

MacCallister was putting on his fresh buckskins when the man with the dark hat came out. "Name's Dawson," he said. "I know you, don't I? Your name happen to be MacCallister?"

"It's a real common name where I'm from," Falcon shrugged. "It's a big family."

"Yeah," the man said. "But only one MacCallister

I've heard of carries iron the way you do. I've got a notion that yahoo Tad come off lucky today."

MacCallister strapped on his gunbelt. "If those boys were riding with you, I guess you broke up."

"Aw, we'll see them again." Dawson shrugged. "We're all headed for the same place. Wolf Creek. Heard there's work there, and not too many questions asked."

"That a fact?" Falcon combed back his straw-gold hair with his fingers and put on his hat. "Didn't know there was much work in No Man's Land. Nobody around to hire a man, the way I heard it."

"Not necessarily," Dawson said. "There just isn't anybody there *legally*. That's because there's no law, no legal ownership of land, and no court jurisdiction. But there's folks there, all right. Way I hear it, the whole Barlow clan is movin' in yonder."

"Barlow?"

"Hill folk. Bad medicine if they're pushed, but they keep to themselves."

"Barlows don't hire hands," one of Dawson's men said. "But somebody's hirin'. Word is, somebody's gonna build a stock spread over 'round the haymeadows, south of the Kansas line. To make a thing like that work, they'll need hands."

"Need more than cowpokes to build a spread in No Man's Land."

"That's what the boys and me figure." Dawson nodded. "Without real law, they're gonna need regulators." The dark hat tilted as the man glanced sharply at Falcon. "Happen you're lookin' for work, you might drift over to Wolf Creek. See Colonel Amos DeWitt."

"Well, I'll keep that in mind."

" 'Course, your name bein' MacCallister, might be you already got work," Dawson said. "Word's out, all along the foothills, that the Kansas Pacific's lookin' for Falcon MacCallister. Somethin' to do with trackin' down a bunch that robbed a courier. The way I hear it, they'll pay top money to get the bunch that did it."

Falcon ignored the pointed comments. "Why go so far looking for work, when they're mining gold a mile from here?"

Dawson cut his eyes upstream, grinning. "Bunch of idiots. Nobody's found gold in Black Mesa yet, nor likely to. And if there's any in the Cimarron, it's so far down in that river sand that the devil himself can't reach it."

Dawson started away, then turned back. "Don't underestimate Tad Sands, Mr. MacCallister. He was drunk today, an' feelin' his oats. But he'll be sober by and by, and he ain't likely to forget bein' humiliated."

"Better than being dead," Falcon pointed out.

When the Indian boy was presentable, Falcon marched him into the store and matched him up with some denim britches, a sheepskin coat, boots, and a couple of ready-made shirts. The new clothes fit the scrawny kid like a tent, but it was still an improvement. The storekeeper brought out steaks, beans, and coffee, and they both ate as if food were going out of style. The proprietor of Outpost, Mose Polan accepted the lame horse in exchange for Woha'li's new wardrobe, and threw in a wide-brimmed hat.

Falcon settled up for his purchases, asked a few questions, and the two saddled up. They would head out—eastbound—when the sun was sinking below dark clouds in the west.

Mose had offered lodging for the night, and Dawson and his bunch were toting their bedrolls to the barn. "We'll see what the mornin' looks like," Dawson said. "Funny spring, this year. Got here real early, but that don't mean it'll last."

Falcon wasn't staying. He could still make a good ten miles before nightfall, and he preferred an honest outdoor camp to sleeping in a mule barn, no matter what the weather.

As he guided Diablo up the slopes, to the high flats above the river, Woha'li rode beside him thoughtful. "You gonna find those *yonegs* with big wagon?" the boy asked.

"Yeah. I'll find them. But I don't know what I'll do about you. You have kin anywhere, boy?"

"I go with you," Woha'li said flatly. "We find those *yonegs*, I kill them."

I do believe you'll try, Falcon thought, glancing aside at the hard narrowed eyes in that young face. He recalled how well Woha'li had used the Winchester, and now it was loaded again—twelve rounds of .32-20 in its magazine, one in the chamber, and the action on half-cock.

He didn't know yet who those six men were, out ahead somewhere with an overland wagon. He only knew what they had done to the people whose wagon that had been. He had seen the remains, buried what was left of them, and he meant to find the brutes responsible. It brought a hard anger welling up in him to even think about what those men had done to that woman and those two little girls.

Falcon had no use for a kid tagging after him, but he didn't argue the point. Woha'li had an even better reason to hunt down the killers. Those same six men had killed his parents . . . for no more reason than that they happened to be there. They had missed the boy simply because Woha'li had been out on the prairie, trying to snare some quail or robins, when they came. He had seen them, but only from a distance, and too late.

Falcon looked again at the Cherokee boy, and kept his peace. Woha'li might be only a kid—probably not more than twelve or so—but those outlaws had made a bad mistake when they overlooked him. The Cherokee, as a people, were generally the most civilized people in North America. But even the wildest Comanche knew that a Cherokee—any Cherokee—was about the worst enemy a man could have.

A few miles from Outpost, fresh scuffs in the bluff above the river caught Falcon's eye. He had almost missed them. Evening light faded quickly as the clouds marched in from the west, and a chilly wind had picked up.

It was wheelprints—three-inch iron tires six feet apart and carrying a load. An overland wagon had jostled down the slope there, angling toward the river flats.

On the sandy flats they picked up the trail again, and followed it. The prints were clear there, even in the dimming light of evening—the five-span team and outriders. The outlaws had followed the river, looking for a good place to put the wagon across.

In last light of evening, Falcon saw firelight—the slightest tiny glow, a few miles ahead. There was a bend in the river there, and the little spark of light was on the high bluff beyond. The killers had crossed the river.

But they weren't all there. He had read the sign, and he counted only four men now in the wagon party. One was driving, the rest trailing along on horseback. Somewhere back there, two of them had left the group.

Woha'li had seen the fire, too. The kid was ready to head out there and kill everybody in sight, but

Falcon held him back. "Two of them are missing," he said. "I want them all. So we'll wait 'til they're together again."

"*Ha-la'ya?*" Woha'li demanded. "When? How far?"

"I think I know where they're going," Falcon said. "Place called Wolf Creek. Something's going on there that's drawing hard cases. We'll find this whole bunch there, I imagine."

He peered into the twilight ahead, puzzled. The fire they saw was at least two miles away, but in the momentary shift of winds he caught just a hint of woodsmoke.

Billy Challis and Tuck Kelly rode into Outpost late that evening. Billy was itchy, like a hungry cat scenting fresh blood, and Tuck was looking for a little fun. They were both disappointed. There were no whores at Outpost just then. The usual little flock of soiled doves that sometimes hung around there had migrated up to Taos some months ago, and no new ones had come in yet.

There was a crowd, though, and it wasn't a crowd that any man—even Billy—wanted to fool with. There were some hard men in the bunch passing through on their way into the strip called No Man's Land, and the few hardscrabble river miners they saw were hard-eyed and close-knit. Even Billy Challis, mean and spoiling for trouble as he usually was, saw no percentage in bucking that kind of odds.

They held their tongues, had a meal, and spread their rolls in a cold smelly loft above a mule stable, apart from the other travelers staying over.

They did learn something, though. There had been another stranger at Outpost, just hours before them, who might have been that Colorado gunslick, Falcon MacCallister. He had been there and gone, but there was speculation about him. From his questions, it was clear he was looking for somebody.

"Whoever it is, I'd hate to be him," a man named Dawson allowed. "What I've heard of that MacCallister, he's pure-dee hell in a handbasket when he's riled."

Tuck had a notion—from the questions the man had asked—who he was looking for.

He was looking for *them*.

The two gunnies were both stone sober when they rolled in for the night. They decided to double back in the morning—follow the north rim of the valley and maybe catch up with the wagon at the bend crossing. If they missed the trace, they would head straight for Wolf Creek, maybe be there when Asa Parker arrived. Asa Parker could decide what to do about MacCallister.

"And don't call him Asa Parker any more," Tuck reminded Billy. "Remember, from now on we call him colonel! He's Colonel Amos DeWitt."

SEVEN

Tad Sands was madder than Pete had ever seen him, and for three miles or more he took it out on everything in sight. The redhead rode like a madman, ignoring cuts and washes along the upper bank, pushing through thickets that he could as easily have gone around, not giving a damn what it cost the horse beneath him.

The sorrel was bleeding from flank and mouth. Its eyes were wild and its ears laid back, and Tad raked it savagely with his spurs as it shied away from a washout.

Pete Monte winced, despite himself. "You're gonna kill that horse if you don't ease up," he called from behind. "How about—" He went silent as Tad swivelled half around in his saddle, glaring at him. The redhead's eyes were pale blue rage, and Pete's hand dropped instinctively to hover at his waist, his fingers touching the butt of his cross-draw Colt.

Tad's glare held him for an instant. Then the redhead turned away and spurred the sorrel again—forcing it to jump, letting it find its own footing on the uneven ground across the washout.

Pete shook his head grimly, hauled aside, and went around. "You're crazy as a loon, you wormy bastard," he muttered.

They had followed the river since leaving Outpost. Mostly staying to the upper bank, they had been clear of the heaviest brush and the nasty little thickets of soapweed, yucca, and prickly pear that grew among the broken slopes. The forbidding portals of Black Mesa were still visible behind them, but Outpost was far back and hidden by the rises.

Pete gave up on trying to calm the enraged Tad Sands. The redhead would just have to ride it out, and if it cost him a horse, that was his lookout. By the time the sun lost itself in rising cloudbanks beyond the mesa, the redhead was out of sight, and Pete didn't particularly care where he had gone.

He found him a mile or so on, though. It was getting dark, and a cold wind was pushing in ahead of the clouds over the breaks. Tad had crossed the river and camped in a cove on the south slopes. Pete followed his firelight in, and the sound of hammering.

The redhead had removed the ejector from his Colt and was hammering on it with a rock, trying to straighten it. " 'Bout time you showed up," he growled. "Give me that nail puller you got."

Pete climbed down, dug the tool out of his saddlebag, and handed it over. Using it as a vise, Tad went back to hammering. Pete brought water, put on a pot, and set some coffee to boil. Then he stripped his saddle and gear, rubbed down his horse, and dug out a tin of liniment. Tad didn't even look up as his partner tended the scrapes and cuts on his sorrel.

When the ejector rod was eyeball straight, Tad reassembled his revolver and jacked the rod through every port of its cylinder. "There," he husked, finally. "Don't look just right, but it works. Thought that son of a bitch had ruined it."

"I thought he'd broke your neck," Pete said casually. "God, that big jasper must be strong as an ox. The way your head was bobbin' around—"

"You just shut your damn mouth, Pete!" Tad croaked. His voice was hoarse and raspy, as if his windpipe had rusted. He glared at his partner. "Son of a bitch is gonna pay for that. An' if I hear one more word about it, you will, too."

Pete shut up. He had ridden with Tad Sands for nearly a year now, and he was about sick of the redhead. They had been drovers together, working a herd. But Tad had changed after a run-in with herd-cutters over in the Outlet. When the powder smoke cleared, Tad had decided he was a gunhand.

He took to strutting and drinking, and seemed to be always spoiling for trouble. He practiced his draw for hours at a time, and when he could afford bullets he put holes in every fence post, bean can, and cactus leaf in sight. The more he drank, the meaner he got. He had a short fuse by nature, and nowadays his anger was frightening.

Getting along with Tad Sands was like petting a badger. Pete just never knew what was going to set him off.

Pete shared out the coffee when it was boiled stiff, and stretched out on his soogans. The cove broke the wind, but there was lightning now in the western sky. "Funny spring," he said. "Started too soon. Prob'ly gonna be a storm season."

Tad didn't answer, and Pete glanced over at him. The redhead had cleaned and reloaded his Colt, and now he was working on his saddle gun, occasionally peering out into the darkness, toward the river. He had an open jug of Mose Polan's rotgut beside him.

Pete felt a chill that wasn't just from the wind.

"What are you thinkin' about, Tad? We're headin' for Wolf Creek in the morning, ain't we?"

"When I'm ready," Tad rasped, coughing to clear his voice. "You notice the flats down there when you rode over, Pete? Notice how there's no cover out there?"

"I noticed," Pete admitted. "What are you aimin' to do, Tad?"

"I got a notion that moon-haired jasper will be comin' this way," the redhead said. "Sometime tomorrow, he'll come ridin' along with that Injun kid. I aim to be waitin.' "

"Have you looked at the sky?" Pete suggested. "If it rains, ain't anybody gonna be ridin' them bottoms."

"Ain't gonna do more than blow a little," Tad said huskily. "They'll come. They'll be right out there where the riverbed's widest. When they get to where I want 'em, I'm gonna teach them both some manners."

"Hell you are!"

Tad turned to face him, a feral glare in his eyes. "If you get in my way, Pete, I'll kill you, too."

Pete Monte finished his coffee, then got to his feet. Without a word he rolled and strapped his bedroll, picked up his saddle, and went to get his horse. He was tightening the cinches when Tad Sands came up behind him, carrying his rifle.

"What the hell do you think you're doin'?" the redhead demanded. "What's the matter with you?"

Pete turned, sighing. "I've said it before, Tad. You're crazy as a loon. And you're a mean drunk. If you aim to bushwhack a man just because he didn't kill you when he prob'ly should have, then you've got it to do, but I don't hold with ambush. I believe I can find my own way from here."

Stepping past the redhead, Pete collected his gear and stowed it aboard his horse. The wind was kicking up some sand now, and whipping the little fire. It was cold, and there was a wetness to the air. The little cove would have been a snug place to spend the night, but he would find another place.

"You ain't goin' anywhere!" Tad spat, his voice a harsh croak. "You unpack that gear!"

"I'm leavin'," Pete said. He snugged the straps on his pack and tossed a rein over the saddle horn.

"You ain't runnin' out on me!" Tad croaked.

"What are you goin' to do, shoot me in the back?"

"You'll face me, Pete. By God, I won't allow this!"

"Gonna shoot the only friend you've got, an' with a bent gun?" Pete's voice was harsh with disbelief. "I'm through, Tad. It's you that's bent out of shape, not your damn gun."

"Face me, you . . . you polecat!"

Pete looked around at him, not turning. "Tad, you know I won't back down from any man. Not even you. But I'm no murderer, either. I'm damned if I'll help you ambush a stranger, and I don't intend to draw down on a crazy drunk." Leading his mount, he walked out of the light, picking his way up the slope toward the flatlands above.

Tad looked after him for time, peering into the darkness long after Pete was out of sight. Then he shook his head and kicked at the sandy ground. "Jesus!" he complained, his voice a harsh whisper. "What's ailin' him, anyway?"

When Tad Sands left the cove fifteen minutes later, leading his saddled sorrel, he passed within a dozen feet of Falcon MacCallister. Crouched in the brush just out of the fire's light, camouflaged by darkness and long instinct, Falcon watched the redhead leave. Then he faded back into the shelter of the bluff and began the walk back to his own snug camp, where Woha'li waited with Diablo and the dun.

Few would have seen him pass, even anybody who had been there watching, but to Falcon MacCallister the stars of half a sky—and the staccato flare of lightning in the clouds to the west—gave light enough to see. As he walked, a slight smile teased the corners of his mouth.

Falcon MacCallister was recalling something he had heard a long time ago—something his own father, the legendary Jamie Ian MacCallister, had said: "The rarest quality in the human critter is ordinariness. Mankind's plain peculiarities never cease to amaze me."

As though God seconded the motion, the low sky flared and a mighty clap of thunder echoed through the hills like cannon fire.

Under the sound of the thunder and wind was another, more ominous sound. Even from high on the south slope, Falcon could see what caused it. The rain that was just commencing had already washed the foothills to the west. The river was rising.

It was one of those springtime storms that struck the high plains in a hundred guises—sometimes as blizzard, sometimes as hail, sometimes as dust, sometimes as torrential rain, and sometimes with tornado ferocity that swept the lands clean and devoured anything standing.

This time it was lightning and a thunderstorm that strode down from the high slopes and swept across the Cimarron breaks. Two hours after sundown the western sky was alive with searing tendrils of lightning. An hour later fitful rain rode the winds, and the whole sky was ablaze with sound and fury.

The little dun was skittish at the first few cascades of thunder. Woha'li had his hands full just keeping the horse attached to his tether. But when he snugged the animal's lead closer to MacCallister's big black, on a picket rope close under a limestone shelf, Diablo's solid presence seemed to calm him. When the first rains hit, both horses crowded the line and edged around, closer to the snug little fire where Woha'li waited.

Great flares of lightning lit the rainy sky, and thunder drummed. The air smelled sweet, and seemed to hum and crackle like a den of vipers—a sky full of brilliant rattlesnakes striking downward.

"Utsonati," the Indian boy sang quietly, looking skyward and speaking to the lightning in the ancient way of his people, *"Anagalisgi, osiyo! Hiwo'ni-a agasga'."* Hello, lightning. When you speak, the rains come down.

Woha'li was impatient and nervous. Though he spoke some English—far more than the man MacCallister spoke *atsalagi*—still he didn't know much about the tall *yoneg* who had befriended him. The man was soft-spoken and polite, yet he was very strong, and he moved with the grace and purpose of a warrior. One had only to glance at those pale eyes to know that he could be deadly. He had hair the color of moon-corn, yet he adapted himself so well to the land and the moment that sometimes Woha'li would have sworn he was Indian.

And he rarely said or revealed more than he had to. Right now, Woha'li had not the vaguest idea where he had gone, or why. MacCallister had simply told him to make camp and wait with the horses, then had disappeared into the shadows.

Woha'li was thinking seriously about breaking away from the white man, going on alone. He was grudgingly grateful for the things MacCallister had done for him, but he didn't see that he needed to follow any *yoneg* around. He had a loaded rifle now, and he knew what he wanted to do.

The frontal rains came in a rush of wind and spray, and Woha'li pulled back into the shelter of the cut bank. Out in the gully beyond, the slope was screened by scrub cedar.

The thickets were alive with windsong and with scurrying small things moving up the slope from the riverbed below. A wilderness in motion, seen from above.

And just overhead, above the rock rim of the ledge, were the rolling flatlands where lightning danced like spider legs walking.

"Anagalisgi," his father had told him. *"Anagalisgi ale Utsonati . . . Tsalagiyahi unali'i gesa."* The lightning, like Utsonati the rattlesnake, is the Cherokee's friend.

In Woha'li beat the heart of a warrior, and vengeance flowed hot in his veins . . . the single-minded resolve to exact retribution upon those who had killed his father and mother. MacCallister was *aniunega*—a *yoneg*. Only a white man. He might return, and he might not. Either way, Woha'li would go on, and he would have his revenge.

The lightning flared, the thunder rolled, and eyes dark as hawks' eyes looked out at the flashing wilderness. In his heart, Woha'li was very much a Cherokee warrior. Still, for the rest of him, he was only twelve years old, and he felt lost, cold, and lonely. All the family he had was gone, and the white stranger he rode with had disappeared into the night.

And down the slope, brush crackled and splintered as the floodwaters from upstream rose steadily in the Cimarron gorge.

Woha'li's loneliness only added fuel to the seething rage that burned within him. Somewhere out there, not far away, were the men who had killed his father and mother. Maybe only a few miles away. Even at night, he could find them. And if he had a very good horse . . .

Hesitantly, he scanned the brush again, then crept to the picket rope. Bypassing the little dun, he approached MacCallister's big black horse and reached for its halter.

The horse laid its ears back and showed its teeth. *"So'qui-li,"* the boy crooned softly. "Horse, I want to ride you." With a lunge, he grabbed the halter and reached high for an ear. Woha'li wasn't sure what happened next, but he found himself tumbling backward, with a powerful hoof whooshing past his head. He came up against the limestone bluff and lay there, stunned.

MacCallister had told him to leave Diablo alone. Now Woha'li knew why.

The boy sat slumped and silent beside glowing embers when Falcon MacCallister slipped soundlessly into the sheltered camp. Exhausted and confused, Woha'li the warrior had gone to sleep with his worn old .32-20 cradled in his arms.

EIGHT

After the lightning came the pouring rain—waves and walls of it, driven by wild gusts of wind. It was a downpour, a real frog strangler, and the slopes below the cut bank flowed torrents. But it ended as abruptly as it had begun, and before dawn there were stars in the western sky and the high-up hills stood crisp against a freshly washed horizon.

By first light, Falcon climbed the caprock to look down across a different river. Normally the upper Cimarron was a gentle sleepy stream meandering along a wide sandy bed between high valley walls. Only now and then, sometimes many years apart, did it reveal its true character. It was doing so now.

From the caprock, Falcon looked out on a wide surging stream a quarter-mile from bank to bank. The flash flood had come down from the high foot-hills and filled the ancient waterway almost to the rim. Here and there up and down the south side, among the inundated scrub brush of the new banks, were scatterings of debris—broken planks, a demolished tent, a dead mule tangled in harness.

Far upstream, something bobbed and swayed on the floodcrest, coming down. Seen through the tele-scope, it became a raft of sorts—a jumble of wood planking, like the remains of a footbridge attached to a placer-mine chute. There were people on it, busy with poles and bits of board, fighting the current as they fought to keep the contrivance upright.

They brought the horses up from the cut bank, and then Falcon made his way down to the floodway. He waved his arms until those aboard the raft had seen him, then set about splicing ropes to make a lifeline. A mile or so downstream, the river made a hard bend to the left. Even without using his scope, Falcon could see the torrent pounding at the banks there.

The makeshift raft coming down from the Black Mesa "mines" might hold together on a straight current, but it would never survive that bend. It and all those aboard would be dashed to pieces if they went that far.

Woha'li appeared from the brush and swung out on a salt-cedar branch to look upstream. "Crazy *yonegs*," he stated flatly, then swung back to firm footing. "Horses ready," he said. *"He-ga.* We go."

Falcon ignored him. Splicing three coils of saddle rope and a length of reata, he had a line nearly fifty feet long. To one end of it he tied a chunk of driftwood, and then he coiled the rest.

Aboard the makeshift raft men were struggling furiously to alter course, edging to the right as they approached. There were seven or eight of them clinging to the debris, all working frantically with plank oars and bits of pole while they struggled to keep their vessel intact. With each shift of current, the mess threatened to split apart, to separate into disconnected flotsam.

As the unlikely thing neared, Falcon waved and shouted. When he was sure they saw him, he stepped as far out as he could, freed the chunk end of his coil, and began swinging it in a widening circle.

Woha'li watched in disbelief for a moment, then picked up his rifle. *"He'ga-ha!"* he demanded. "We go now!"

Falcon was busy. He ignored the kid. He completed his swing, gauged his distance and trajectory, and let the chunk fly. It arced out over the muddy waters, trailing its rope, and fell directly ahead of the raft. Men aboard scrambled to grab it, and secured it somewhere. Falcon wound the free end around a squat cedar bole, looped it, and tied it off. Gripping the line then, he set it across his shoulders, held it as a sling, and braced himself.

With men heaving at both ends of the line, the ungainly raft veered sharply, veered again, and began to disintegrate in the current.

Eighty yards from water's edge, up the tangled brushy slope where the canyon wall met the wide limestone shelf called caprock, erosion had formed a narrow trail angling up to the prairie above. For long moments, as the people below worked to swing the motley raft ashore, a horse and rider were skylined, watching.

Woha'li the Eagle, last survivor of what had once been one of the proudest families of *Ani-wa'ya*, the wolf clan of the eastern Cherokee, had run out of patience. He watched for a moment as *ani-unegas* below him struggled against a rampaging river. He was only twelve years old, but there was work now for a man, and no other man remained in his family.

He raised a hand in quick salute. *"Donada'gohui, Towo'di,"* he murmured. "Man named Falcon, goodbye."

There were more people on the raft than it had appeared. As the thing came closer, Falcon could see glimpses of people everywhere in the wreckage. He could not tell how many, or even how many of them were alive, but all of them were in pitiful condition. Considering the wall of water that must have swept down on that mining camp in the river bottom upstream, it was a wonder anyone had survived.

The raft bumped and scraped against other floating debris, and bit by bit it continued to come apart. One entire section of the thing—something that looked like a wrecked buckboard wagon and some lashings—veered off into the current and floated away. There were two or three people aboard it, none of them moving. As it rolled and turned, beginning to submerge, Falcon saw two faces and a disconnected arm. Two men and a woman, he guessed . . . all dead.

By the time the raft grounded, just a few yards out into the stream, there wasn't much left except a section of what might have been a footbridge, a broken rocker-box still holding bits of gravel from a mine, and a few kegs and barrels lashed into the mess with rope.

It was full morning by the time Falcon got them all to shore and counted them. Fourteen men, three women, and the bodies of two more dead men. Falcon muttered his amazement. Twenty-two people had ridden that torrent on a frail lash-up of floating debris that they had somehow assembled when the first rush of flood hit them.

Five had not survived, but somehow seventeen had!

He revised his count when one of the men waded out to the wreckage and brought back a wriggling, unhappy bundle in a wet quilt. A young woman screamed when she saw it, and ran to take it.

"Make that eighteen," Falcon said.

It was only then, when he herded them all up the slope to caprock—some of them being supported or outright carried—that he realized the Indian boy was gone. Diablo stood alone up there, still tethered, but the dun was missing along with its saddle and Woha'li's belongings. Woha'li had gone on alone, and left no sign where he was going.

The flood survivors were a dismal lot, battered and drenched. Several had injuries, but none appeared to be dying just yet.

"We tried to get out of the water at Outpost," one of the men—a dark-bearded beanpole named Iverson—told him. "They came out with lanterns, and threw ropes to us, but we were . . . just going too fast. All we could do was hang on."

"You were crazy to be in that riverbed when you could see it was storming in the foothills," Falcon said. He dipped his head for a moment, remembering something Woha'li had said to him the day before. *"Hade'ne-a equone unegadihi,"* he muttered.

Iverson blinked. "What?"

"It's Cherokee." Falcon shrugged. "It means something like, 'that's how the river kills crazy white people.' "

Morning had passed into evening by the time Falcon MacCallister had the refugees tended and secure. Some of the injured rested in the shelter of the cut bank where Falcon and Woha'li had camped the night before, all the rest on the caprock shelf above.

They were a pitiful lot, cold, hungry, and exhausted. One of the men had cracked ribs, and he coughed up blood each time he awoke.

Falcon helped them as much as he could. He

bound some of their wounds, set a broken arm, shared his little stock of foods, and saw to the setting of signals—a bright-colored blanket to wave and a ready bonfire for the night. He helped them bury the dead from the raft. Then he saddled Diablo and rode out, southward into the breaks.

He was gone for an hour and came back with a dressed-out mule deer and two antelope. He rode up to the refugees' fire and dropped the meat, then unsaddled Diablo and turned him out to graze. It was too late to travel, and they still needed help. He would stay for the night.

"The water should begin dropping by morning," he told them. "There'll be people coming down from Outpost when they can, I guess."

"They won't come," one of the miners said glumly. "Why would they? They probably think we're all dead by now."

"They'll come," Falcon said.

By first light of dawn he rode west, upstream along the high south ridge. It was three hours' ride to the breaks across from Black Mesa, and it took another hour of signaling across the flooded river before they understood what he wanted. When he saw riders heading east from Outpost he fired two shots into the air, mounted, and headed east again.

It was past noon when he returned to the survivors' camp. "They're coming from Outpost," he told them. "They'll be on that ridge over there in an hour, and they'll cross when they can. One of them's a gent named Dawson. Tell him MacCallister said to help you. Tell him I'll make it worth his while, if he wants to look me up."

Seeing nothing more that he could do there, Falcon MacCallister rode away, not looking back. He set his course east along the south rim of the Cimarron canyon, with the quartering sun and the crisp wind at his back. He paused only briefly at the cove where the two ex-cowboys—Tad and Pete—had stopped, then went on. Once he saw faint impressions that might have been the prints of Woha'li's dun, but only briefly. The Indian boy had chosen to go his own way, and Falcon couldn't fault him for that. The kid was hardly more than a lanky child, but who was to say when a boy became a man?

The thought brought back memories of his father. Jamie Ian MacCallister had been a man at Woha'li's age. Raised by Shawnee Indians, he had learned the warrior's way and learned it early.

Jamie Ian MacCallister had become practically a legend—a man feared by many, loved by some, and respected by all who ever knew him. But to Falcon, the living legend had been, simply, Pa. Pa might have said that a boy becomes a man when he chose to.

And Pa had said some things about the Cherokee. To the Shawnee, they were "the ones who came before" or "those who were always here." In Kentucky, the two peoples had fought for centuries, and they knew each other very well. "Spirit people," the Shawnee called the Cherokee. The Shawnee were masters of camouflage, yet a Cherokee warrior, they said, could disappear—even from Shawnee eyes. Disappear . . . then strike with deadly force.

Woha'li was hardly a Cherokee warrior. The kid was only a cub. But then, a boy became a man when he chose to.

"Donada'go-hui, Woha'li," Falcon said. "Good-bye. Take care of yourself."

He found where the wagon party had camped, up on the crest above the river's bend, but the trail was cold now and he lost it a few miles east, above the breaks where stony gray-red clay defied tracks, and drift sand shifted with each breeze as it dried from the last night's rain.

There were still only four men in the bunch. He knew that two had broken off, but had no idea where they had gone. He could only speculate that they were off on some errand, and might rejoin their buddies later.

He hoped they would. The images of that desolate gully up in the foothill slopes, and what he had found there, haunted him. Like an old scar, the memories of his beloved wife lived in him. Now these newer images were a torment, reopening the old wound, renewing the pain of it.

He shook his head, trying to clear his mind. Those six men . . . those brutal men! Somebody had something they wanted, so they took it.

The forlorn silence of that gully haunted Falcon. Five people had been murdered there—two men killed outright, three women raped and brutalized, then finally killed. And two of those had been young girls!

Six men had murdered those people, and six men should answer for that. Falcon didn't intend to settle for four. The constant ache of Marie's memory, he knew, was partly because he'd never had a chance to avenge her. Her killers were dead now, but Falcon had had no part in their deaths.

He felt a need to somehow atone—to set things right—and that need drove him as he rode the lawless land, heading east.

A dozen miles east of the Cimarron's bend, he made night camp beside a little stream and shook out his soogans under a deepening sky where stars were coming out.

He had lost the trail of the overland wagon some-where back, and had not found it again. But he knew the direction they were going, and he knew what was there. Somewhere ahead, in the prairies of the neutral strip called No Man's Land, was a tallgrass region known as the Haymeadows. And somewhere in that region was a place called Wolf Creek.

A lot of people seemed to be heading for Wolf Creek. If there was a spread being built there, as Dawson said, there'd be a settlement. And a settle-ment would be a good place to look for the killers he was hunting.

Again he reviewed his images of the six, as Woha'li had described them. Two big men. Big! One of them was bald on top, above wide jowl-length hair, and wore his clothes like a city dude. The other big one had a full rust-blond beard and pale eyes. A little skittery man with snake eyes, big guns, high boots, and a lot of silver trim. A hunch-shouldered buzzard with an overcoat and a shotgun. A cowboy with jug-handle ears and a mashed nose. A squinty nervous rooster with a tied-down Colt.

Falcon could almost see them, just as the kid had. Again and again he had added details from obser-vation, and from what the boy said.

By last light of evening, he looked skyward to see a nighthawk circling high—a swooping predator, graceful and deadly, spotting the nests of lesser fliers so it would know where to find them when the morning came.

"*Towo'di,*" he muttered, then sighed with irrita-tion. Even though he was gone, the scrawny Chero-kee kid still deviled him.

Falcon didn't expect to meet any travelers along this lonely stretch of prairie, and he certainly didn't expect company. But even before he had saddled up the next morning he saw movement a couple of miles north.

Curious, he angled that way. For a time he saw nothing, the rolling lands hiding the distances. Then from a high swell he saw riders—a passel of them, moving southward in a hurry. It might have been twenty men, or sixty. They were spread far out, mostly in groups of three or four, and he could see they had covered some ground.

He was just scanning the terrain, trying to count them, when a bullet whined off stone twenty feet ahead of him and the ground there erupted in a shower of sand. Then the air seemed full of bullets, none of them close but all traveling in his direction. The crackle of gunfire sounded like both rifles and handguns.

With a kick he bailed out of his saddle, hauling out his rifle as he did, and hit the ground with its sights aligned. He could barely make out the forms of the shooters across veiled expanses of grass and sage, but he sent them some responses. The .44-40 spoke with authority, and though Falcon doubted he had hit anybody, the shooting stopped. Distantly he heard shouts and curses, and the drumming of hooves.

He stood, and saw no one where the shooters had been. A moment later, though, he saw a dozen or so riders hightailing it away, keeping low and making distance.

Whoever they were, they had changed their minds.

Diablo was nervous and skittish. None of the shots had touched him, but their whine had been like hornets, and he was in no mood to be reasonable. It took Falcon a while to coax him to lead, croon him down, and convince him that it was time to travel again.

He had barely settled himself into his saddle when the crest to his left sprouted soldiers. A dozen uniformed men thundered down on him, carbines at the ready.

It was a cavalry patrol—a lieutenant and eleven men. The regimental colors were unfamiliar to him, but the red bands on their sleeves said state militia. Atop a grassy rise he reined in and waited for them.

They slowed as they approached, and fanned out a bit. When MacCallister made no move, they closed in. When they reined up, he was neatly flanked by nervous young soldiers to right and left.

The lieutenant—a bright-eyed young man with freshly shaved cheeks and polished boots—eyed him carefully, then walked his mount closer and looked him over again. A weather-seamed sergeant came to join him. The two of them eyed MacCallister like cats eyeing cream. They huddled together for a moment, leaning from their saddles to exchange whispers, and then the shavetail stepped his mount forward. "MacCallister?" he asked. "Is your name Falcon MacCallister?"

"I'm MacCallister." Falcon nodded.

"I knew it," the lieutenant said. "I glassed you, about the time those hooligans started shooting. The description fits. I'm Colegrave, sir . . . John Colegrave, Lieutenant, Company A, Second Kansas. I have standing orders to locate you, sir, and escort you to Captain Burroughs. You're to come with us."

Falcon's eyes narrowed at the youngster's imperious tone. "Come with you where, lieutenant?"

"It's about three days' ride northeast of here, sir. Fort Dodge, in Kansas."

"I'm no longer under obligation to the army,"

Falcon said. "I completed my contract eight months ago. And I'm a little busy at the moment. I have other things to do."

"That will just have to wait, sir." The shavetail gestured, and carbines came up all around Falcon.

"What's all this about?" he demanded. "What standing orders?"

"You'll have to talk to the captain about that, sir. Now will you come with us voluntarily, or . . ."

Falcon had learned long ago the uselessness of trying to argue with fresh lieutenants. With an exasperated shrug, he flicked his reins. Diablo advanced on the smaller cavalry mount and the lieutenant was forced to back away. "Let's go see your Captain Burroughs, then," Falcon said. "And tell your men to rest those carbines before I get irritated."

"Best do as the man says," the sergeant said, quietly. "Don't pay to push a man too far."

NINE

The way to hide in a forest, Woha'li knew, was to *be* the forest. This bit of wisdom required some adapting, of course, for in all of his twelve years Woha'li had never seen a forest. Born just south of the Kansas town of Baxter Springs, he had been an infant when drunken *yonegs* came up from Texas with their cattle and their guns and their hatred of Indians.

Night riders killed Woha'li's two older brothers and drove his family from its little farm in the rolling hills. For a time the family had lived among the tame Pawnee, while Woha'li's father, Wili Hasusgi—known to the whites as Will Fisher—taught English at the Indian school. In the boy's fourth year, though, wild Kiowa raiders led by Satank had caused much trouble. In the ensuing turmoil, Will Fisher was again driven away.

The only life Woha'li had ever really known was the catch-as-catch-can existence of a frontier scavenger going from job to menial job and gathering buffalo bones between employments. Though his father had taught him much of the old ways of the proud *Tsalagi*, Woha'li had little practical experience.

To hide in the forest, *be* the forest. To hide in sage and grass, then, he must *be* sage and grass. His rifle was small, and its range limited. To kill the *yoneg* murderers he must be close to them.

Belly down on the prairie, the boy called Eagle let his senses lead him as he slithered from dip to shallow swale, from clump to cluster. He was almost naked, and smeared from head to toe with gray mud. His dun horse and all his belongings were at least a mile away, hidden in a grassy gully. He wore only his old tar-soled moccasins and a swatch of feed sack belted as a loincloth. He carried his rifle, and had a handful of extra loads in a makeshift pouch.

A chill breeze played waves in the pale endless grass, and he moved with the waves, becoming part of them . . . *being* the grass. His small size helped him in this. Only his mud-streaked hair and narrowed eyes showed above the grass as he slithered forward, closer to the path of the trundling overland wagon approaching from the west.

He had spotted the wagon hours before, when the sun was still ahead of him. A covered overland—a prairie schooner—its hind wheels as tall as a man and its rearmost bows twelve feet off the ground. The big wagon was nearly fifteen feet long and distinctly swaybacked, like an old horse or the gunwales of a boat. Ten dray horses in harness—two to a span—pulled the rig as easily as one horse might draw a surrey, although the wagon's total loaded weight could exceed ten tons.

Woha'li knew it was the same wagon, and he closed in on it cautiously. There were four men with it—three outriders and the driver. From more than half a mile away he recognized the men. They were four of the six who had killed his parents. Woha'li knew from MacCallister that the men had killed others, as well. The wagon they drove was a stolen wagon, and innocent people had died when they took it.

That was why the man called Falcon now hunted them. Woha'li had his own reasons.

He stalked the wagon as a wolf stalks wary prey—staying well away until he knew the lay of the land, then circling ahead to take advantage of the best ground.

Time was his friend, and the vast emptiness of the rolling prairies his ally. Calling up all the inherent skills of his ancient ancestors and the bits of lore he had learned from his father, the son of Wili Hasusgi let white ways fall from him like molting feathers and became as *Tsalagi* as any twelve year old could. As nearly as he could, in his mind, he tried to become a *danawa'yehi*—a warrior, like the formidable *didanawa-i* of ancient times.

The gentlest of people, it was said, were the Cherokee. Yet the thought of *didanawa-i*—Cherokee warriors—even now could freeze the spirit of the fiercest Shawnee, the wildest Pawnee, or the most savage Comanche, and make their blood run cold. Like the mystic *Leni Lenape*—the Delaware—the *Tsalagi* were Spirit people. Other tribes and other peoples had learned the cost of underestimating them.

Woha'li knew little of all this. But as he eased up behind a clump of sage, atop a slight rise where wind and rain had etched the land in shallow gullies, he became the grass and the sage—so much so that a big diamondback rattler coiled in a shallow crevice six inches from his shoulder was no more aware of him than he was of it.

As motionless as the earth itself, Woha'li watched the men approach. One by one, he identified them. One of the two big ones—the *an'da'tsi* with the moon-straw beard and the pale blue eyes—was up on the wagon, driving the team. Three others—the bat-eared one with the flat nose, the long-coat buzzard, and the second big one, who seemed to be in charge—rode saddle mounts.

Carefully, Woha'li eased his rifle to his shoulder. Windsong covered the slight rasping sound at his side as the rattlesnake reacted to the movement, tightening its coil. Its dark tongue flicked in and out, sensing the body heat of a living creature close by. The snake's tail twitched once, tentatively, as it readied itself to strike.

The boy knew, from the way the men were spread out, that he couldn't shoot them all from here. But he might shoot two, or maybe three. He must number his targets in advance. The first shot would bring the rest down on him, and he must be ready for them.

The only one who couldn't react instantly was the one driving the wagon. He was therefore the least dangerous. He would be target number four.

The nearest rider—bat ears—was farthest from the wagon, and the big man with the slick clothes was nearest, riding alongside. Woha'li decided his best chance would be to shoot bat ears first, then take the other riders out as they came.

When bat ears was a hundred yards away, the boy sighted carefully, dead center on the rider's chest, and eased back the hammer.

At its click, the rattler in its crevice raised its head, opened its gaping mouth, and buzzed.

Everything was a blur after that. Woha'li felt and heard his rifle discharge, but he knew his aim was off. He saw the rattlesnake beside him, recoiling to strike, and reacted instantly.

* * *

Folly Downs never saw where the shot came from. He was just riding along, thinking about all that money in the wagon back there, and suddenly something whacked him alongside the head and the world turned upside down. He heard the shot, but couldn't think what it was. He felt his horse shy, felt himself hitting the ground. Then he was looking up at empty sky.

Asa Parker and Casper Wilkerson heard the shot and saw Folly Downs slide off his horse. Above them on the wagon's bench seat, Kurt Obermire yelled and pointed. He had seen a flicker of movement in a sage stand just as the shot rang out. As one, Asa and Casper spurred their mounts. Asa leaned low over his saddle and pulled his big Winchester from its sheath. Casper veered toward him, brandishing his big stub-barreled greener.

Leveling his .44-40, Asa fired, worked the lever, and fired again. Dust and debris flew from the sage ahead. He held slightly left, fired again, then put a fourth shot just to the right.

Fifty yards out, Casper rode beside him, his hands full of shotgun and his eyes full of murder. At thirty yards he let go with both barrels, right into the sage patch Asa was shooting, and the little thicket seemed to explode. Dirt, gravel, and sundered sage flew, raining down like a cloud on the devastated earth below.

At full gallop the riders entered the sage, thundered past the fringes where their guns had been at work, and plunged on—thirty yards, forty, sixty— before reining in and circling, watching for any movement, any slightest hint of a target.

With one hand full of rifle and the other full of furious rattlesnake, Woha'li lay facedown in a tiny gully no more than a foot deep. Braced on his elbows, he clung desperately to the neck of a very large and very angry viper and felt debris raining down on his back. The snake beneath him writhed and surged, and he strained desperately to hold it still. Even while the debris was falling a thunder rose, and horsemen were right on top of him. Pounding hooves pummeled the earth inches from him . . . and went right on by.

Not even daring to breathe, Woha'li lay frozen still and listened. An inch from his nose, the rattlesnake hissed and gaped, its fangs dripping venom on the hand that held it imprisoned. His other arm, the right one, was almost numb with a searing pain that shot clear to his shoulder. The snake had stung him as he was grabbing it—a glancing blow, like two short scratches, but it hurt like fire. He ignored it as horsemen thundered toward him unseen.

The riders went right over him! He heard them receding, heard their voices as they circled and searched, looking for him. Then he heard again the roar of the shotgun, and men seemed to be shouting all around.

With every ounce of his strength, Woha'li held himself still in the tiny trough that hid him, held the writhing rattlesnake imprisoned beneath him, held its seeking fangs away from his flesh and held his breath. To hide in a forest, one must *be* the forest.

"Be the prairie," the Indian boy commanded himself. Nine pounds of powerful rattlesnake writhed and twisted, trying to free itself from the desperate fingers clutching its neck and head, and Woha'li did not move. He lay as still as the prairie.

* * *

A covey of bobwhites exploded from cover as Casper Wilkerson circled his horse, peering closely at the concealing underbrush. Almost underfoot, seven or eight quail flushed in a flurry of wings, and Casper's shotgun came up and roared.

Four birds dropped, and Casper heard Asa's angry shout, "What are you doin', you fool? It's only birds!"

"Prob'ly all it ever was!" Casper shouted back. "See anythin' else?"

"Not a damn thing! But that was no quail that shot Folly! Keep lookin'!"

From a distance, the bull voice of Kurt Obermier roared, "What is it? Did you get him?"

"Haven't seen anybody! How's Folly?"

"He's bleedin' like hell!" Obermier shouted. "His cheek's gouged wide open! God, I can see into his mouth through it! An' he's got a hole through his left ear! Somebody come help me with him!"

For long minutes the search continued. Then Asa said, "Whoever it was is gone now! Let's get back to the wagon!"

Once again, the riders passed within yards of Woha'li without seeing him. Half-buried in gravel, sand, and shreds of sage, he was as invisible as a Cherokee can be.

When he was sure they were gone Woha'li raised himself carefully, keeping his tight grip on the rattlesnake. His right arm throbbed, swollen and awkward. The men had returned to the wagon, where bat ears was on his feet now, staggering around and moaning, holding his head with a bloody hand.

Carefully, Woha'li rolled out of the little depression, bringing the snake with him. The creature was as big around as his forearm, and almost as long as he was tall. Powerful coils writhed around his arm, compressing the flesh cruelly, and the extended fangs were like curved ivory needles, nearly an inch long.

Watching until the men were turned away from him, he freed his arm of the rattler's coils, then turned and flung it away from him. Landing among sage clumps, it coiled and buzzed, then stretched out and disappeared into shadows.

"*Utsonati,*" Woha'li whispered. "*A'ali'i a-awaduli.*" Rattlesnake, be my friend. You are in my blood now. I have your spirit. "*Utsonati, unali'i,*" he added. "Go in peace."

His rifle was clogged with sand, and when he tried to jack a shell into its chamber it jammed. The boy suddenly felt very small, and very tired. His arm hurt like fury, making him dizzy. His gun was useless now, and he hadn't killed anybody. He felt like crying, but he cursed himself and fought back the tears. *Didanawa-i*—Cherokee warriors—did not cry.

Half an hour later he watched the prairie schooner lumbering eastward, and when it was safely away he headed south. He moved slowly, weaving drunkenly and dangling one arm. He would clean himself at a little creek, retrieve his horse and belongings, clean and reload his rifle . . . then he would rest. He needed to rest, until *Utsonati*'s poison wore off.

That might take a day, or several. And he would be sick. But the snake had shared its spirit with him, and it would strengthen him if he knew how to make it his own. He would rest, treat his swollen arm with a poultice of sage and mud, and then he would just wait it out. When he could, he would start again.

He had found his prey—four of them, at any rate—and drawn first blood. True, he had not hurt them much, but next time it would be different. Next time . . . next time they would wish that they had never come across a bone cart operated by peaceful harmless Cherokees.

Woha'li had a war name now, like the *didanawa-i* of old. Next time those men were in his sights, it would not be just the boy Woha'li they faced. It would be *Utsonati*, the rattlesnake.

MacCallister's ride to Fort Dodge was one of the strangest journeys he could recall. Except for one crusty veteran with topkick chevrons, the cavalry patrol consisted of one shavetail state militia officer as green as new clover and a gang of rosy-cheeked State of Kansas recruits who didn't know horseshit from high ground.

The second time Lieutenant Colgrave refused to divulge the reason for Falcon's impoundment, Sergeant Lyles eased the civilian aside. "He don't know why he's got you," he explained. "He's just actin' on orders, an' don't know what it's about. You wanted for somethin'?"

"I am not," Falcon stated.

"Well, all I can suggest," the sergeant said, "is just make the best of it. You're lucky he hasn't took your guns—"

"He'll play hell trying!"

"I suggested as much. Anyhow, you're not under arrest, but the lieutenant does mean to bring you in.

"He's taking me to Kansas, and he doesn't even know why?"

"That's the new army," Lyles shrugged. "Just like the old army was. Never tell anybody anything, just give orders. These boys here couldn't wipe their butts if somebody hadn't issued standin' orders how to do that. Not bad young'uns, some of 'em, but they're green as crick moss."

Falcon made the best of it. There was nothing to be gained by provoking the lieutenant or any of his green troops. The problem with shavetails and recruits, he had learned a long time ago, was that when confused they became trigger-happy. Many a man had died of no hard feelings, in scrapes with unenlightened soldiers.

He did set the pace, though. With every mile northward, Falcon pushed ahead, riding alongside Colegrave and easing ahead of him, forcing him to increase his mount's pace to keep up.

For Falcon, it was a mildly amusing way of passing the time. He had encountered his share of Colegraves in the past—fresh young lieutenants plucked prematurely from the cradle and solemnly designated as officers and gentlemen. In the field, a lieutenant's function was to be a "leader of men." In exact military protocol, this meant that he was expected to always be in front of his charges, never behind them. Among army scouts, it was considered almost a duty to enlighten lieutenants as to how the real world worked.

Unobtrusively, the plodding march became a sort of race, with Colegrave pushing harder and harder to stay at the head of his column and soldiers spurring their mounts to keep from being left behind. The lieutenant's furious glances now and then assured Falcon that Colegrave understood what he was doing, but just didn't know what to do about it.

They crossed the Cimarron at a place where the bluffs outlining the wide valley were more than a mile apart. All along the bottomlands were the smokes, tracks, and marks of settlers settling into a new land. Within view, Falcon counted three distinct settlements scattered across the miles.

"The 'great American desert,'" Lyles commented, observing a farmstead from a distance. "Fifty, sixty years ago this whole region was declared uninhabitable. Look at it now. Fillin' up!"

"Well, they've got their work cut out for them," said Falcon.

Behind him, Private Finch muttered to Private Lester, "So have we . . . just keepin' up with our prisoner."

It was no great workout for Diablo. The big black took the forced march like a Sunday stroll, but for two days the cavalry's horses had been near exhaustion each time they stopped to rest.

Of them all, only Sergeant Lyles seemed to enjoy the sport. Falcon noticed how the old topkick's eyes sparkled with constrained mirth each time Lieutenant Colgrave spurred his horse to regain the lead position in his patrol.

For anyone watching as the unit filed across Crooked Creek and lined out toward the distant smokes of a sizeable settlement ahead, just who was bringing in whom would have been a good question.

TEN

Trails by the dozens converged toward the old ford of the Arkansas River and the seething little settlement beyond. North of the Cimarron had been sand hills, but once past them there was more and more settlements. Every creek and gully, it seemed, was lined with fresh soddies and hardscrabble little steads. There were even patches of raw soil where the grass had been broken out for plowing.

In the distance, on the River's south bank, were several sizeable farmsteads. On the nearest one, the charred remains of a burned-out barn stood stark against the background.

Where there were people, there was always trouble.

And it all seemed to concentrate toward Dodge. Falcon could almost smell the place, even from upwind. A pall of smoke hung in the air—smoke from dozens of cook fires, blacksmiths' forges, tannery embers and stoves—before catching the wind above the low hills to feather off to the east.

Along the main trail, at the edge of town, bales of overripe winter hides were stacked before lowslung sheds, awaiting cartage. Great mounds of sunbleached bone sprawled roof-high along wagon paths, and every kind of shack, shed, hovel, and tent crowded the well-marked line where the city limits began. Beyond were more substantial buildings, many of them still sapwood new.

The main street was a drover's lane, close to a hundred yards wide where it entered the town, narrowing beyond a maze of slat-fenced pens and cattle chutes. The railroad depot there was as varnish-new as the iron rails coming in from the east. This was the new railhead for the Texas herds, replacing Newton and Ellsworth in that trade.

Most of the structures in the town were squat soddies and dugouts. But where the street narrowed, high buildings faced across a busy thoroughfare, many of them dressed up in garish false fronts.

The buildings on the south side of the street backed up to river flats where a wagon camp stood like a second town at the edge of town. Falcon counted at least thirty prairie schooners out there, sharing space with an array of lesser vehicles and a pair of huge Conestogas that dwarfed all the rest. The associated livestock—draft horses, mules, and oxen in various enclosures along the river—numbered in the hundreds.

"Homesteaders." Lyles pointed. "First spring flock, headin' west."

There were people everywhere—men in eastern finery rubbing elbows with frontiersmen in buckskins, grizzled buffalo hunters clearing their own space as they walked, duded drummers and gamblers lounging in the morning sunlight beneath railings where half-dressed women hung out their wash and their wares. Here and there were furtive defeated-looking Indians in ragged white man's clothing, a few sauntering drifters sporting sidearms, and a collection of wagon travelers keeping to themselves.

The rutted streets were a riot of wagons, surreys, drays, carts, and pedestrians, where bonneted women scurried across from produce market to general store and grimy children played tag among the wheels and hooves of the traffic. Two livery barns, a rattletrap hostelry, a newly opened hotel, a bathhouse, several gambling halls, and fourteen saloons—Dodge City seemed to have just about everything a seven-year-old town might offer.

Along the south fringe of the settlement were the stout pens, counting chutes, and branding corrals of a cowtown awaiting the summer herds.

"Dodge by God City," Sergeant Lyles proclaimed. "Hardly manind's finest achievement, but the whiskey here flows more reliably than the river usually does."

The sprawling little city, in its snug pocket on the plains, was indeed a sight to behold as Lieutenant Colegrave took imperious command of his troops and paraded them up Trail Street. Even in this season, the place crawled and bustled with coinciding humanity. It was anybody's guess how many people actually lived in and around Dodge City on any permanent basis. Probably no more than two or three hundred. But compared to the empty prairies he had crossed, it was a metropolis.

With early spring and all the trails open, the count of people was several times the permanent population. Rail and stage traffic from the east, drovers from the south, pack trains from the west, and the sprawl of commerce pushing down from Hays and Great Bend all collided at Dodge. The place was a brawling volatile powder keg where law and order were as fragile as a whiskey whim but just as determined.

They plodded through the town as a parade

might, with crowds gathering to watch them pass. There were catcalls and derisive comments from men in the crowd, and some explicit suggestions and invitations shouted by dance hall women on the upper balconies, but no real incidents.

Falcon had the feeling that hard eyes were on him as he rode by—that sensation of hostility that can make a westerner's scalp tingle like warning flags. Here and there he spotted familiar faces—men he had seen at other times and other places, though none he could put names to.

It wasn't unusual, in any western town where men gathered in passing, to see faces one had seen before. The West was filling up, some said wryly, but there weren't all that many people yet in the vast land. Roads were few and trails were known, and those who went from place to place often encountered each other many times.

Eyes accustomed to seeing what must be seen in wild country developed a knack for seeing everything, all the time. And Falcon MacCallister had such eyes. Scanning the crowds as they passed, he saw and catalogued a dozen or more men who looked familiar. And some of them recognized him, too.

"We're not stopping here?" he asked Colgrave.

"No, sir," the lieutenant rasped. "Not when we're on duty. Fort Dodge is just five miles east."

A mile or so out they passed another burned-out place, just off the road. Both house and barn had been destroyed, and a field of kitchen greens trampled.

"Night riders did that." Sergeant Lyles pointed. "That was the bunch we chased down to the border. Just across, in No Man's Land, we saw a big camp of outlaws, and the lieutenant went after all of them."

"The ones that I saw?" Falcon asked. "There were more of them than there are of you."

"Nobody ever said these greeners didn't have sand." Lyles shrugged.

"I swear to God!" Captain Abe Burroughs sputtered as he pumped Falcon's hand in the little adjutant's office at Fort Dodge. "You *are* Falcon MacCallister! Jamie Ian's son! It's an honor, sir! Heard about the job you did in the Apache campaigns. Nice bit of work, that."

"Thanks," Falcon said. "Now would you tell me what I'm doing here, captain?"

"Oh, that." Burroughs looked embarrassed. "I'm afraid some of our younger officers are . . . well, overly enthusiastic at times. Please accept my apologies. Lieutenant Colgrave's detail wasn't looking for you. They wouldn't have even been over there in the Neutral Strip, but for hot pursuit of a gang of night riders. But there they were, and there you were, and . . . well, you understand. There's been a great deal of reassignment since Kansas became a state, and things get confused."

"Obviously." Falcon sighed.

The cavalry at Fort Dodge was a far cry from the U.S. Cavalry Falcon had scouted for. This was state militia, and cut from different cloth. The soldiers were still soldiers, but their officers were often a motley collection of political appointees and clerks from Topeka.

Falcon knew a clerk when he met one. "I'm a hundred miles from where I intended to be right now," he said coldly, "and I still don't know why."

"I'm not sure I do, either." Burroughs shrugged. "There is a general notice from Topeka. Every post on the line has been looking for you, Mr. MacCallister. The same notice has been issued in the territories. You are to be found, and the U.S. Bureau of Railways notified."

"Bureau of Railways? What do they want me for?"

"I'm sure I don't know. The notice just says to notify a Mr. Sypher, in care of one of the bureau's division points. I've sent the notification, by wire. I attended to that when Lieutenant Colegrave wired from Hardwoodville."

"So what does he say?"

"Who?"

"This Mr. Sypher!" Falcon growled. "What response did you get?"

"Why, none. Mr. Sypher is away, on an extended tour of bureau projects, with the bureau's division chief."

"Then what am I supposed to do? Cool my heels until he gets back?"

Burroughs seemed flustered. "Well, I . . . I suppose you're at liberty to do whatever you want. We've done what we were asked to do. Oh, by the way, there is a telegraph message for you. It's from Denver. I believe it's at the purser's office."

Falcon stared at the officer. "I was hauled all the way up here to pick up a telegraph message?"

"Well, I suppose you could say that, as things turned out."

The few well-chosen words Falcon uttered then made Burroughs cringe. "I'm sorry, sir," the officer said. "I suppose it is an inconvenience."

"That's putting it mildly," Falcon growled. "All right, I'll take my telegram."

Burroughs hastened out and returned with a

folded sheet of yellow paper. "This must be important," he said. "It's from Mr. Horner. That's James Russell Horner. He's—"

"I've heard of him," Falcon said. "The railroad magnate. He's a partner in the Kansas Pacific Railway Company. Some would say he *is* the Kansas Pacific. What does he want?"

"The telegram is addressed to you, sir." Burroughs handed it over. "It's in some sort of code."

Which you couldn't decipher, Falcon thought, sardonically. *You tried, though, didn't you?*

"It must be very important," Burroughs repeated, "I've never seen a telegraph message sent all-points general delivery like that."

"I was detained and escorted a hundred miles out of my way because of a telegram? It had *better* be important." Falcon's glare was thunderous.

"Yes, sir." Burroughs shook his head apologetically. "Well, as I've already explained, that was a simple error. Lieutenant Colegrave is new here, his first posting. He's an eager young officer . . . possibly a bit overzealous."

Falcon sighed. The buck had just been passed, in good military fashion. "I'd say so. Captain, are you the commanding officer of this garrison?"

"Temporarily, sir, yes. The post commandant is Colonel Mahlon Grace. But he's on extended leave, to Topeka. As his executive officer, I'm acting commandant."

Falcon nodded. Recruits and greenhorns, with a clerical functionary in charge. A typical state militia installation—situation normal: all fouled up.

Falcon had noticed that four civilians—hard-looking men who had been lounging around the sutler's store when Colegrave's patrol rode in—made haste to saddle up and ride out soon after. From Burroughs' window he saw them leave, and he put names to two of them.

Jack Cabot and Sandy Hogue had carried iron for Nance Noonan up in Wyoming. They were among the hard cases who pulled out when MacCallister burned out the Gilman place, but he had always wondered when they might surface again . . . especially Cabot. Cabot was kin of the Noonans. Word was, he was one of the nephews who had taken an oath on the Bible to see MacCallister dead.

By way of apology for detaining him, Falcon was offered the hospitality of the fort. That meant a cot at the BOQ and breakfast in the mess hall. He settled for a sample of the cook's pottage and a shave and bath, after tending to his horse. The idea of Diablo at the mercy of remount wranglers didn't appeal to him. The big black horse did not take kindly to strangers. Falcon rubbed him down, gave him a bait of grain, and carefully inspected his legs, hocks, and shoes.

Soaking in a tub of hot water, Falcon lay back and read his telegrams. The general notice from the U.S. Bureau of Railways was just as Burroughs had said: a simple inquiry for information on the whereabouts of Falcon MacCallister. It was from one A. Sypher on behalf of a bureau official named Stratton. It requested information be wired to a coded relay at Topeka.

It had already been answered, he knew. The post telegrapher had advised "A. Sypher" a full day before MacCallister was at Fort Dodge.

The general delivery message, though Burroughs had puzzled over it, was clear and concise:

TO FALCON MACCALLISTER FROM WYLIE AF JRHORNER KPR DENVER STOP *SVC RQ* STOP *KPR AGT RBMD 9MAR81 SE DENVER* STOP *SPCT ASA PARKER PLUS 5* STOP *CN Y ASST* STOP *FEE PROP RCVY* STOP *ADV WYLIE KPR DENVER* STOP

It read like gibberish, but Falcon recognized the language. Apparently Mr. Wylie had some experience on riverboats—or with surveyors. To anyone not familiar with semaphores, the cryptic message might have seemed an elaborate code. But it was simply a shorthand—signal-flag shorthand set to the telegrapher's Morse code.

Six men, one of them named Asa Parker, had robbed and killed a Kansas Pacific Railroad agent southeast of Denver on the ninth of March. James Russell Horner and the Kansas Pacific wanted their money back. They were offering Falcon a reward for recovery.

"That's what reputation does for a man," he told himself sardonically. "All of a sudden I'm in demand . . . to be a policeman."

Still . . .

March the ninth. That was only a few days before the slaughter of those homesteaders he had found. The location could have put the robbers there, then, and men on the run eastbound—in that country—might have truly coveted a prairie schooner.

It was a plausible connection, and the count of outlaws was interesting. Six men! There were six in the bunch he had been trailing into No Man's Land.

Asa Parker. The name didn't mean anything to Falcon, but it obviously did to somebody. It wouldn't be hard to find out more, by wire.

He didn't intend to contact Mr. Wylie, and he didn't intend to use the post telegraph at Fort Dodge. Too many people had access to military messages, and nosiness made him edgy. The general inquiry about him, the one that had led to his escort to Dodge, had obviously come about because somebody, somewhere, had read his name in the "coded" telegraph from Horner's man.

Who was A. Sypher, and why did a private message to Falcon MacCallister make him so curious . . . unless he knew something about the subject of the message?

"The post telegrapher can send your response, if you like," Captain Burroughs had offered. Falcon decided to decline.

Bathed, shaved, and fed, Falcon headed for the stable carrying his saddle gear and his pack. Sergeant Lyles and three of the greenhorns from the patrol were waiting for him inside, at the feed stalls. Falcon stepped out of the daylight and eased aside, letting his eyes adjust. It was long habit, this gathering of advantage in an uncertain situation.

But the soldiers showed no hostility. Seeing the cautious move, a couple of the recruits grinned and turned away, and the third spread his hands to show that he was not armed. Of the four, only Lyles carried a sidearm. The rest had carbines, but the guns were stacked aside, away from them.

"Thought you might not stay the night, Mr. Mac-Callister," the topkick said affably, crossing his arms on a rail. "There seems to be a whole lot of interest in you around here."

Falcon said nothing, just returned the sergeant's gaze.

"Telegrapher's a friend of mine," Lyles said. "When the captain sent his answer to the railway bureau, a couple of boys from Dodge—they haul meal for the quartermaster from time to time—they managed to have a look at it. Then they lit out for Dodge City with a pair of drifters. They work for the land drummer, O'Brien."

"I saw them leave," MacCallister said. "Is there a good farrier in town?"

"Eugene Paul's about the best there is." Lyles grinned, cutting his eyes toward Falcon's big black horse waiting in a feed stall. "He's got the little barn behind the livery. I don't know if he's ever put shoes on any son of a bitch as mean as that, but I reckon he'd try."

"And a hotel?"

"Dodge House, I guess. It's open all the time. Ah . . . these boys and me, we're goin' to town after a bit. I could show you where the smithy is."

"I'll find it," Falcon said. "Thanks again." He led Diablo from his stall, spread a folded blanket on the black's broad back, and threw his saddle atop it.

The three privates had hung around, listening. Now one of them, an eastern kid named Finch, said, "I read about you back home, Mr. MacCallister. The papers say you're sure and sudden with those guns of yours." Finch glanced at the big .44 at Falcon's hip, and at its twin thrust into his belt. "Do you really shoot like they say?"

"I don't know what the newspapers say." Falcon shrugged, cinching up the saddle. "But I don't consider a revolver an ornament. In this country, a man carries guns because he might need them. Happen he does need them, he'd best know which end to point."

"Yes, sir." Finch grinned. "I guessed that's how you'd see it. We've got day leave, an' we heard the talk. There's always a few hard cases looking for trouble in Dodge. Do you think you might need any help?"

"They mean that," Lyles assured him. "These boys may be green to army life, but I'll vouch for all three of them in a social situation."

Falcon removed Diablo's tether and set his headstall, easing the bit into his mouth. The horse was as fresh and ready to run as though he had been on pasture. "I'll keep that in mind," he said. He turned to Lyles. "Who's O'Brien?"

"Land drummer," the sergeant said. "He's been around lately, hawkin' squatter plots in the Neutral Strip."

"No Man's Land?"

"Sure," Lyles shrugged. "Folks are land hungry. Some come to homestead, some with booster patents. Buy acreage sight unseen, anyplace somebody'll issue a title. Lately it's been foothills claims over in Colorado. Folks back east buy land from some riverboat drummer, then they haul out here thinkin' they'll settle on their property. The latest bonanza is the Neutral Strip. Some speculator's claimed a land patent down there, south of Hardwoodville. O'Brien's sellin' town lots an' parcels."

Falcon's eyes narrowed. That was what had happened to those massacred travelers he found. They had been on their way to the foothills to prove up on a land deed bought back east.

Apparently the land sharks were becoming more brazen now. There was no legitimate claim land in the Neutral Strip. It was a lawless zone—no law, no legal residents, no claimable land.

"Who's doing the selling?" he asked offhandedly.

"The deeds are issued by a Colonel Amos DeWitt. They're patent claim deeds. Don't have any weight in a court of law, but then there's no courts in the

Neutral Strip. Anybody can sell anybody anything down there, if anybody wants to buy."

"So what makes them valuable?"

"O'Brien claims there's a town down there, past the line, with a railroad headin' for it."

Shouts and a clatter of harness chain came through the open doors. Outside on the parade ground, a dozen soldiers were piling aboard a wagon. When they were aboard, the driver hied the mule team out through the main gate and turned west.

"Looks like you fellows missed your ride to town," Falcon noted.

Lyles shrugged. "We'll get there," he said.

The sun rode low on the western horizon when Falcon MacCallister headed out of Fort Dodge, bound for the brawling little town five miles away. Up ahead, where the trail dipped into rolling hills, he could still see the furlough wagon—a rocking dusty silhouette against the horizon. Even there, along a traveled road in settled country, the land was vast and lonely.

He tipped his hat low, shielding his eyes from the headlong glare of sunset. With sunset, the wind turned chill and a million stars emerged in the sky. From the first rise, he could see the sprawling lamplit stain that was Dodge City, straight ahead.

It would be full dark when he got there, but Dodge didn't look like a town that would close when the day ended. He could smell the place on the west wind, and a mile out he could hear it.

With that sixth sense that a man develops when he's outlived some who tried to kill him, Falcon read the wind and knew that there were men nearby whose eyes were on him, and their intentions weren't friendly.

In any trail town—particularly a boomtown like

Dodge where men came together in the most volatile conditions—there were always those who hungered for gold, those who thirsted for blood, and those who dreamed of power. There were ambitious men, driven men, hell-raisers, and bullies. And among them, always, were the hard-eyed predators whose lust was for combat—to prove and prove again, by provocation and duel—that they were better than other men at the art of killing.

Falcon was used to that. His size, his appearance, and the big gun he wore in open leather made him a natural target for those fools who wanted to try their luck. And for any who recognized him, his name and reputation magnified the attraction.

The trouble with having a reputation as a gunslinger was that every fool kid, crackbrain, and mean drunk with a six-gun just ached to test that reputation if it was the last thing he did.

ELEVEN

Trail Street was quiet when Falcon rode in from the east. The general stores, millineries, shops, and markets were locked and boarded, the stage depot and bank dark, the dozen or so land offices, law offices, and hide brokers closed for the night. Most of the locals had gone home to their suppers and their beds. It was early yet for the night crowds, though the number of horses at hitching posts outside the town's saloons and eating places showed that they would begin spilling out into the streets soon enough.

In the lingering twilight of the high plains Falcon spotted two tin stars—a deputy marshal carrying loaded trays across from the nearest beanery to the jail, and a second one standing guard for him in the doorway there. He passed them by, headed for the sprawling outline of the livery barn, and found the smith's cabin just beyond it.

There was lantern light in the windows, and Falcon rapped at the door. The man who opened it, Eugene Paul, was young, dark-bearded, and husky.

"I need a stall for my horse," Falcon said, gesturing, "and a span of shoes when your forge is hot."

"That'll be morning," Paul told him. "But I can board him for the night. You want to leave him?"

"I'll give you a hand." Falcon smiled. "Diablo doesn't often tolerate strangers."

In the rear of the livery barn, Falcon stripped off Diablo's saddle, rubbed him down, and gentled him into a stall by lantern light while the smith forked winter hay into the trough and added a bait of sorghum grain.

As Paul closed the gate, another lantern appeared at the barn door. Falcon eased into shadows, then stepped out again when the new glow revealed a tin star.

It was one of the deputy marshals—the one who had been standing outside the jail. He stepped forward, squinting, and held his lantern high. Behind him came a taller older man with bushy eyebrows and a big mustache. "You're MacCallister, aren't you?" he asked.

"You know me?"

"You're a known man. And I've heard some talk." He stepped past the deputy, nodded at Eugene Paul, and came near, peering at Falcon. "The name's Stroud," he said. "Sam Stroud. I'm the city marshal here."

Falcon relaxed a little. The eyes and the tone said he was an honest man—a worried one, but fair. "This here's my deputy," the marshal continued. "Name of Bud Wheaton. You *are* Falcon MacCallister, aren't you?"

"I am," Falcon said. "Any problem with that?"

"Well, there could be," Stroud said. "You have some enemies, MacCallister. There are people looking for you around here."

Falcon shrugged. "I wouldn't be surprised. I saw a couple of hotheads coming this way, from the fort sutler's store. I know them, and they know me. But I wouldn't worry too much about them. Jack Cabot and Sandy Hogue aren't the kind to stand up to a man face-to-face, and I don't think they'd try back-shooting where there are witnesses."

"Cabot and Hogue?" Stroud squinted. "Those must be the drifters that came in with the Carlyle boys. They're around here someplace, and so are the Carlyles. But you've got more trouble than that. Some jasper put out a wire on you today. Half the gunnies in town have probably seen it. It offers five hundred dollars for your head."

Falcon stared at the lawman in disbelief. Even in a place like Dodge, a little helltown two hundred miles from anyplace, offering a public bounty on a man was almost unheard of.

"A private bounty?" he demanded. "Who did that?"

"Well, that's an odd thing. The telegram was sent from Newton, but the only name on it was the letter S. It was sent to the land drummer, August O'Brien. He must have shown it around. By the time I heard about it, half the fools in Dodge had read it. I know it don't hold water, Mr. MacCallister. A private bounty's ridiculous, this day and age. But there are some around here who don't show good sense when they're liquored up. There's just no telling what might happen as long as you're in town."

"What about this O'Brien? Have you talked to him?"

"He isn't here. Bud thinks he lit out this after-noon, heading for the Neutral Strip."

"His horse is gone," Bud Wheaton said. "Real nice sorrel racer. One of the hide traders across the river saw him going southwest. I guess he's headed for the Neutral Strip, because there sure isn't much else in that direction."

Falcon cut his eyes toward the deputy, then back

to Stroud. "So what do you want from me?" he asked.

Outside the barn, a racket arose as two buckboard wagons passed slowly, both loaded with talking, laughing men. "Potatoes?" a jovial voice whooped. "You plan to grow potatoes in Colorado? Blanchard, you're crazy as a loon!"

"Tell me that when I'm rich, Tom!" a man answered, "I'm tellin' you, that's the best cash crop a man can have. Sell direct to miners an' railroaders! I'll sell potatoes by the long ton, you watch!"

"I'll put my money on corn and beans!" another offered. "Potatoes take sandy loam, and regular water. You won't find that just ever'place!"

"It'll be there!" the one called Blanchard said. "My brother's already out there, pickin' and choosin'. He left early to get us the right claims!"

The wagons passed, and from somewhere else nearby a chorus of taunting voices erupted: "Squatters!" "Live good while ya can, fools!" "You'll starve on dry-land claims!"

"We'll be there when you're gone, cowboy!" someone responded. "We won't be starved out nor burned out, neither!"

Slowly, the mounting hostilities receded up the street. "I've got me a handful of town here," Marshal Sam Stroud said. "Settlers and speculators, gunslingers up from No Man's Land, grudge fights and brawls. Night riders burnin' barns for twenty miles around, and the damn lawyers and land sharks always stirrin' things up. I just try to keep Dodge as peaceful as I can. I'd appreciate your cooperation."

"I don't aim to start any trouble," Falcon assured him. "I'm here for a meal and a night's sleep, and to use the telegraph when the office opens. Then I'll be on my way."

"That sounds all right," Stroud nodded. "I'd let you bed down at the jail if you want, but that's just an offer. I don't have cause to insist." He glanced at the big .44 at Falcon's hip. "Word is, you're mighty sudden with that iron. What if somebody takes a notion to try you on for size?"

Falcon smiled coldly. "What would *you* do, Marshal, if somebody shot at you?"

"I'd shoot back, of course."

"Then you understand my inclinations. I appreciate your offer, but I don't believe I want to spend the night in jail. I'll make do."

"Palace Hotel," Bud offered. "You can get a meal there, too. They'll have the kitchen fire goin' 'til midnight."

Out on the street, the noise level was rising. Some riders had come in—men from the farms downriver and from the wagon camp out on the flats—and the sounds of voices carried into the barn. Somewhere a piano was being tuned up.

The saloons were serving, the dance halls were open, and the gaming tables were getting some use. There was talk on the street of night riders and squatter disputes. There were some powerful grudges out there. It was going to be a typical Dodge evening.

"Oh, Lordy." Stroud shook his head, listening. "Drifters, land sharks, politicians, mean drunks, and lawyers. First sign of spring, they pop up like ragweed. Not to mention the hell bein' raised over those rawhiders butcherin' stolen cattle down around Hardwoodville."

"That's a little outside your jurisdiction, isn't it?"

"It would be." Stroud sighed. "Except they bring their beef to Dodge and sell it. The Sawlog and

Smokey Hill ranches are out to put a stop to that, sure enough.

"I don't mean offense, Mr. MacCallister," he added, "but I'll rest easier after you move on." The marshal turned and strode out of the barn, followed by his grinning deputy.

Eugene Paul hadn't said a word through the entire discussion. Now he watched the law depart, then turned to Falcon. "Jamie Ian MacCallister was your father, wasn't he?"

Falcon turned. "He was."

"Then you have a friend in me," the smith said. "And some others, too, if you want them. Hadn't been for Jamie Ian MacCallister, my family would never have made it through the war. I don't recollect much of it, and I never quite sorted out all of Pa's stories about what happened in sixty-seven, but I know I owe your daddy my ma's life, and maybe my own and my sister's."

"He got around some." Falcon nodded. "I guess none of us ever heard all of it. Your family's name is Paul?"

"It was Paulson, back in Tennessee. Pa changed it when he got to Missouri."

"I heard the name Blanchard a bit ago. You know any Blanchards?"

Paul thought for a moment. "None here in town. Maybe out at the wagon camp. Want me to ask around?"

"Never mind. Just take care of Diablo."

The smith stuck out a hand, and Falcon clasped it. It was a good honest hand, as hard as the metal it worked. "You need anything around here, you just sing out," Paul said.

"Obliged," Falcon told him. "But I'm just passing through." He walked the few feet to the open door and peered out into the deepening dusk. In the distance, eastward along Trail Street, several buckboards full of hungry men—and a few women among them—had pulled up in front of a two-story building. Lanterns on posts lit the sign that said *Palace Hotel Dinah's Fine Food.*

Eugene Paul stepped into the stall with Diablo and patted the horse on the neck, then worked his way to the black's nose, murmuring to him. He came out a moment later. "Your horse will be ready when you are," he said. We'll get along fine."

As Falcon picked up his gear the smith said, "Keep an eye out for a big buster named John Moline, Mr. MacCallister. He's a local bully, hangs around the Palace and Spiro's looking for trouble. He's gunned down a couple of drunks, and thinks he's a bad man."

A cold wind was blowing from the west when Falcon MacCallister stepped into the warmth and glow of the Palace Hotel lobby. The lobby occupied one fourth of the ground floor of the two-story building. The remaining three-fourths, opening off the lobby through a wide open archway with a gilt sign proclaiming Dinah's, was a big dining room served from a busy kitchen.

The place was packed with people of all descriptions. At every table and bench men, women, and children dined on beefsteak and fresh bread while others stood along the walls, waiting. A dozen or so harried-looking women with starched bonnets and long aprons hurried in and out through the back serving door, carrying platters.

Falcon's stomach growled appreciatively at the wafting aroma of freshly baked bread. It was a while, he realized, since he had eaten any decent cooking but his own. But he had things to do, first.

At the lacquered desk, a night clerk watched him approach and opened the registration book. Any man carrying saddlebags, duffle, bedroll, and a rifle was obviously a customer.

"I need a bed for the night," Falcon said. "Private room, if you have it. And I'll want one of those beef steaks in there."

"Room's a dollar," the clerk said. "Clean sheets and two oil lamps. Privy's just outside, and there's water on the washstand. Dinah's charges separate."

Falcon signed in, glancing at the names on the register. "You know any of those people who just came in?"

"Those are wagon people." The clerk shrugged. "Homesteaders, mostly. They come in all the time, but just for a meal. They don't sleep here."

A big smudge-faced man lounging at the end of the counter had been looking Falcon up and down. Now he said, "That's big iron you carry there, Mr. Know how to use it?"

"Well enough," Falcon said, not looking around. He paid over his dollar and picked up his gear. "Which room?"

The clerk handed him a skeleton key on a brass ring. "Two-oh-five," he said. "Upstairs, on the left."

Falcon turned toward the stairs.

The smudge-faced man scowled and straightened. "I believe I was talkin' to you, Mr."

"Go talk to somebody else," Falcon muttered. Without a backward glance, he went to find his room.

The Palace Hotel, like every other plank-built structure in Dodge City in 1881, was so new its timbers still creaked and settled. But behind its elaborate false front it was a sturdy structure, built by a crew of German immigrants out from Mound Ridge.

Falcon glanced around the little room, then tested the bed and judged it acceptable. He stripped down, washed himself at the washstand, then put on a fresh shirt from his pack and cleaned his hat and boots. The dark broadcloth suit in his duffle was a pleasant change from worn buckskins. He shaved, and put it on. Finally, he cleaned and oiled his .44s, strapped one on, and shoved the second into his waistband.

By the light of an oil lamp he retrieved a little oilskin package from his saddlebags, unwrapped it, and sat for a moment gazing at its contents. Then he dropped it into a coat pocket and went downstairs.

What must be done now was not going to be easy, but he had it to do.

At the foot of the stairs he paused for a moment, then walked through the archway into Dinah's. It took him only a few seconds to spot the wagon crowd. They were seated at three tables near the front, working on platters of steak and potatoes.

"Is there someone here named Blanchard?" Falcon asked.

At the nearest table, someone turned—a young man, sturdy and clean-shaven, accompanied by a young woman and a little boy. "I'm Tom Blanchard," he said. "Who are you?"

"Falcon MacCallister. Are you Owen Blanchard's brother?"

"That's right."

MacCallister hesitated. He hated what came next, but there was no alternative. Removing his hat, he handed Blanchard the oilskin package. "I guess this is yours."

The package contained all that Falcon had salvaged from the massacre out in that Colorado gully—a Bible with names and dates, a piece of a map, a battered clasp knife, a scrap of lace, and an ornate locket of inset ivory hearts in a gold oval. They were things the outlaws had somehow overlooked. Every other personal thing he had found out there was either bloodstained and ruined, or destroyed. He had buried all that with the victims' remains.

Tom Blanchard stared at the mute salvage, his shoulders going stiff. Beside him, his wife gasped and started to cry.

"I'm sorry," Falcon said. "I found them. What was left of them. They were . . . robbed and murdered, by outlaws."

"Owen . . ." Blanchard murmured. "My God!" He turned stricken eyes to the stranger. "Where? When?"

"All of them?" The woman sobbed. "Ruth and . . . and the children, too? And Bob Simms?"

In a quiet corner of the hotel lobby, Falcon related what he had seen and what it meant. The Blanchards sat huddled, too stunned yet to grieve, while others from their wagon party gathered around. The clerk was asleep at his counter, and there was no one else around at the moment except people coming and going from Dinah's.

"I buried them proper," Falcon said, finally. "Then I picked up the trail of their wagon. I think I know where those men were going."

"How about the law?" one of the men demanded. "Aren't there sheriffs or . . . or somebody, to deal with those monsters?"

Falcon shrugged. "Law's spread real thin out there in the slopes," he said. "And where those men went, there's no law at all. I'll send a report to the authorities in Denver as soon as the telegraph opens tomorrow, and you can contact them, too. Don't expect much, though. There isn't much they can do."

"But those men!" Blanchard insisted. "You say you know where they went?"

"I think so, and I'm going after them. I'll need to know how to contact you, if I can recover your brother's property." He stood and put on his hat. "I'm real sorry about what happened to your brother and his family," he said. "Nothing's gonna make that right, but I promise you those owlhoots won't get off scot-free."

At the door, a couple of the homesteaders caught up with him—young men who could have been brothers. Both had the sloping shoulders and big hard hands of farmers, and both carried sidearms. "Why are you goin' after those men, Mr. MacCallister?" one asked. "What's your business in all this?"

"It's personal," Falcon said. "I have reasons of my own."

The answer wasn't good enough. "Do you know those murderers?" they asked. "Did they do somethin' to you, too? Is that it?"

"I don't know them," Falcon shrugged. "Let's just say I've seen way too much of their kind. I guess I just can't tolerate any more."

The cold night wind was as bleak as Falcon's spirits when he stepped out into the night. There was music and laughter coming from a place across the street, and he headed that way, wanting to shake off the dismal memories of lonely graves on the Colorado plains, and of the grief his news had brought to the Blanchards. The memories were pitfalls, leading down to the aching emptiness that his wife's death had left.

Spiro's Saloon offered a raucous rowdy haven of gaiety in a cold hard world, and Falcon needed a drink.

He spotted a few familiar faces in the crowd. Jack Cabot and Sandy Hogue were at a gaming table off to one side, with several other men. And he saw a little knot of soldiers from the fort, keeping to themselves in a far corner.

As he stepped to the bar and ordered whiskey, a snarling voice came from behind him. "Why, here's the gent that don't talk to common folks!"

Falcon turned. It was the tough from the hotel. "You turned your back on me once before, Mr.," he said. "Nobody insults John Moline a second time."

The man was braced, just spoiling for a fight, and ready to slap leather. Falcon gazed at him levelly, then stepped away from the bar. "I've had enough of you," he said.

Whatever Moline may have been expecting—bluster or a move to draw—he wasn't ready for what came next. Falcon stepped away from the bar, then stepped again, and abruptly Moline found himself doubled over a fist that exploded like a mule's kick into his belly. He went white and bent over, and another fist came from down around the knees to cartwheel him backward.

The tough sprawled on his back, bleeding from broken lips and nose, and Falcon stood over him. With a quick swoop he hauled Moline's gun from its holster, emptied its chambers, and cast it aside.

"You picked a real bad time for a chat, fella," he said.

The room had gone dead still, and every eye was on him. Falcon looked around, sizing up the crowd one by one, then rested his cold gaze on the side table where Cabot and Hogue sat.

"Anybody else?" he asked. When there were no answers he went back to the bar and downed his jigger of rotgut. He really ought to thank John Moline, he told himself. He felt a whole lot better now.

They dragged the unconscious Moline out of the place, and the piano player went back to his work. When Falcon looked around again, Cabot and Hogue were gone, and maybe a dozen others. Three tables had emptied.

Sergeant Jack Lyles was pushing through the crowd with a couple of his fledglings, signaling for a hand in the game the former Noonan riders had left.

"You sure know how to make an impression, Mac-Callister," the sergeant said.

Billy Challis and Tuck Kelly were miles southwest of Dodge by the time dawn touched the prairie sky. They had gone up to Dodge on a whim, to nose around and maybe get drunk. But at Spiro's Saloon they heard the talk—a big yellow-haired man with a big gun was on the warpath. He had blood in his eye, and he was looking for the men who took a prairie schooner over in Colorado.

They heard it from an eavesdropping hotel clerk, from talk among homesteaders. From Sandy Hogue and Jack Cabot, from fort gossip, they heard about Falcon MacCallister.

Then, abruptly, they heard what happened to John Moline, and put two and two together.

Falcon MacCallister was a legend. But now the legend was real, and taking a personal interest in Asa Parker's game. And he knew just where to look.

The owlhoots rode toward No Man's Land, and others joined them for the ride. At Crooked Creek Billy Challis turned upstream, where a bare-limbed cottonwood grove offered some shelter. "Let's hole up here a while," he said. "I'd like to get a look at that yahoo Cabot's been talkin' about."

TWELVE

. . . JRHORNER KPR DENVER STOP *ATT
WYLIE* STOP *MSG RCD* STOP *SEE AUTH DEN-
VER RE RBMD BLANCHARDS* STOP *SIX MEN
STL RIG BND SE WOLF CREEK NTRL STP* STOP
IN PURSUIT STOP *FALMAC* STOP *DODGE
CITY* STOP

From the Western Union terminal at Denver, the
message was rekeyed to Kansas Pacific's private wire
and received at the division land office in the Waring Building. A garter-sleeved clerk delivered it to
Sebastian Wylie. Wylie composed a list of questions
and dispatched runners to the Denver Constable's
office, the courthouse, and the resident federal marshal. Within the half hour, he had a copy of Falcon
MacCallister's telegram reporting the burial of murdered homesteaders in the southeast foothills.
Armed with this, he took MacCallister's latest message and rapped at the door of J.R. Horner.

Together, they peered at the message, and Horner
said, "Translate, please."

"It's from Falcon MacCallister," Wylie explained.
"We can be fairly sure it's authentic, because of the
survey code shorthand. It was sent from Dodge City,

Kansas. He says six men and a stolen conveyance are bound for someplace called Wolf Creek, in the Neutral Strip. He is pursuing them. He says to see the authorities in Denver regarding robbery and murder of someone called the Blanchards. I've done that. The federal marshal confirms a report—from MacCallister—of finding a family of movers dead and robbed."

"Does this have something to do with our missing land money?"

"I can only assume it does, sir." Wylie shrugged. "Otherwise why would he tell us about it?"

"Then the six men he reports are the same who stole our money? Asa Parker and his men?" Horner's voice was a deep growl. "Do the authorities verify this?"

"I don't see how they could, at this moment." Wylie removed his reading glasses and cleaned them with a pocket kerchief. "Apparently MacCallister thinks they are. But what if they are, sir? How do we proceed? There are no legal authorities in the Neutral Strip. That's No Man's Land."

"We're a railroad, Wylie. Private enterprise, with government sanction to conduct our business as we see fit. We don't have the limitations of law. If there is no law, we make our own." Horner turned to a big section-gridded map on the wall. He stooped to peer at its lower right corner. "The Neutral Strip . . . south of both Colorado and Kansas . . . buffer between Kansas and Texas . . . runs from Black Mesa and the Cimarron breaks on the west, over to the Indian territories east . . . there's nothing shown here, Wylie. No features at all."

"No, sir. As I said, the Neutral Strip is No Man's Land. There's nothing there . . . officially."

"Well, it's all outside of our grants and bounds.

That region is all C.R.I.P territory. Julius Randolph's domain. Lordy, wouldn't that son of a bitch love this, if he heard about it! Nine thousand dollars in Kansas Pacific currency straying over into his claims! I guess to protect myself, I'd better notify the U.S. Bureau of Transportation . . . about the robbery, and all."

"They already know, sir. We've had an inquiry from a Mr. Sypher about it. He also inquired about our broadcast alert for Mr. MacCallister."

"Oh, he did, did he?" Horner frowned. "Nosy functionary, isn't he? I assume we haven't responded?"

"No, sir. Private dealings within the company are none of the bureau's business. Not unless we choose to make them so."

Horner nodded. "Very well. Establish contact with Mr. MacCallister, Wylie. Advise him that—"

"Sir, I don't know how to contact him. He's left Dodge City, and the only working wire beyond there is someplace called Hardwoodville. Out on the Cimarron. There's nothing in the Neutral Strip."

Horner's scowl was like a thundercloud. "Then find him! Find him, Wylie. I want this matter resolved, before the transportation bureau calls in federal marshals. My God, Randolph could swing votes with this! He could make me a laughing stock!"

"Sir?"

"Our stock would drop by half if word got out that we had set bounty on persons or properties within the claimed jurisdiction of another railroad. The C.R.I.P. would love to take over our land rights. So would A.T.S.F. They're both bargaining right this minute for transcontinental privileges."

"But this is simply a matter of recovering stolen property, sir."

"That stolen money came from public funds,

Wylie. Right now, it is unaccounted for and out of my control, and this MacCallister has no more credentials than a bounty hunter out for a posted reward! I want you to find him and get him on our payroll. Make it clear that he is working for the Kansas Pacific in this matter!"

Wylie shrugged, shaking his head ruefully. "I'll try, sir. Do you really think he'd trade a finder's share of nine thousand dollars for railroad wages?"

"Damn the wages," Horner sighed. "He can have the whole nine thousand if he recovers it. Just don't let the bureau or Randolph get to him first! Find him, Wylie. Do it! In the meanwhile, I'll notify Julius Randolph and the C.R.I.P. that we have an agent in pursuit of felons somewhere between Dodge City and Texas. *Our* agent, an employee on legitimate railroad business."

Falcon MacCallister was completely unaware of the political turmoil seething in his wake as he topped out on the great swell of grassland south of Crooked Creek and headed into the sand hills above the Cimarron's north bend.

He had covered nearly forty miles since leaving Dodge City, and his eyes ached from hours of squinting into bright skies across distant horizons. The land was wide and empty, with the illusion of featureless prairie that always confounded so many travelers.

Since leaving Dodge City he had not seen a sign of civilization. It was as though the westward advance of progress ended where the rails did. Mile after endless mile, there had been no sign of humanity. It was illusion, though. Out here a man could see forever, but much of what was there was hidden.

He had known for at least ten miles that he was no longer alone. For the past hour there had been riders to his left and behind, moving with him across the miles, being careful to stay out of sight. To the hunter's eyes of Falcon MacCallister, though, they were discernible. Flocks of birds, hints of dust, even the telltale stance of a little group of antelope far away were like signal flags, saying where the riders were.

He didn't how many there were, but he guessed who they were—a bunch of drifters, toughs, and bounty hunters who had left Dodge some hours ahead of him. They must have holed up somewhere, waiting for him to pass. Whoever they were, they sure weren't friendly. For most of the ride, up on the flat plains, that they were there had been just a fact to note—a matter of curiosity. They had kept their distance. But it was sunset now, and the sand hills offered more cover than the empty prairies. The riders were crowding in, too, still furtive but getting closer.

He knew they would show their hand soon, and it would be at a place of their own choosing.

He knew that Cate and Hogue were among them. It didn't matter much who the rest were. What did was staying alive.

He had let Diablo set his pace, pushing the followers hard. They would be expecting him to stop soon. Forty miles was a long day's ride. In the sunset he saw the sand hills spreading before him—ancient dunes now covered with sparse surface grass but still contoured by centuries of ceaseless wind. They would be marking time out there, guessing at how far he would go before making camp. And they would be thinking about an ambush.

He saw the spot they would likely choose. A mile

ahead, shadowed in slanting sunset, rose a high crest that stood like a slanted wall across his trail.

He would head for that dune. A tired rider on a tired horse, he would decide to rest there rather than make the climb tonight. So they would figure.

And if they got around behind the ridge, they could pick him off with braced rifles, or at least pin him down and come at him without warning whenever they were ready.

Making camp below that dune—out of the night wind—was what any tired man might do. And setting an ambush there was what any outlaw bunch would do. Neither was what Falcon had in mind.

Whether or not they knew him, it was unlikely that they really knew Diablo. Most folks didn't expect a horse like Diablo.

Full seventeen hands and in his prime, the big black was a mix of racer and warhorse. And from long experience, Falcon knew that he had more stamina than any two ordinary horses. He was tired now, of course. But his shoes were new, his legs sound, and he had not yet begun to show a lather.

"Let's make this interesting, sport," Falcon muttered as the rising of a dune hid him from any spotters to the east. "Let's see if they mean business."

To anyone watching from the surrounding crests, the rider disappearing behind the lone dune was a weary traveler plodding one last mile before supper camp.

But what came into view on the other side, half a mile south, was a fresh racer at full gallop, showering sand in little sprays at each long stride.

Falcon had covered three hundred yards in full view and was still gaining speed when he heard the first distant shouts off his left flank. "Let it out, boy," he urged Diablo as he bent low over the black's neck. "Show those buggers how it's done."

Like black thunder, Diablo flew down the trail and the rising dune came to meet them.

The old dune was eighty feet high—a slipping sliding ridge of compacted sand barely clad in thin sparse clumps of grass. In the flare-light of sunset, shadows faded and features were obscured. Falcon let Diablo have his head, to select his own path.

At a sharp angle they climbed, rivulets of sand cascading behind them. Falcon let the horse climb nearly to the top of the dune, then tightened the reins and turned him. Bounding and skidding, they descended the slope, straight down its face, and Falcon guided to the left.

He had left plain trail to the top of the dune. But in the dimming twilight his descending trail—several hundred yards to the west—left no visible track at all.

Twenty minutes later Falcon crawled on his belly to the crest of a scoured-out dune and looked toward the long ridge. There were at least fifteen riders over there, a few at the top, the rest scrambling upward. By fading evening light they were hardly more than moving shadows against the ancient sands.

Those at the top had halted, milling here and there, straining to see into the darkening valley beyond. Their voices drifted back on the wind: "Where'd he go? I can't see a damn thing!" "He's down there someplace! Somebody get out a glass! Look toward the river!" "Hell, Billy, I don't see anything out there! The son of a bitch just disappeared!"

One by one the shadows converged at the crest of the dune, then disappeared over it.

As evening became night, Falcon MacCallister passed the time resting himself and his horse. There was little graze in the sand hills, but a handful of grain and a hatful of water kept Diablo content for a time. MacCallister's supper was pemmican and water. With darkness the winds turned cold, but he made no fire. With Diablo tended, he wrapped himself in his soogans and allowed himself a hunter's nap—dozing an hour with his senses alert.

Two hours after the riders had passed, MacCallister crossed that same rise—the rim of the sandy lands—at a different point and paused at the crest. It was full night then, but the silvery glow of brilliant, high plains starlight lighted the land. From the high crest he could see vague patterns in the sandy swales below—pale patches where hooves had gouged the grass and stirred the sand in passing.

Even by starlight the trail pointed like road sign, saying where the riders had gone. Falcon nudged Diablo down the incline. At the foot of it he cut west, then southwest again. Only a fool would ride a fresh trail of men who hunted him. He followed the trail, all right, but he took his own path and it was aside—taking advantage of the terrain for natural cover.

A mile or two along, he found them. Their night camp was pitched in a trough among the sand hills. Beyond, the starlit land sloped away into distance, toward the valley of the Cimarron.

He left Diablo in a little cove just above and west of the gang's camp, and went in on foot.

Most of the gang were asleep, around the embers of their cookfire. A small group at the fire was talking quietly, all facing the low-burning flames.

Fools, he thought. They felt the safety of numbers, and had set no guards outside the camp. Using the

cover of the rolling, windswept dunes, Falcon
slipped close. At thirty yards he could make out a
few faces in the firelight, and hear a few words carried on the cold erratic wind. The few still awake
were staring into the fire, speaking now and again
as men do when they mistake darkness for shelter.

Just a few years ago, Falcon thought, *this bunch
wouldn't have lasted the night out here. Any band of rov-
ing Kiowa or Cheyenne who happened along could have
walked right in on them and killed every last one while
they were still fire-blind.*

He recognized a few of them, faces he had seen
at Dodge. One of them he knew by name. Sandy
Hogue was still awake, near the fire. Falcon knew
that Jack Cabot was there, too.

Watching the men around the fire, it was easy
to spot the one who dominated this gang. A short
barrel-chested young man with the shoulders of a
wrestler and the eyes of a snake made it clear by
his every move and glance that he was in charge.
Falcon studied him closely. Long cornsilk hair
hung wild below his flat-crowned hat, and the firelight lit a face that might have been a child's—a
round-cheeked beardless face with only a little stub-
ble, a face that seemed designed for laughter until
one looked again at these cold slitted eyes in it.

Instinct told Falcon that this was no show-off kid.
This was a dangerous man, with a flaring temper
that could be wild and lethal. Despite his youthful
appearance, this one was no child. This was a dangerous man—far more dangerous than most of the
toughs and saddle tramps around him.

In the shadows just away from the fire, another
one who didn't seem to fit lay sprawled on a sand
slope, resting on a saddle as if it were a forty-pound
pillow. This one didn't join in the talk, but Falcon

had the feeling that these two were partners. Where baby face went, the quiet one would be there, too.

Then he heard a few words of conversation on the faltering wind, and learned a name. Baby face was called Billy.

Falcon catalogued them all in his mind. Billy and his quiet shadow, Jack Cabot and Sandy Hogue, two or three more from the tables at Spiro's. The rest were saddle bums, fiddle-footed badmen along for the ride, and maybe a share in whatever came to hand. There were thirteen in all.

Falcon spent an hour in the gang's camp, slipping from one point to another, listening and sizing them up, before he decided he had learned all he could.

Cabot and Hogue might have set this bunch onto Falcon's trail, or some of them might be thinking of that private bounty that someone with the initial S had advertised. Mostly, though, the bunch was heading for No Man's Land, to sign on for wages with someone called The Colonel. Billy and his partner were encouraging them, and directing them.

Someone in No Man's Land was paying top dollar for gunhands, and among the words Falcon heard were Wolf Creek and Paradise.

Falcon was watching from a distance when the gang headed out at dawn. They scattered out and circled for a time, looking for his trail, then began drifting southwestward by twos and threes, toward the Cimarron Valley. He lost sight of a lot of them for a while, and when he saw them bunched again they were half a mile away—tiny figures of mounted men heading away.

Patiently he lay concealed atop a dune and counted them. Then he counted them again. There were only eleven now. He scanned the surrounding lands, and watched the gang until they were out of sight, but saw no sign of the missing two.

He was on his way back to where he had left his horse when something whisked past his ear like an angry bee. Even before the sound of the gunshot reached him, he was crouched and running, heading for the only cover in sight.

A second bullet kicked sand in his face as he dived into a shallow wash screened with sparse bone-white grass. He tried to see where it had come from, and something hot scorched his shoulder like flying fire.

He flattened himself, counted six heartbeats, and rolled aside, belly-down and several feet from where he had been. Hanging his hat on the muzzle of his rifle, he held it at arm's length and raised it slowly, only a few inches. Hard sand erupted six inches from its brim, and this time he saw where the shot came from.

The shooter was a hundred and fifty yards away, firing from behind a comblike ridge. Now he knew where the missing outlaws had gone.

Without returning fire, Falcon edged farther to the left. Winds had scoured out a little shelter here, a foot-deep depression under the shallow swell of the sand. He kept low and out of sight, digging in, giving himself a little cover. Then he waited.

Moments passed. Then, on that comb ridge out there, a shape changed. Aligning his rifle, Falcon pumped three quick shots toward it and saw the dust spray as his bullets struck.

He didn't think he had hit anybody, but he had given them something to think about. He rested his rifle on cold earth, braced himself, and waited. They would have to show themselves to shoot, and now he was ready.

When the shots came, though, they were from his left, and the first bullet almost flattened him as it smashed into his ribs just above the canteen slung there. Like a coiling snake he swivelled, belly-down, and emptied his magazine at the disappearing silhouette atop a rise a hundred yards away.

Long wild hair waved beneath a flat-crowned hat as the sniper disappeared from sight in a shower of spraying sand and singing lead. The man was hit, but moving. He stumbled, swayed, then was gone.

Another shot from the north buzzed over Falcon as he struggled to reload his .44-40. The gun felt unusually heavy, and his fingers were awkward. Glancing down, he saw dark blood spreading, seeping through the cold sands beneath him. Too much blood.

With a dry curse he thumbed the last shell into the rifle, worked the lever, and began a methodical fire-and-fire-again—first at the knoll to the north, then at the rise to the west, then north again. Big lead bullets tore up the ground out there, and his shots echoed like rolling thunder.

The morning didn't seem as bright as it had. His vision was dimming from shock and lost blood. But he kept it up. He fired, waited a heartbeat, and fired again, as flitting shadows flicked along the crest of the north dune and disappeared.

Falcon was hit bad, and he knew it. His only hope now was that the ambushers didn't know how bad.

Staying flat, he got out his knife and cut a wide strip from the bottom of his buckskin shirt. He rolled over, wrapping the cured hide around him. He could feel the hole in his side, way around to the back, and could see the one in front—a gaping, bleeding tear just above the waist. Holding the bandage tight, he fired again, with one hand, toward the north ridge. There was no response.

Awkwardly, he levered another round into the chamber, then laid the rifle down to pull the bandage tight with all the strength of both hands. It was slippery, soaked with his blood, but he managed a tight knot. Drawing his belly gun, he pushed its muzzle under the buckskin on the right side, then twisted it there. The pressure of the binding sent flaring agonies through his left side, almost blinding him with pain, but he held the twist in place. Then he gave the gun one more cruel push and snugged its butt into the loop of his belt.

Falcon couldn't tell whether the hint of movement behind the little ridge to the north was the brim of somebody's hat, or just the grass waving in the wind. He managed one more shot from the .44-40. A cloud of dust scudded above the distant grassy dune.

He was still trying to work the lever for another shot when darkness closed in on him, shutting down like curtains all around—a darkness full of the sound of guns.

THIRTEEN

The buckboard wagon was no ambulance, but Jude Mason handled it like one. A blacklands farm boy grows up handling teams, hitches, and loads. He learns the feel of the leads, the sway of the bed, and how to avoid sudden bumps. From the first crossings of Cumberland through the war of Yankee aggression to the great migrations westward, those who handled the rigs and guided the wheels were always those whose roots were in the rich soil.

With strong sensitive fingers he manipulated the traces, guiding the buckboard up the long undulating slopes with the river behind them and the high plains still miles ahead. He eased around a washout while Jubal clung to the plank seat beside him. Behind, the horses on leads skipped this way and that, finding footing. Just behind the seat, Jonah crouched in the wagon bed and yelped, "Easy, easy, Jude! Lordy, you just goin' out of your way to hit every bump there is?"

"You can get out and ride your own horse if you don't like it," Jude said stolidly. "I'm doin' the best I can."

There were six of them in the party. Brett Archer was out ahead, riding lead and setting the pace. Two others, Johnny Lawrence and Buck Tyber, rode flank, keeping pace with the buckboard. Jubal and

Jonah had tied their mounts on behind, with the found horse, and now rode the pitching wagon with their brother. Of the three Mason boys, only Jonah, the youngest, was distinguishable, mostly because of his age. Jude and Jubal, the twins, were alike as peas in a pod—two sunburned farm boys cut from identical cloth.

Now Jubal turned to look back at their kid brother. "Just hang on, Jonah," he said. "And try to keep that feller from bleedin' any more. We still got a ways to go, but it'll smooth out once we're past these wash banks."

Muttering, Jonah relaxed a little and turned his attention to the sleeping man sprawled among the expedition's luggage. A big man, his straw-blond hair matted around his ears, he lay untroubled by the bumpy ride. The fresh linen wrapped around his middle showed a little blood, but no more than before. And though he looked as pale as death, his breathing was regular. He had been deathly pallid at first, and they had feared he would die during the night. But he had held on, somehow. He was still breathing shallowly, and gasping with each breath, but at least he was sleeping.

A smaller bandage covered a bullet burn on the man's shoulder, and a dozen small scabs were forming on his face, neck and the backs of his hands, where flying pebbles had nicked him. The main wound, though, was high on his belly, just left of the breadbasket. A bullet that had struck him low in the left back had come out in front, leaving a jagged hole that bled profusely. He had lost a lot of blood by the time they found him.

"Why were those jaspers shootin' at you, Mr. Mac-Callister?" Jonah muttered to his sleeping patient. "They run off when we showed up, and we never saw where they went. Brett figures they were some of that crowd that pulled out of Dodge last mornin' early. Why do you suppose they took you on that way?"

The sleeping eyes twitched as though the man might wake up, but then he settled again into sleep.

His head rested on the saddle they had taken off the black horse, and the horse plodded along on lead, with their own mounts. Brett Archer had thought he might ride the big black today, to rest his own horse. He had changed his mind about that. The stranger's horse didn't intend to be ridden.

At their noon stop, where cottonwoods grew along the streambed of the Cimarron, they had debated turning west for a few miles, to deliver their burden to the settlers at Hardwoodville. But they decided against it. The man called MacCallister was still alive, and all they could do at Hardwoodville was bury him. He stirred a little now and then, struggling, and they got some thin stew into him. He went back to sleep.

"We'll go on with him," Brett had decided. His dark eyes went moody and fierce as he fingered the little inlaid and ivory gold locket in his hand. "Maybe he'll come around before he dies. From what we heard in Dodge, Mr. MacCallister's our best hope of finding those . . . those damned snakes who killed Dorothy and her family."

Jonah squinted. "That blacksmith at Dodge said something about a medical man who had staked a claim at Horse Spring, right near the Strip line. I say we stop there, and get this gent looked at. Lord knows I'm no doctor, but if we need him alive, let's get help."

It wasn't so much concern for their passenger that

guided them toward Horse Spring, as it was the notion that he could help find the killers.

It was the goal they all shared in common now. Of the six of them, five were kin. The Mason brothers were cousins of Tom and Owen Blanchard. Hardly a word had passed among them that evening when they stood by as Falcon MacCallister delivered his news to Tom Blanchard. Owen was dead. He, his wife Ruth, their daughters Dorothy and Tess, and Ruth's brother Bob Simms. Outlaws had killed them. And MacCallister was going after the outlaws.

The three had made up their minds at that moment. Where outlaws could go, *they* could go, and their guns would be loaded. They might not be able to keep up with the moon-haired man on the black horse, but they could follow.

Buck Tyber and Johnny Lawrence were cousins of Simms, and they went, too.

Of the six, only the Virginian, Brett Archer, was not kin to any of the victims. But what drove him was strong. His reason was Owen Blanchard's oldest daughter, Dorothy. The locket the stranger brought—ivory hearts in gold—was Dorothy's. Brett Archer had given it to her before her family set out from Neosho, and he'd promised her that he would follow.

So now they turned south at Hackberry Ridge, and Archer rode ahead. Jubal and Jonah took turns nursing the wounded man while Jude drove the buckboard. They had set out from Dodge, thinking to follow his tracks. Now, without his tracks to follow, to lead them to the killers, they needed him.

As the wagon cleared the rutted wash to smoother ground, Jonah looked again at their passenger. The man looked more dead than alive, but he was still breathing. "You got the fortitude of a stud bull, Mr.

MacCallister," he muttered. "By rights that back-shot shoulda killed you, but it looks to me you're still fightin'."

They found Horse Creek, and they found the medical man—a horse doctor named Linsecum who changed the dressings on MacCallister's wounds and shook his head. "Reckon he'll be dead by night," he pronounced. "If it was me, I would. But if he sets out to mend, get him back here an' I'll take another look. An' tell him to come back if he commences bleedin' again."

At midafternoon they topped out on the south-west rim of the valley, and Brett Archer came riding back to call a halt. As always, his presence was a sobering influence on the rest of them. Even though he was barely past twenty, the dark-haired Virginian was an educated man, with the touch of sophistica-tion that The College of William and Mary provided. He had a smooth maturity about him, and a manner that made a man keenly aware of the pair of Dra-goon Colts that lurked beneath his dark coat.

Rumor had it that Brett Archer had killed a man—maybe more than one—in a stand-up duel back east, before migrating to the Neosho Valley, where the Blanchards met him. Certainly there was a dark brooding quality about the young man from Virginia.

Still, although the ominous rumors persisted, the people on the Neosho found no reason to shun the easterner. His manners and appearance were above reproach. Quiet and solicitous, Brett was a decent enough young man. He had a fine manner, and was always courtly in his dealings—a gentleman through and through. But not a man to be pushed.

Archer reined in beside the buckboard and looked down at the big man sleeping there. "He's still alive," he noted. "Keep him covered with those quilts, Jonah. The wind is cold. Has he said anything?"

"Not a word." Jonah shrugged. "Thought a couple of times he might be comm' around, but he just lays there."

"Loss of blood." Brett nodded. "It's like shock. Lord's wonder he's still twitching. Keep feeding him that beef stock whenever he'll take it." He stepped down from his saddle and looped the reins on the buckboard's wheel rim. "While we're resting here, let's have a look at that map the blacksmith drew. The state border is along here somewhere. Beyond is the Neutral Strip. Let's see if we can determine where Wolf Creek is."

Falcon awoke to the sight of starry skies seen through a broken roof, and the smell of coffee. He turned his head, squinting at what seemed to be the remains of a crude sod cabin. The roof was partly caved in, the strap-hung door was aslant, and the two little windows gaped shutterless into the night. The soddy looked as though a conquering army had marched through. The only shelter it offered was from the cold wind, but the baked mud hearth still kept a fire.

Falcon lay beneath piled quilts on a rickety canvas-and-stick cot. The only light was the fitful glow from the hearth, where several men huddled together.

He tried to raise himself, to sit up, and groaned when pain lanced his midriff. Beside the cot a figure stirred and said, "I think he's awake, fellers."

A moment later there were young men all around him, looking down at him. "You'll be all right, Mr.

MacCallister," one said. "Do you remember getting shot?"

The memories came back, and he nodded, gritting his teeth against the pain that seemed to envelope his entire left torso. "Where are we?" he rasped. "Who are you?"

"We were there when you told Tom Blanchard about his brother's family," the same one said. "We're kin. This place is an abandoned soddy. Looks like squatters built it, then moved on. We're somewhere in No Man's Land. Do you know who shot you?"

"I've got a name and a face," Falcon said. "A hard case named Billy Challis. I guess the one with him was his pard. What happened to them?"

"Don't know," another of the group said. "I guess we interrupted them. When we came up, they fired a few shots our way and we shot back. Then they ran off. One of them was saggin' like he'd been hit."

One of them pushed through with a plate and a spoon. "We got hot stew, Mr. MacCallister. Best you eat some of it if you can. I'm Jude Mason. These are my brothers Jubal and Jonah. That's Brett Archer there, and Johnny Lawrence an' Buck Tyber. Right now let's see if we can get some stew into you."

"Did you find my horse?"

"He's in the corral with the rest of the stock." Brett Archer's smile was just a quick pull at his cheeks below dark serious eyes. "The beast tried to kill me. Why do you keep him?"

"Don't take it personal." Falcon sighed. "Diablo doesn't tolerate anybody much. But I like him."

The spring of 1881 was a peculiar season, even by high plains standards. The thaws came early that year in the lands east of the Rockies, earlier than anybody could remember. With them they brought windstorms, sudden rains, flash floods and whirlwinds, topped off by unseasonably warm weather that brought the buds out on the cottonwoods and gave a greenish hint to the pale eternal grass.

Then, in late March, as though to emphasize that this was still the high plains, it turned around and snowed.

There was a patch-up roof on the soddy by then, and oilcloth laced over windows and door. There was even a shed of sorts for the horses, though the snow that fell was only "mush" snow—big wet flakes out of an overcast sky with almost no wind.

The wound in Falcon's belly was scabbed over and healing, but he still felt as though he had been kicked by a mule. "I expect you've got a cracked rib or two," Jonah Mason had diagnosed. "Prob'ly gonna hurt like hell for a month." With a bucktoothed grin, the kid had proceeded to prod and poke until Falcon could have strangled him. "You're lucky," Jonah added. "Most men'd be dead from a wound like that."

Day by day, the aching—the sharp pain every time he moved—diminished. By the end of a week he was up and about, sweating in the cold as he gathered winter hay on the meadows above the stead. By the time the snow fell he was breathing easier, and had a cribful of hay stored in the shed.

But sometimes sharp pains shot through his chest when he turned abruptly or moved in some wrong way. Sometimes the agony doubled him over and left him pale and shaky.

Big flakes were drifting down when Brett Archer rode in from a long scout. The Blanchard kin were scattered around, tending stock and hauling deadfall wood from a lightning-felled cottonwood by the creek. Falcon sat on a fence rail cleaning and oiling his .44s.

Brett hauled rein near him and stepped down, glancing at the sky. His hat and shoulders were white with snow. "I've been to Wolf Creek," he said. "They're there."

Falcon loaded the cylinder of a clean .44 and thrust it into his belt, picking up the other one. "You're sure?"

Brett nodded. "I know Owen Blanchard's wagon, and I know who's got it."

"You're determined to take a hand in this?" Falcon ran a scrap of cloth through the .44's barrel, scrubbed oil into its cylinder, and reloaded.

"We all are," Archer said. "Those animals killed Dorothy." His narrowed eyes were as cold as the snow falling around them. "When you found the remains, back there in Colorado . . . when you found Dorothy . . . they raped her, didn't they?"

Falcon looked away. Some things were better not described. "There's some yucca pods on that broken rail over there." He gestured. "Can you see them? How good are you with that gun? See if—"

The Dragoon's sharp bark cut him off. Glancing away, he hadn't even seen Archer draw. But on the rail fifty feet away a yucca pod exploded into dust.

"That good," Archer rasped. He slid his Dragoon into its holster. "How about you?"

Even looking directly at Falcon MacCallister, the Virginian couldn't be sure of what he saw. The big man had been lounging against a fence rail. Then suddenly he was on his feet, crouching like a big cat, and the .44 in his hand roared and bucked like a wild thing. On the rail, pods in a row became little clouds of dust. Archer gaped at the sight, and when he looked around MacCallister's gun was empty and he had a second one in hand, still crouched and ready.

"My God," Archer whispered.

Falcon took a few deep breaths, then limped over to a stump and sat down. His tanned face was drawn with pain, his eyes squinting, and his brow wet with cold sweat. He was weak and shaky. The effort had cost him. But when he thrust a hand inside his shirt it came out dry. He wasn't bleeding.

"It isn't fancy duels out here," Falcon gasped. "It's last man standing. When you start something, finish it."

Masons and cousins came from everywhere at the noise, guns out and ready, then hauled up in confusion.

"What the hell's goin' on?" Jubal Mason demanded. "Sounded like a war!"

"Mr. MacCallister, you look like hell," Jude observed.

"Just getting acquainted." Falcon shrugged. He reloaded his belt gun and put it away. "Brett's been to Wolf Creek. Let's boil some coffee and hear about it."

They gathered in the soddy to hear the news.

"Wolf Creek is southwest about ten miles." The Virginian pointed. "There's a settlement there—mostly lean-ups and tents—but there are some real buildings going up. Couple of false fronts with a mercantile and a beanery, and a two-story hotel. All kinds of soddies and cabins. I saw a couple of new corrals, a hay barn, and a big pole barn that's being used for an office. Half a dozen plank-and-barrel saloons, a canvas-top gambling hall, and a whole cluster of whore cribs."

"A real town," Falcon allowed. "Does it have a name?"

"I heard the land agent call it Paradise." Brett shrugged. "Must be a hundred, two hundred men around there, just in the town. Border trash mostly, I guess. Twenty or thirty of them are local law of some kind. Yellow bandanas. Vigilance Committee, they call it.

"The head man is a big slick gent by the name of Colonel Amos DeWitt. He headquarters at a covered wagon right in the middle of everything. There's another bruiser, by the name of Obermire. He heads up the vigilancers, him and a buzzard called Casper. There's a hard case named Folly Downs that's in close, and a couple of others I didn't see. But the six of them—DeWitt, Obermire, Casper, Downs, and the other two—they all arrived together a few weeks ago. It's their town now. They just moved in and took over.

"The rest around there are hired guns, drifters, and a few settlers looking for land."

"I expect they've got gunhands," Jude allowed.

"They do. Real hard bunch. They all wear those scraps of yellow to mark them . . . like a uniform. This place draws hard cases like honey draws flies. Those vigilantes would as soon shoot a man as look at him, and they look like they come from all over."

"Any place there's law and order, probably," Falcon mused. "They drift here because there isn't any law."

"You've got that right." The Virginian nodded. "There's probably dodgers on every one of them. I recognized two or three. One of them is Jean Paul Calumet. You've heard of him?"

"Canadian," Falcon said. "A slick man with a gun. He was hunted out of Canada for murdering half a dozen men. He drifted down the Mississippi, ran with the Lawler bunch for a while. Calls himself a duelist, but the law calls him a cold-blooded killer. What's their game here?"

"Selling land," Brett said. "The pole barn is a land office, and the agent is a flimflam type named O'Brien. Looks like DeWitt intends to build quite a town there on the creek. They're selling town lots and steads, and DeWitt's promising a railroad."

"What kind of covered wagon did you see?" Jude asked. "Overland?"

"Yeah. A big prairie schooner. Rigged for five-span, and he has the stock for it. It's Owen's rig, fellas. Right down to the gouges on the gate."

"That's them, then." Jonah's gaze was bleak as he cradled his shotgun in his arms.

Brett's voice went hollow as he nodded. "It's them. There was a quilt airin' on a line. It was the same quilt Dorothy and Tess were working on when they left Neosho."

"You went right in?" Buck Tyber pressed. "Right in close?"

"I moseyed all over the place," Brett said. "They probably took me for a homesteader or a buyer. You're right, the murderers are there. I'm sure DeWitt's one of them, and Obermire and Folly Downs and Clarence. With the two I didn't see— they call them Billy and Tuck—that makes six."

"Land sharks," Falcon muttered thoughtfully. "Speculators turned pirates. DeWitt . . . that could be Asa Parker. That ties in with O'Brien and the patent deeds he peddles. No Man's Land . . . no legal ownership of anything, so who's to say who can sell what, as long as the seller has possession."

"Yeah," Brett said. "They don't have to buy land to sell, they just take it. But it's more than just a land swindle. Judging by the money DeWitt's laying out for guns, I'd say it's a high stakes game."

"This place . . ." Falcon indicated the abandoned stead they occupied. "Did you see any neighbors around here anywhere?"

"Nobody close." Archer shook his head. "Down along the creeks there are squatters, some of them pretty well dug in. But not up here. Mostly just places like this. Abandoned cabins, a lot of them empty. Some of them burned out. Some places that might make good farms, but the squatters who started them are gone. Nobody around."

"Vigilantes," Falcon said. "Hired thugs and assassins. They scout the territory and clean out occupants so the land shark will have farms to sell. It only works if the shark has a good base of operations and plenty of bullies on payroll."

"And good bait to bring in customers," Brett added. "DeWitt's selling town lots and quarter-section plots, but the railroad is what brings them."

"No better bait than that," Jubal noted. "You own property where a railroad goes, you're a rich man."

Jude frowned at his twin. "You see anybody rich in Dodge City?"

"No, nor any original owners, either, I bet. They took their profits and headed for better places."

"Wolf Creek sounds like a big operation," Falcon said. "He'd have to have somebody inside the railroads to back it up. And plenty of capital. Did the Blanchards have money with them?"

"Not much, I guess." Jude shrugged. "Owen sank everything he had into that prairie schooner and his draft team and supplies."

"Well, there's money at Wolf Creek," Brett said. "I saw more cash money floating around there than I've ever seen outside a bank."

"Railroad money," Falcon muttered, thinking about the telegraph message that had been waiting for him at Dodge. "Stolen money, from the Kansas Pacific. It's their investment capital."

"And Owen Blanchard's family just happened to get in the way." Brett nodded.

"So what are we going to do about it?" Jubal and Jude demanded in unison.

"We go to Wolf Creek," Brett said. "We leave now, so the snow will cover our tracks."

"Yeah, and get yourselves killed." Falcon grunted. "You said yourself there are guns all over the place. And only four of the six are there."

"We can get them!" Brett Archer protested. Then he frowned. "You're right, though. There are guns all over the place, most of them working for DeWitt."

"Find the rest," Falcon nodded. "You only saw four of the bunch. Four's not enough. Let's put them all down. We'll look around some more."

"You aren't up to it, Mr. MacCallister," Jude said. "We've seen how you are. Something's busted inside you, and it hasn't healed yet. Besides, some of those hooraws will know you on sight. You can't just blend in down there. You'd stand out like a sore thumb."

"You boys won't," Falcon said. "You go in. I'll be around. I want to see those claimed places down on the creeks, maybe get to know some of the neighbors."

FOURTEEN

Where God puts water and the means to subsist—no matter how meager—no act of congress will keep people away.

The Neutral Strip between Kansas and Texas—that long rectangle of land that would someday be known as the Oklahoma Panhandle—was created by oversight. Some said it was to pacify the Indians forced into the Territories to the east. Some said it was intended as a buffer between Texas and Kansas following the War of Northern Aggression.

And there were some who held that in the blood frenzy of postwar federal politics, the U.S. Department of the Interior simply overlooked it when the plainslands were designated for settlement.

Whatever its origin, the Neutral Strip was a rectangular void in the spreading cloth of United States dominion. A hard day's ride across from north to south, closer to a week from east to west, it straddled the central plains from the Indian Territories to the breaks of the Purgatoire, and was entirely devoid of any semblance of law.

For some, it was a land of opportunity. Where there is no law, a man can take what he wants, sell what he can deliver, and hold what he can defend. South of western Kansas was such a place.

They called it No Man's Land.

Fresh and wet, melting snow lay a foot deep along Wolf Creek when Colonel Amos DeWitt—the man once known as Asa Parker—opened the hind flap at the tail of the prairie schooner and looked across at a freshly whitewashed building. Even with its paint, it was little more than a converted barn with a high loft, but it and the new hotel just down the way were still the most impressive structures in the squalid little town sprawling around him.

Quick-eyed men with yellow scarves on their shoulders and shotguns across their arms—men whose appearance would have marked them as trouble in any civilized place—glanced toward him as he buttoned up his coat and snugged his hat tighter around his head. Near the off rear wheel, where stretched canvas made a roof over some benches and a chimneyless potbellied stove, Folly Downs glanced up from his whetstone. DeWitt wrinkled his nose in disgust.

Folly had never been much to look at, but he was hideous now. The scabs had peeled away from his ruined cheek and ear, but that was no improvement. The bullet scar across his cheek gaped like a second mouth, off to the left of his nose, and Clarence's needlework only emphasized it.

Folly had a hand-sized piece of rough hairless hide laid out on a bench, and was slicing it to make a hatband. He called it "squawhide." He wouldn't be the first to decorate himself with pieces of dead Indians, but a hatband cut from a squaw's breast was unusual. At DeWitt's frown, Folly nodded, sneered, and went back to sharpening his knife.

DeWitt disappeared inside the wagon for a moment, and the sound of a bolted-down strongbox being closed and locked echoed from there. Then he reappeared, righted the wagon's gate ladder, and descended to the ground. Guards in yellow scarves around the wagon cradled their guns and nodded, and the two nearest the tailgate moved aside for him as he stepped down. "Afternoon, colonel," one greeted him. "Looks like the snow's stopped."

Here and there other heavily armed citizens touched their hats, raised their hands, or otherwise saluted the big man in the fine coat. Most of them also wore the yellow cloth of the Vigilance Committee. In only a few weeks since his arrival, Colonel Amos DeWitt—Asa Parker—had staked his claim on everything within thirty miles of this place, and made it stick.

It wasn't just the fact that DeWitt owned everything around there by right of force—or that he paid most of them good wages to protect his interests—that earned him this show of respect. As much as anything, it was fear.

The former Asa Parker was a big man, more than six feet tall and as broad and solid as a woods boar. Despite his natty attire, he had made it well-known around there that he brooked no insolence. Among men who understood violence, he had made a point to establish himself by doing his own chores when it came to punishment.

A smashing fist was something these men understood. A six-gun was something they understood even better. Colonel Amos DeWitt had demonstrated both in lining up his organization at Wolf Creek.

DeWitt paid well for the services he bought, and he paid in cash. But over by the bluff, just across the creek, were mounds of freshly turned soil testifying that Colonel DeWitt was a man who accepted no excuses, tolerated no interference, and didn't hesitate to maim or kill.

Still, dressed in the finest broadcloth suit, starched linens, and spotless outerwear, he was a match for any banker or politician in finery.

With a brief nod, DeWitt acknowledged them all and squinted in the bright gray light of day. Across the rutted street men on ladders were hoisting a big canvas pennant into place on the front of the pole barn, and Dewitt studied it critically. Its bright paint was a nice theatrical touch for the drab building and the motley snow-covered piles of salvage that surrounded it—stacks of lumber, piles of battered furniture, mounds of rusty hardware and stained tools, limestone blocks, and a huge stack of cut cedar posts with a sign on it: Fence posts 5 cents ea.

On the building front, workmen hammered nails into the canvas banner, stretching it taut as they went. The sign read:

PARADISE LAND COMPANY—TOWN LOTS—BUILDING SITES—COMMERSHAL INVESTMENTS—COL. AMOS DEWITT PROP.

DeWitt studied it carefully as they began nailing it up. "Is that how you spell commercial?" he asked the nearest gunman. "It doesn't look right."

"I guess so, colonel." The man shrugged. "I'm no hand at spellin'."

"And what's this 'Paradise' business? I thought we were callin' this place Prosperity."

"O'Brien changed it," the thug said. "I don't know why."

DeWitt scowled at the sign once more, then turned as Kurt Obermire and Casper Wilkerson walked toward him. Obermire was as big as the colo-

nel but of a far rougher cut, and even the paid con-
stables and Vigilance Committee members who did
DeWitt's bidding tended to stay shy of him and his
ever present sawed-off shotgun. Obermire was, plain
and simple, one big mean son of a bitch, and he
looked it.

Wilkerson, by contrast, was a hawk-nosed beanpole of a man, more draped than covered by the
long coat he always wore—a coat that concealed
considerable armament.

"Riders comm' in," Wilkerson said as they approached. "Maybe some more boys from over in
Kansas."

DeWitt shaded his eyes. Riders were just pulling
into the far end of the settlement—three young men
on tired horses. With the distance, and the collars
and mufflers they wore against the cold, he could
see no faces. They seemed like ordinary drifters,
young bucks on the run or on the prowl, and not
particularly noticeable.

"They're nobody," he decided. "If they're lookin'
for work, they'll find Kurt." He glanced at Obermire. "What about the bunch Billy and Tuck
brought in? Can we use them?"

"They'll do for gang work," Obermire said. "Most
of them can use a gun. I've got Calumet drillin' 'em.
I'll try some of them out tonight."

"All right. They're up to you. Anybody else new
today?"

"The usual," Casper said. "Couple of immigrants
with O'Brien's deed plasters. A few drifters, sight-
seein'. Only one looks like he might have money.
Young fellow named Archer. He was around here a
day or so ago, and now he's back. He's over at the
post, last I saw."

"Archer," DeWitt noted. "Well, see if you can

herd him toward the land office. Maybe O'Brien can sell him something." He turned slowly, full circle, surveying his domain. "What was that ruckus I heard awhile ago?"

Casper sneered. "Oh, that squatter Coleman, that had the cedar camp out on north rim. He thinks he's a hard man or somethin', raisin' hell about the boys runnin' him off that land last week. Shoulda shot him out there, 'stead of just runnin' him off."

"Damn squatter should have just moved on," DeWitt rumbled. "What did we get from his place?"

"Mostly those cedar posts yonder," Casper pointed. "O'Brien had 'em hauled in. Thinks he can sell 'em." He grinned—a grotesque expression on his bony face. "I bet it took that squatter a year to cut that many posts."

"We got us some planed lumber, too," Kurt added. "Maybe a wagon load. An' some wolf hides. There was a pair of mules out there, but they weren't worth chasin' so the boys shot 'em."

"And the squatter's still around?" DeWitt sneered. "Some folks just don't get the message, I guess. Stupid. Where is he now?"

"He was out here hollerin' about bein' robbed," Casper said. "Don't know where he is now. Maybe down in the cribs, or holed up in one of those soddies. He's still around somewhere, I guess. Want somebody to go find him?"

"I don't want him shootin' off his mouth when there's customers in town," DeWitt snapped. "Just tell the boys to keep their eyes peeled. And speakin' of customers, I don't want Billy on the street for a while. The way he's been carryin' on since he killed that gunfighter . . . what was his name? The legend? Oh, yeah. MacCallister. Tell Tuck to keep that rooster under wraps for a while. He's bad for business."

"Billy's out at the spring place, sleepin' it off. He's got a bullet burn that'll keep him tame for a day or two. Tuck's watchin' him."

Turning his back on them, DeWitt walked across the slushy street to the land office. Inside, Clarence O'Brien was tacking up a big hand-drawn map. It was a gaudy thing, full of official-looking lines and notations, covering an area of perhaps nine hundred square miles, with a painted star in the center. Beside the star, in detailed calligraphy, was the word PARADISE. Angling down toward it from the northeast was a wide red line with the caption: ATLANTIC TO PACIFIC CENTRAL RAILWAY.

A separate map, on another rough wall, was an elaborate detailed drawing of a sizeable city, lined with streets and alleys—none of which existed outside the minds of the speculators—and all blocked out in rectangular segments representing town lots. Its label read PARADISE.

O'Brien was a slick-looking, nattily dressed jaybird with a huge waxed mustache and an air of courteous authority. He could, they said, sell anything to anybody and make them truly believe—for long enough to part with their cash—that they had made a good deal.

"Impressive as hell," DeWitt admitted, looking at the new map. "Why PARADISE?"

O'Brien explained, "I had to call it something. All the town deeds have that name, and the country tracts are Paradise Valley." He opened a drawer, pulled out a stack of official-looking document forms, and displayed them. "I picked these up at Newton. Printer there does nice work."

"Whatever it takes." DeWitt shrugged. "Let's just

get the damned acreage sold. Sypher needs documented landowners to swing the railroad this way."

"No problem." O'Brien grinned. "There's a sucker born every minute. Soon as the roads thaw there'll be customers showing up. I've got a cash buyer coming from Winfield, interested in that bottomland section south of here. Hackberry Meadows. I hope it's . . . ah . . . unoccupied when my buyer gets here."

"It will be," DeWitt growled. "Obermire's going out there tonight. We're through tryin' to reason with the Barlows."

"Good. I'll mark it clear. And you might tell those hoodlums of yours . . . sorry, those Vigilance Committee gentlemen . . . to keep it quiet around here, colonel. Cash buyers don't like to hear people holler about being robbed. Makes 'em nervous."

DeWitt was inspecting the maps when a ruckus erupted outside. Men were shouting and running. Followed by O'Brien, he stepped out onto the narrow plank walk. "What's goin' on?" he shouted.

Across the street, his guards had pulled in around the wagon as men ran past them, heading west. Beyond the crowd, Folly Downs waved at him and shouted, "Fire, colonel! The hay barn's burnin'!"

"Well, go put it out!" DeWitt roared. "I'll keep watch here!"

The fire was clearly visible—a writhing column of smoke two hundred yards to the west. Within moments the street in front of the land office was practically deserted as crowds gathered around the blazing sheds.

DeWitt stepped down from the walk, shooed O'Brien back inside the land office, and glanced around. He was almost alone in this section of street now.

Almost, but not quite.

A ragged figure had appeared beside the cedar stack and stepped toward him. "DeWitt!" the man rasped. "You owe me . . . you owe me for my land, my cabin, my mules, my cart, and for these cedar posts! You're a thief and a robber, DeWitt. You and your men, you're nothin' but night riders! You owe me, and I expect to be paid!"

DeWitt glared at the man. "You must be Coleman," he said.

Coleman's fingers twitched above the butt of the big gun at his belt. "I want to be paid!" he snarled. "You . . . you damned sharks have ruined me! Now you owe me!"

"I don't carry cash around with me," DeWitt said quietly. "The money's all locked away. Maybe we could discuss this later—"

"Pay up now, or by God I'll kill you!" Coleman snapped. "Even that's better than you deserve!"

DeWitt stared at him. "I don't owe you anythin', squatter. You squatted on land that wasn't yours, cut posts that didn't belong to you—"

"Well, none of it belongs to you, either!" The fingers clawed nervously, closing around the gun butt. "Now pay up! I won't say it again!"

"I guess not." DeWitt shrugged. Carefully, his arms spread wide, away from the .45 at his belt. It was a gesture of surrender, and Coleman responded. His hand dropped away from his own gun.

Then, with a movement too quick to follow, DeWitt's right arm swung forward. His hidden derringer slid from his sleeve into his hand, and he pointed and fired—two shots.

Coleman staggered and gaped as a heavy slug tore through his chest. He tried to pull his gun, but failed. The second shot took him through the wishbone. The man was dead before he fell.

At the sound of shots, faces turned in the crowd two hundred yards away, and yellow scarves flashed as several of Obermire's Vigilance Committee regulators came running. They all had their guns out, and two or three fired excited shots into the air. Echoes rebounded from the bluff across the creek, seeming to multiply as they sounded. In the noise and confusion, it seemed that the echoes of gunfire went on and on.

For a moment, many of the men glanced around in confusion. It sounded as though there had been a lot more shooting than there had been. But DeWitt roared at them, and they gathered around him.

In the background crowd half a dozen men— hard-bitten farmers who had been hanging around town—exchanged glances and drifted away.

"Clean up this mess," DeWitt told them, standing over the bleeding corpse of the squatter Coleman. "I suppose he's the one who set the fire. Has Folly got it put out?"

Several of the thugs stepped back, looking around. "Folly?" someone said. "I thought he was here with us."

"Guess he's still at the fire," another suggested.

They found Folly Downs an hour later, behind the burned hay barn. He lay face down in the muddy slush churned up by earlier crowds, his body riddled with bullet holes.

It was no casual shooting. It was a methodical execution. Small precise holes decorated the corpse— throat, groin, shoulder, knee, and chest. It was as though each shot had been planned, each bullet intended to punish before destroying.

An execution . . . but there was no trace of the executioner.

"I ain't goin' out tonight, Asa," Kurt Obermire said flatly, his eyes level with the angry glare of Asa Parker. "Billy was right. There's been somebody trailin' us since Colorado, and now he's here!"

Casper Wilkerson hovered nearby, backing him up. The three stood alone, just behind the closed gate of the overland wagon, while yellow-banded vigilantes kept the traffic away from them.

"You're spooked," Parker growled. "You're downright scared! You can't even remember to call me Colonel DeWitt, you're so scared!"

"I ain't scared!" Obermire said. "But you saw what happened to Folly. That wasn't any natural shootin'. I got a bad feelin' that we're bein' stalked! And it's just the three of us here now, with Billy laid up and Tuck with him. I don't intend to go ridin' out to let some sniper get me."

"He might be right, colonel," Casper said. "We ought to keep close 'til we get to the bottom of this."

"I'll send Jackson and Calumet out with the vigilantes," Obermire stated. "They can handle those Barlows. I say we stay close together for now, and here in town where we can watch one another's backs."

"You're both damn fools," Parker/DeWitt scoffed. "Whoever killed Folly is gone."

"We'll stay, anyway," Casper said, his thin voice grim and determined, his gaze leveled at DeWitt. "Maybe Kurt's right, maybe not. But I'd hate to see anybody left all alone with this wagon . . . and the money that's in it. Might be just too much temptation there."

DeWitt knew when he was outvoted. "Do Jackson and Calumet know what's to be done?"

"They can handle a few damn squatters." Obermire nodded.

"Then send them! But I want that claim cleared . . . and I want Billy and Tuck back here as soon as possible."

"Billy's stove up bad, Colonel. That bounty man he shot put a bullet into his butt. Tuck's stayin' out there with him."

"Billy and his *private business*," DeWitt growled. "Well, get them back as soon as they can come!"

FIFTEEN

"This place is a pure hellhole," Jubal Mason announced when Brett had joined the brothers at the Paradise Hotel. "I tell you, boys, I seen about enough of it." Pacing the plank floor, he glanced out of the smudged little window. Beyond, evening light across the bluffs cast a bleak smoky glow over the town of Paradise. Out by the corral, Sam Jackson and the man called Calumet were assembling some of the vigilantes. It looked as if at least twenty riders would be pulling out soon, heading south.

"Obermire's not goin'," Jubal growled. "How we gonna get to him . . . and those others . . . if they stay inside their guard circle?"

"Well, we got one of 'em, anyway," Jude said. He cut his eyes toward the somber Brett Archer, who was just shucking his coat. "Nice goin', Brett."

Archer frowned. "It wasn't me," he said. "Wish it had been, but it wasn't. I don't know who killed that son of a bitch. Thought maybe one of you boys got him."

The three Masons exchanged surprised glances. "You didn't kill Folly Downs? Then who did?"

"I sure don't know."

"Well, how about that fire at the hay barn? Didn't you set that?"

"It wasn't me," Brett repeated. "I was over by Owen's wagon, trying to get a look inside. Couldn't get near it, though."

"Then who did all that? It wasn't any of us."

Brett shook his head. "Place like this, it could have been anybody. But I never saw anything quite like it. Did you all see that corpse? That jasper was shot to pieces."

"Yeah," Jubal said. "I had a good look. Back home, I'd have said somebody used him for target practice . . . with squirrel guns. Those weren't pistol shots in him. Those bullets were small caliber, high power loads. Like a squirrel rifle. God, back home the law'd have posses out combin' the country. But all those vigilantes did was drag him off across the creek, along with that feller their boss man shot! They're both layin' in the snow out there, waitin' for somebody to bury 'em. What kind of law is that, anyway?"

"Law?" Brett smiled sourly. "There's no law here, Jubal. No law at all. Just the criminals in charge, and I'd say they make up near half the population. Did you all see DeWitt gun that settler down out there? That was nothing but cold-blooded murder . . . with a hidden gun! The settler never had a chance."

"I listened around," Jonah said. "Way I heard it, Obermire's vigilantes ran that fellow off his land and stole his posts. When he came in to complain, DeWitt shot him. DeWitt carries a .45 in plain sight, but he never touched it. He shot Coleman with a sleeve gun. Like you said, the poor fool didn't have a chance."

"No Man's Land," Jubal muttered. "No damn wonder it's called that! This whole place is nothin' but a hellhole!"

"You been out to the place? How's MacCallister coming along?"

"He's on his feet," Jude said. "I don't see how, but he's talkin' about takin' a hand at the Barlow place. Swore he'd get a saddle on that big black if it killed him. Maybe it did. We left him there."

Outside, the light was dimming. It would be dark soon. With a final glance from the window, Jubal put on his coat and hat and drew a yellow scarf from his pocket. With Jude's help, he fastened it to his lapel.

"I better make tracks if I'm gonna catch up with the vigilantes," he said. "Wish me luck."

Jude was fishing out his own yellow banner. "I'll be along directly. I'll try to stay back; see if I can find some way to back your play, Jubal."

"What play?" Jubal frowned. "Nobody we're after is goin' out there tonight! Best we can do is maybe even the squatters' odds a little."

High clouds hid the stars and a chill wind whined through dark canyons as the Paradise Vigilance Committee picked its way down ragged slopes toward the bottomlands called Hackberry Meadows. In near-darkness where only the dim glow of snow and caliche ledges gave view, they led their mounts single file and stepped carefully.

The best in the gang at seeing at night, swarthy Calumet and the Kiowa half-breed Osa, led the way, with the outlaw Sam Jackson close behind and the rest following.

Dim points of light glowed faintly a quarter-mile away. In the darkness, from that distance, they couldn't see the limestone-braced soddy, fenced corral, and pole barn of the Barlow claim. They could barely see the little grove of cottonwoods behind it. They could see the lamplight in the slit windows, and the faint glow atop the low chimney.

It was guidance enough. Some of them had been there before.

"Old man and a brood of grown-up boys," Jackson told them when they gathered at the base of the ridge. "There's some women with 'em, and a few urchin kids. Hill trash from back east. They had their warning. Now the colonel wants 'em cleaned out."

"This the bunch that Palmer's men tried to drive off last fall?" someone asked. "I heard they put up a hell of a fight. Palmer and three of his boys dead, two more shot up. Then, when they finally took the place, there wasn't nobody there."

"Don't know if it's the same ones," Calumet purred. "These Barlows, they're a whole tribe, not just a family. That Palmer, he said he didn't know there was so many."

"Palmer was a fool," Jackson rumbled. "These are just squatters, no better than any others. This time I don't want them getting away. We surround them, kill them, and burn the place down. That'll put an end to that."

"What about the women?" a man in the ranks asked. "We s'posed to kill them, too? And the kids?"

"That's what happens to squatters," Jackson said. In the darkness he couldn't see faces—only shadows and the pale swatches of their yellow scarves. Most of them he knew, from a season or two of holeing up in the strip. A few others were newcomers that Obermire had recruited into the Vigilance Committee.

"I ain't gonna be no part of killin' women an' kids," one of the men muttered.

Jackson turned to glare at the man. "That's up to you," he said. "Kill 'em or drive 'em off. They all had their chance to go away. Anybody here think he ain't got the stomach for this?"

There were no answers. Jackson hadn't expected any. "Then saddle up," he ordered. "It's flat grassland from here. Stay together 'til we get close, then divide up. Calumet will lead five of you around back, to the trees. I don't want anybody skinnin' out of that cabin when we hit it. Keep 'em pinned down inside, and keep your guns pointed at that cabin. Any son of a bitch that gets excited and sends a shot my way is gonna die right then and there. You understand me, Calumet?"

The swarthy gunfighter's nod was lost in the darkness, but his voice was as soft and cold as a snake's hiss. "I'll tend to it personal," he said.

Halfway across the dark open prairie, the halfbreed Osa reined back and fell in beside Jackson. "Somebody back there," he said, pointing back the way they had come.

"Back where?" Jackson turned, squinting toward the faint line of limestone bluffs behind them. "I don't see anybody," he said.

"Was somebody," Osa said. "See . . . look back there."

Calumet was also looking back. "I see," he said. "I see yellow, too. He's ours. Prob'ly stopped to pee."

Jackson glared at Osa. "You drunk again, Injun? You just get on out there ahead and watch for trouble. If there's guards out, they'll be at the barn or the corral, not out on the damned prairie! Now move before I take a boot to your sorry ass."

A hundred yards from the corral, they could make out the lay of the place. It was quiet, with not even a barking dog to alert the inhabitants. Leotus Barlow had been proud of his dogs—five big mountain hounds that he used for hunting and for herding livestock. All five were gone now. They had disappeared weeks before. Two of them the Barlow boys had found, hanging from ropes in a cottonwood tree. Jackson's scouts and their rifles had the others, as well as a milk cow and two horses.

Osa rode back again, a shadow in the darkness. "Barn's empty," he said. "Nobody at the corral or the sheds. They're all forted up in the cabin."

Jackson swung toward the nearest men. "You five," he said, "you go with Calumet. Get around the far side and spread out. Cover the woods and the breaks. The rest of you, get down. Leave the horses here with two men. The rest of us go in on foot."

The riders dismounted, drawing rifles and shotguns from their saddle boots. When they were ready, Jackson beckoned. "Let's go," he said. "Fast and quiet. Spread out, but not far. Get close. When I hit that door I want lead pourin' in through the windows. Let's make this quick and sweet."

Jean Paul Calumet led his riders along a dry slough, out of sight of the Barlow cabin. Circling around, they made their way into the maze of erosion gullies that zigzagged across the breaks where Little Creek met Wolf Creek. The slope there dipped away gradually, then abruptly, where old floods had shaped the limestone scours.

Where a close-in cliff offered a good view of the squatters' claim, Calumet paused and signaled in the dark to a rider. "You, Dobie," he ordered, "you stay here. Anybody comes out, you use your rifle."

One by one in the darkness they dropped off to take positions where they could see the cabin and barn. Only Calumet and the breed reached the dark grove of leafless cottonwoods. The half-breed Osa had not been assigned a vantage point. Instead, he followed along with Calumet.

The Canadian knew that Osa was no good in a fight. The breed was about as reliable as a snake, and was as likely to turn tail or change sides as to stand and shoot. But he had night eyes, and Calumet had often found him useful.

They picketed their horses in the creek bottom below the house, where they could reach them quickly, and moved into the sparse winter-bare cover of the grove.

Jackson's strategy for clearing the bottomlands of Barlows was simple and direct. Hit them hard, hit them fast, take them by surprise, and take no prisoners. The Vigilance Committee's raid was hammer and anvil—an overwhelming strike force from the north to surround and annihilate, and a line of snipers on the south to pick off stragglers.

The little stead showed no sign of alarm as the attackers on foot started across the fields, toward the squat cabin and ramshackle barn. They made their way in silence, the only sounds their footfalls breaking through crusted snow to the moist mud beneath.

Two hundred yards to cover. The gang spread and advanced, dark furtive forms crouching in the near-darkness. Ahead of them the only sign of life was the soft muted glow of the cabin's little windows.

Bodie slipped a rope halter onto his mount and climbed a few feet up the cold crusted face of the gully wall. When he had a good view of the cabin's windows he found footholds and dug his boots in, checking the loads in his repeating rifle. Secure in his perch, he glanced around, slowly scanning the darkness behind him. He could barely see his horse a few yards away, and beyond it the creekbed and the driftline beyond. It was cold and quiet, and he was alone. Eyes attuned to the Missouri hills, senses honed from his live or die life as a renegade in harsh country, he missed little.

But those eyes, those senses, had never dealt with the reality of ancient Shawnee discipline—called the Warrior's Way. Fugitive, renegade, and survivor, Bodie was as tough as they come and as wary as a badger. But in his scan of the area behind him he missed the obvious.

Only a few feet away, where the limestone bank jutted outward, the snow crust and shadows combined to form a shape like that of a man crouching—a big man with moon-blond hair. It was the kind of illusion that darkness lends to shapes and shadows, and even as Bodie noticed it he dismissed it. His hooded eyes flicked past, searching for hidden menace, and found none.

Bodie turned back toward the cabin. He never saw the form he had not noticed as it uncoiled silently and launched itself at him.

Falcon MacCallister had never lived among the Shawnee of the eastern forests, but his father had. Jamie Ian MacCallister, some said, could out-Shawnee any Shawnee in the arts of camouflage and misdirection. And Falcon MacCallister had grown up with the lore his father taught him. The real trick of covert approach, he knew, was in the timing of movement and the blending of surroundings. It was the Warrior's Way. The trick was not to be invisible, but simply not to be noticed.

Bodie didn't know he had company until that company had him pinned at the base of the limestone rise, helpless and gurgling, with a knife point prodding him under the ear and an arm like an oak bole around his neck.

"I've got some questions," Falcon MacCallister's low voice purred in his ear. "Now I want some answers. So talk to me, night rider."

Out in the darkness, across the field, gunshots flashed in the night and their reports crashed and echoed among the breaks. Somebody had opened the ball at the Barlow claim. A shot, then three more, and the night erupted in chaos. With the crash of gunshots, whine of bullets, and the intermittent scream of richochets singing off into the distance, it sounded as if war had been declared.

In the cottonwoods, Jean Calumet ducked low as a ricochet whined over him, then eased up to where he could see the back side of the spread. There was gunfire where there should have been none—over by the barn, near the hay chutes, from the cover of a drifted fence. And from the cabin windows, spits of angry flame shot outward, toward the north field where Jackson's night riders advanced. They had not reached the cabin, as expected. Someone on the stead had opened fire before the place was surrounded.

"It's an ambush!" Calumet growled. "Those damn squatters . . . I can't see from here." He turned his head. "Osa, where are you? Pass the word back down the line, saddle up and follow me." There was no response. "Osa? Osa! Where'd you go?"

The breed didn't answer. Cursing, Calumet eased

down the embankment and crouched. "Osa! Bring up the horses, damn you!"

Still, there was no answer. Squinting in the murk, Calumet headed downslope, into the trees, then stopped abruptly. Osa sat hunkered against a drift bank, legs crossed, rocking slowly and cradling his head in his hands. Even in the near-darkness, Calumet could see blood on the Indian's face.

"What happened here?" he demanded.

Osa just kept rocking, moaning softly, and shaking his head. *"Da'huida . . ."* he groaned. "Ghost. Big ghost. Came right out of the ground." Dim tracks showed where the breed had been jumped . . . by someone not six feet away from him. Osa's old Dragoon Colt lay on the ground, where he had dropped it.

Calumet raised his eyes, squinting into the thicket. The little opening where their horses should have been was empty—just dim snowdrift and trampled ground.

With a growl, the Canadian sprinted eastward, gun in hand, skirting the grove. He found two more of his vigilantes where they had fallen. One had a caved-in skull. The second was dead of a broken neck. There was no sign of the others, and no horses.

"Mon Dieu," the Canadian hissed, then ducked as a rifle ball sang past him. Up on the ridge to his left, a shot flared and a voice called, "Yonder's one of 'em, Omer! See him? Down in the slough!"

Twisting and ducking, Calumet headed for the crusted creek, running as though the very devil were on his tail.

In rolling hills northeast of the Barlow claim, Falcon MacCallister wheeled Diablo at the top of a rise and looked down at the ambling herd of saddle mounts passing below. The clouds had broken overhead, and wan moonlight gave him a good view of the scene. Twenty or so horses, all wearing saddles, trotted eastward in good order, hazed by a single rider.

Falcon took a deep painful breath, feeling dizzy for a moment. Back there, when he put the second of those night riders down, something had twisted inside him—a gut-wrenching pain that almost doubled him over. But it had passed, a little. What remained was a throbbing ache that pulsed with each breath, each beat of his heart. Still, his wounds had held. He was not bleeding. He put the pain back where it belonged—in the back parts of his mind.

As the herd neared, Falcon waved, and the rider waved back. Circling, Falcon picked up his four spare horses and angled them down the slope to join the herd.

Jude Mason grinned as Falcon pulled in beside him. "You do get around for a dead man. We got us a nice herd here. Saddles an' all. See you got a few, too. Learn anything?"

"Names," Falcon said. "Brett was right about the six men who murdered your kin. They're the same ones running that town. Colonel DeWitt's real name . . . or at least another name he uses . . . is Asa Parker. The ones with him were Kurt Obermire, Casper Wilkerson, Folly Downs, Billy Challis, and Tuck Kelly. The reason Brett never saw the last two is that they're laying up at a place south of here. The Spring place."

"I know where that is," Jude said.

"Well, they're the two that waylaid me out on the plains. I guess I winged one of them."

"That all fits," Jubal nodded. "But there's only

five of them now. Folly Downs was killed in town. Did you do that?"

"Not me," Falcon said. "I haven't been in."

"Well, somebody sure enough made him dead. He was shot to pieces. Small-bore rifle, used real mean."

"That leaves five, then," Falcon said.

"I guess so, but there's no way to get to DeWitt and Wilkerson. They never leave town. And Obermire's stayin' there now, too . . . surrounded by his hoodlums."

"So they're spooked." Falcon looked back. "Sounds like a war back there. Where's Jubal?"

Jude's teeth glinted in a grin. "I saw him cut off halfway here, head out on his own. Guess he had an idea. Those vigilantes never got to where they meant to go. I'd say those squatters saw 'em comin'." He squinted, looking back. "You know, half the vigilantes are out here right now. We could ride back and . . ."

"And pick a few murderers out of an armed camp?" Falcon shook his head. "I want to get all of them, Jude, not just one or two. And I want the man behind them, too. I won't settle for less."

Jude frowned. "You sound like hell, Mr. MacCallister. And the way you're hunched over . . . are you bleedin' again?"

"No, I'm not."

Jude shrugged. "You still look like hell. What are we supposed to do with all these horses?"

"Well, this is No Man's Land," Falcon said. "No law here, so the rule is finders keepers. I'd say these horses and saddles all belong to you boys now."

"That's nice," Jude allowed. "But what do we do with them?"

"Take them home," Falcon decided. "Back to the

haymeadows place. It'll take the vigilantes a while to sort out where their horses went, and give Asa Parker something else to wonder about. With a little luck, the Barlows and their neighbors have set back his plans for Paradise. Take these critters home, Jude. Then you and the boys wait there for me."

Jude peered into the gloom and shook his head. Even in darkness, the big man looked half-dead, but he was riding. "Where're you goin'?"

"I've got some scouting to do," Falcon said. He was thinking about the weird death of Folly Downs—how the man was "shot to pieces." He was thinking of that . . . and wondering.

"Might sell these saddle mounts for a good price," Jude mused. "There's a town yonder that's probably real short of horses right now."

"Just take 'em to the Haymeadows," Falcon repeated. "Wait for me there."

"We're gettin' a little tired of pussyfootin' around, Mr. MacCallister," Jude said, reining his mount around. "We know who it was that murdered Owen Blanchard's family, an' we know where they are. We're tired of waitin'. I guess we can wait around 'til you get to the haymeadows, but my brothers and me are about ready to open the ball."

Jude hesitated, expecting an answer, then turned. Like a shadow in the night, Falcon MacCallister had ridden away—a hunched shadowy figure on a big black horse.

"Cripes," Jude muttered. "Anybody else'd be flat on his back, trying to get well. Not him, though. He don't even know he's hurtin'."

SIXTEEN

Jonathan Boles Stratton's private rail coach arrived at the Dodge City railhead in late March, in time to see the last snowfall of winter blanket the bleak hills along the Arkansas River. The gilded coach was shunted onto a dedicated siding where pennants whipped in the wind.

The rowdy cowtown at the gateway to the plains had put on its best finery to welcome the representative of the United States Bureau of Rails. Fresh paint glistened on doorways and storefronts, and temporary deputy marshals were out in force to keep the commercial area off-limits to its usual occupants.

Stratton was escorted in style to Dodge's best hotel, the Palace, by a contingent of smartly attired Kansas State Militia under the command of Captain Abe Burroughs himself. Marshal Sam Stroud's deputies prowled Trail Street and the intersecting ways, establishing a deadline against drunks, drifters, grubline cowboys, and anybody else who might appear in any way unsavory. Even the Dodge House had been spruced up. For the duration of Stratton's stay, and for the benefit of the flood of railroad investors who would follow him, the West's roughest little city had put on its Sunday face.

Along Trail Street all eyes were on the great man as he stepped from Harold Bolin's best carriage to the boardwalk in front of the Palace, where dignitaries, photographers, and visiting capitalists gathered beyond a cordon of state guardsmen. Few paid any attention to the little flock of honorary bodyguards and servants who followed Stratton into the new hotel—least of all to the gray little man who brought up the rear of the parade.

Sypher was very good at not being noticed. Years of close association with preening politicians and pompous tycoons had honed his skills. In the circles where he moved, protective coloration was the best job insurance. In the bureau of rails, as in any federal mechanism, the Strattons came and went with each new tide of political patronage, but the functionaries—the unnoticed Syphers—went on and on, adapting grandiose legisation to their own agendas, running the country as they saw fit.

When Stratton was comfortably ensconced in the Palace's best and only dignitary suite, surrounded by fawning opportunists, Sypher went off on errands of his own. He spent an hour arranging for his employer to be provided with a discreet and plentiful supply of Dodge City's best liquor, cigars, and whores, and spent ten minutes at the local Western Union office catching up on his correspondence. He dropped in at the town marshal's office and listened to the conversation there while he thumbed through stacks of warrants and claims. Then he made his way to the big livery barn at the lower end of Trail.

Sergeant Jack Lyles was there, talking with Eugene Paul, when the functionary came in.

"I want to rent a carriage," the little gray man said.

Paul nodded. "I have some rigs. Where do you want to go?"

Sypher squinted at the liveryman. "I don't believe that's any of your concern," he snapped. "I shall require a good carriage . . . a surrey will do, if it has a supply box. And a strong horse. I shall be gone for possibly a week."

"Well, that'll cost you," Paul said. "I charge daily, in advance, and a deposit to cover loss."

"Loss?" The stranger bristled. "Sir, I am an employee of the government of the United States of America!"

"Most would charge you extra for that." Paul shrugged. "Not me, though. But I'm no fool, either. We're at the end of the world out here, Mr. You'd be surprised how many rigs just take a notion to keep right on goin' once they're out of sight. And bein' a government man gives you about as much credibility as a top hat gives a gopher."

"I don't intend to steal your carriage," Sypher growled. "Only to rent it."

"To go where?"

"If you must know, I have business south of here, in the Neutral Strip."

Paul grinned. "Lot of rigs never come back from No Man's Land," he said. "Nobody there to say they have to. I can fix you up with that surrey out back. It's sturdy and sound. And I've got a couple of good horses to choose from. I'll need, ah . . ."—he paused, considering—" . . . I'd say three hundred and thirty dollars will cover it."

"That's highway robbery!" Sypher growled.

"No, sir. That's what I figure the rig's worth. Rent will come to six dollars a day, for the horse and the buggy. If you bring my property back I'll refund your money minus the rent. Take it or leave it."

Fuming and glaring, the gray man drew a wallet from his coat. He fingered in it, partially withdrew a printed leaf, then shoved it back and produced cash money. He counted out goldbacks and handed them over, and Paul gave him a receipt.

"I'll pick up the rig in an hour," Sypher said. "And I'll need some provisions. Blankets, a tarp . . ."

"I know what you'll need in No Man's Land." Eugene Paul nodded. "I'll have you stocked and ready. And I strongly suggest you get yourself a rifle if you don't have one. It gets real lonesome out there, without protection."

When the easterner was gone, Jack Lyles said, "That's one of the people that came in with that bigshot Stratton. Could be he's scouting right-of-way."

"Could be." Paul shrugged. "But he sure didn't look like any surveyor I ever saw. And that was railroad scrip he flashed when he paid me. I'd give a dollar to know what he's up to."

"Prob'ly never know unless he don't come back," Lyles said.

"What do you mean by that?"

"Well, if he don't show up in a week like he said, you could file on him with the marshal. Then, if Buck sees fit, he might request a search for stolen property. Captain Burroughs would likely send a patrol out, since he don't know any better, and I'd likely be with that patrol."

"But he wouldn't be stealing anything," Paul pointed out. "He's already paid me the price of the rig and a good horse."

"Didn't notice him payin' you for the provisions, though." Lyles smiled. "Just keep it in mind. My bet is, that feller's headin' for the same place Falcon MacCallister went."

The first shot at the Barlow place came from the shadows beside the barn. It didn't hit anybody, but it was the bait that sprang the trap. Its muzzle flash was bright in the darkness, and eight or ten men in the advancing vigilante line returned the fire.

The blaze of gunfire from the creeping attackers was all the Barlows needed. Guns in the loft, guns on the roof of the house, guns in the cover of the corral, and guns at various other points raked Jackson's vigilantes as they ran for cover in the open field.

Jubal Mason was on the right flank, near a runoff wash that angled toward the brushy breaks. He dived into cover, then watched as the battle progressed. He had no intention of shooting any Barlows, but he didn't want to get shot by any of them, either. He had planned to put on the yellow band in hopes of getting a shot at Kurt Obermire or another of DeWitt's top dogs. But now he knew Obermire wasn't there, and an owlhoot named Jackson was heading the strike force.

So Jubal eased aside, watched and waited, hoping to help the squatters and wasn't really surprised when the surprise raid on the Barlow place turned out to be no surprise at all.

For a time, the affair was a battle in darkness—mostly just a lot of noise as people on both sides pumped lead blindly at people they couldn't see. But within minutes, distinct patterns emerged. Jubal had spotted a sharpshooter not far from him, in brush at the edge of the draw, and now he saw that someone else had spotted the same thing. Fifty yards away from him, he saw movement in the broken cover of the sloping field. A man was advancing there, crouching and dodging, flitting from shadow to shadow, closing in on the concealed shooter with each flash of gunfire.

The sharpshooter fired again, and in the field a hundred yards away a man screamed and fell, cursing as he thrashed about in pain.

No more than thirty yards from Jubal's cover, the moving vigilante sprinted across an open break and sprawled belly-down behind a sage stand. In that moment, Jubal recognized the attacker, and knew that the hidden sniper was in real trouble. It was Jackson himself, closing in.

As silently as possible, Jubal crawled out of the wash and got his feet under him. Cradling a sawed-off ten-gauge, he crept forward just as the sharpshooter opened up again from the draw and Jackson broke cover with his hands full of .45s.

What came next all happened in an instant. Jackson bounded to the edge of the draw, his revolvers leveled point-blank at the concealed shooter there. With a high-pitched squeal the shooter saw him— too late—and tried to roll aside to bring the rifle up. And Jubal cut loose with both barrels.

The twin roar of the ten-gauge was deafening, and the twin charges of buckshot cut into Jackson and threw him head over heels, right over the sniper and into the brush beyond.

Jackson's .45s, triggered by dead hands, fired harmlessly into the air, and a rifle bullet sang past an inch from Jubal's ear. With a yelp he dived and lost the empty shotgun. He landed smack on top of a squirming, kicking form that tried to brain him with a rifle butt while screaming curses in his ear—

words that nobody who felt and sounded like that form should even have known, must less used.

For a moment, Jubal was fighting for his life. Then, with an effort, he pinned the girl's arms, shook loose her rifle, and rasped, "Will you shut up, damn it? You're gonna have every yahoo out in that field over here tryin' to kill both of us!"

He could barely see her, but what he could feel was interesting. "Just simmer down, girl!" he ordered. "I'm on your side . . . I think!"

"You're one of *them!*" she spat. "Let go of me!"

"Not 'til we're better acquainted," Jubal said. "My name's Jubal Mason, and I'm here on my own business. Hell, I just saved your life, didn't I?"

"Mind your language!" she demanded, but the struggles eased. "I'm Becky Barlow," she admitted. "And you're gonna be dead if Pa and the boys get you in their sights."

Cautiously, Jubal raised his head to look around. The gun battle was still raging, but it was too dark to see who was shooting at whom. He lowered himself, pressing her down, away from the gully rim. For a second or two, he really hated to leave. But there might be Barlows—or vigilantes—all over the place any minute now. "How do I know you won't shoot me in the back when I turn away?" he demanded. "I mean, you didn't sound too much like a lady a minute ago."

"I just might," she admitted. "But I'll have to find my rifle first. Where are you going?"

"North of here," he said. "Ten, twelve miles, I guess, north and a little east. There's several of us with a mind to do some horse farmin' after we hang or shoot the fellers that run Paradise. Might be we're all interested in the same notions, us and your folks. Come see us up there if you want to. We can talk . . .

and I'd like to find out what you look like in daylight, Becky Barlow."

It took MacCallister most of a day to pick up the
trail of Woha'li. It would have taken longer if the
boy hadn't been still suffering from snakebite. The
wound had reddened, swelled, and ached at first,
then festered in an angry sore. Only a drop of
venom had gotten into his system from the fang
scratch, but the lasting infection took more time to
heal. Even though most of the swelling was gone,
the Indian kid was still weak sometimes, and careless.

"A cripple chasing a cripple," Falcon muttered as
he followed cold trail south of Paradise. It was an
easy track, or would have been if he felt better. He
still got dizzy sometimes, and though he wasn't spitting up blood any more he was weak and light-
headed.

But he pushed all that aside, impatiently. Like the
searing pain of his deep wounds, it was something
he could ignore.

The pony's prints were familiar, and the efforts at
concealment clumsy. He wondered what had happened to make the Indian boy so careless. Somehow
the kid had crept right into an armed town and shot
a man down in broad daylight—a dangerous man,
at that. In Falcon's mind there was no doubt who
had killed Folly Downs, and the feat was awesome,
considering the odds.

But out here, having eluded pursuit, his day-old
tracks were those of a weary horse with a careless
rider. Had the kid been wounded at Paradise? Falcon didn't think so. But there was something wrong.

He was nearly ten miles south of DeWitt's town

on Wolf Creek when he spotted the tendril of smoke ahead—across half a mile of grass prairie—and knew where Woha'li was.

But he didn't expect what he found there. Deep in a brushy gully, the camp was almost invisible until he was right on top of it. And it wasn't the camp of a sick, desolate fugitive. In a tiny cove created by a bend in the gully, cuts of freshly butchered cow hung on a willow rack in the smoke of a well-tended little fire. A cowhide stretched across a pocket and camouflaged with clumps of sod, made a snug nest against the wind. There was water in a snow-fed seep, and a battered saddle lay against the cut bank. Further down the draw, on sheltered silver grass, the boy's horse grazed contentedly.

"All the comforts of home," Falcon muttered, leaning on his saddle horn. He raised his voice. "Woha'li! It's me! MacCallister! Can I come in?"

The voice that answered him was scant yards away, to the side and behind him, and Diablo sidestepped nervously as sagebrush there whispered with movement. "I'm right here, *Towo'di,*" the boy said quietly. "Saw you comin' long ways off. Want some meat?"

The boy seemed older somehow—more assured and more contained than Falcon remembered. Still just a lanky half-grown kid, but the resolve in his eyes was that of a man. Over a meal of hot beef and biscuit, they studied each other across the fire. The kid's scrape with a rattler had left its mark—a deep ugly scar that he might carry always. And the kid saw Falcon's careful posture and knew that the big blond man had been injured too. But both of them were recovering, and neither was crippled.

"You killed a man in that town up there, didn't

you, Woha'li?" Falcon asked. "Shot out his voice, then made him hurt dying."

"I'll kill five more, too, if I can," the boy told him. "They're there, the ones that killed my parents. I know them. And don't call me Woha'li any more. I have a new name now." He indicated the snakebite scar. "It's Utsonati. Means rattlesnake."

"You know I'm after that bunch, too," Falcon said. "So are some others. You've made them harder to get. They'll be spooked now. You go in there again, they'll likely kill you. Why not let us handle it?"

Utsonati gazed at him, a level gaze with no expression. "No," he said. "I'm not through."

"Then throw in with us, boy. It's the only way."

"Who did they hurt of yours?"

"People just as innocent as your father and mother were," MacCallister said. "People I never knew, but I buried what was left."

"Why do you care if you didn't know them?"

"Same reason I care about your folks." The man gazed at the little fire, thoughtfully. "What would you do if you saw wild dogs trying to drag down a child?"

"I'd shoot some dogs," the boy said. "Make 'em stop."

"Even if the child was nobody you know?"

Utsonati didn't answer then, but later he said, "I'll go along, *yoneg*. Far as I want to. Then I go alone. Where are we going?"

"Place up north of town." Falcon cut another strip of meat from the roasting loin. "Where did you get this cow?"

"Found it," the boy said. "It was a stray."

Falcon was studying the stretched hide. "This

animal's trail marked," he said. "It's from a Texas herd."

"Some of those Texas drovers catch an Indian near their cows, they'll string him up for a rawhider," Falcon warned. "I'm surprised they'd drive into No Man's Land at all. Best cow trail's along the scarp, past Fort Supply."

"Drovers didn't have this one," Utsonati said flatly. "It was yellow-bands, from the town. They had sixteen cows. Now they have fifteen. How you think all those white people over there stay fed, *Towo'di?* Half the jaspers in this strip steal cows when they can."

It was quite a crowd that Asa Parker—or Colonel Amos DeWitt—had gathered around him in No Man's Land, Falcon mused. The worst of the lawless: killers and robbers, fugitives from all over. The Neutral Strip was full of them. Now a lot of them wore yellow bands and rode for Parker. With cash in hand, Parker and his buddies had built themselves a little empire in almost no time.

Parker was in charge of the big swindle—selling land that wasn't his to sell. And his hirelings were helping themselves to whatever was offered. And that included rustling cattle.

Some changes had been made at the haymeadows when Falcon rode in with the Cherokee boy. A nice little herd of horses grazed on the lush winter grass, and Archer and the boys had put up a sign: A&M LAND AND CATTLE HORSE RANCH.

"You're looking better, Mr. MacCallister," Brett Archer said as the newcomers dismounted. "Not so much like you're going to die."

Falcon shrugged. "You've been working on the place."

"Yeah, fixing it up. Maybe we'll stay a while. Go into the horse business."

"Might sell those vigilantes their own horses," Jude Mason agreed, "or trade 'em for a prairie schooner with a few well-chosen corpses hangin' from its tongue."

"It's a slap in the face to that bunch at Paradise," Jonah chimed in. "Like a challenge."

"You think those outlaws will stand still for this when they hear about it?" Falcon shook his head. "How long do you think it's going to take them to find you here?"

"Not very long," Archer grinned. "We were just waitin' for you to get back before we rode down there and introduced ourselves. That land office in Paradise has a map of available claims, and this place is on it. Listed as four quarter-sections of improved uninhabited property. We need to set them straight about that. Most of the improvements here are ours, and we're staking claim by right of presence."

"You'll have a war on your hands."

"Fine. While they're out here fighting us, we can be down there settling accounts with the men who killed Dorothy."

"Might keep things interesting," Falcon said. "But whoever set that bunch off will show up sooner or later. That's the time to get them all."

Jubal studied him through narrowed eyes. "No offense intended, Mr. MacCallister, but it seems like you're grinding different axes than we are. We know where the murderers are, and we're plumb tired of waiting."

"So you think you'll just force a showdown and take them all out?"

Brett pursed his lips thoughtfully. "Maybe we won't have to fight the whole gang," he said. "I have an idea some of those vigilantes might be interested in a better deal."

The Mason brothers were eyeballing the Indian boy curiously. "Who's the papoose?" Jubal asked.

The kid started to bristle, but MacCallister waved him down. "His name used to be Woha'li," he said. "Now he's Utsonati. He's after the same men you fellows are, for his own reasons. And don't let his size fool you. He's the one who killed Folly Downs."

The kid hung close, listening to the talk, and he shared a meal with them. He was around for a day or so. Then he was gone, and not a one of them had seen him leave.

MacCallister had been hoisting a saddle onto Diablo when sharp pains lanced through him and he noticed that the deep wound in his belly was bleeding again. Jude Mason noticed it, too. Without a word, the youth went and hitched up the buckboard and brought it around.

"Get in, Mr. MacCallister," he said. "Let's go for a ride."

Falcon squinted at him. "Where?"

"Across the line. You might not recollect what Dr. Linsecum said when we took you there, but I do. He said come back when you need tendin'."

"I'm all right," Falcon glared. "It's just a hole healin'."

"Well, 'til it does, I aim to have you see that doc when you bleed. I don't know if you care about livin', Mr. MacCallister, but I care if you do. I put too much fuss into haulin' you down here to have you fold up on me now."

SEVENTEEN

On a spring day as soft as warm velvet, the Mason boys rode in to Paradise and went directly to the land office. Their arrival caused no stir, though the town now swarmed with yellow-banded hoodlums, like bees around a disturbed hive. Following the aborted raid on the Barlow claim, the only safe place for known vigilantes was in town, and there was even some doubt about that.

Even while the remnants of Jackson's raiders were racing for home, harassed by angry squatters, several Barlow kin had raced through town, firing at whatever moved and shouting curses.

Fourteen of Obermire's hoodlums had not returned from the raid. Since then, Paradise had been an armed camp. Vigilantes patrolled the perimeters and prowled the street—surly unruly little gangs of gun trash held in check only by the promise of wages in return for services. Colonel Amos DeWitt stayed close to his wagon, ready to defend it and the cash it held. Casper Wilkerson patrolled the nearby street with his shotgun cradled across his arm. Kurt Obermire strode up and down the street like a big thundercloud, muttering promises and shouting threats, reorganizing his Vigilance Committee.

The Jackson raid on the Barlow place, and its disastrous outcome, had set DeWitt's scheme back. A lot of yellow-bands were taking another look at their hole cards.

The results were visible in the townspeople's cautious arrogance—those who were not part of the "Paradise plan"—and in the eyes of the squatters coming into town to trade. By brute force and gun wages, DeWitt's bunch had come to Wolf Creek and taken over the settlement. Now the Barlows had shown that DeWitt could be backed down. Days passed, and there were no more night raids on homesteads in the Wolf Creek valley. All around was a feeling of barely repressed anger.

Paradise was now a restless and surly little town. The vigilantes still controlled the street, but there was spirit in the glares of those who resented their being there. Still, business went on as usual. Each day a few more land-hungry westers arrived looking for claims, and O'Brien's land office was doing land office business. The land shark frowned and cursed each time a customer arrived who might have paid cash for the choicest property, but he was careful now to issue no deeds to claimed steads.

DeWitt had cursed him for his cautiousness, but O'Brien drew the line at putting his neck into a noose, and in his estimation the demoralized vigilantes were poor insurance.

Brett Archer had become a familiar figure in town. Smooth and striking in high boots, a black tailcoat and flare-brimmed hat set at a rakish slant, the Virginian strolled casually along Paradise's only real street, calling attention to himself, distracting the loungers by his presence while Jonah, Jude, and Jubal Mason surreptitiously tacked up hand-lettered signs in several conspicuous places.

For several days, Brett had been in and around

Paradise, becoming part of the scenery. His presence drew attention, as he intended. Nobody was quite sure who he was, but everybody local had seen him around. Among newcomers and townspeople he made a point of getting acquainted. On this morning he roamed the squalid town, exchanging friendly greetings here and there and tipping his hat to the ladies.

He made a splendid diversion. Not once in the time it took the Mason brothers to post their signs did anyone so much as glance their way.

Jubal and Jude were furtive at first. They could not be sure that some of the vigilantes might not recognize them from the night of the raid. Unlike his brothers, though, Jonah had been no part of that. Now, with his flop hat pulled down to his ears and a harmless grin on his face, he was a nobody who could have been anybody.

Gongs rang at the beaneries at each end of the street, and crowds started drifting toward the places. The Masons met at the land office and waited patiently until O'Brien was alone. Then Jonah stood guard at the door while Jubal and Jude braced the land agent.

"We've found the land we want," Jubal said, stepping around O'Brien's desk to the plat map tacked up on the wall. "These four quarter-sections right here, where this creek forks. We call it the Haymeadows Ranch. I guess you can issue clear deeds to this property?"

O'Brien glanced at his map. The place was some distance out, and had no warning X on it. It was one of the older claims, with no Barlows on it. "Oh, indeed I can," he assured, narrowing his eyes as he calculated the worth of the young drifters. "Of course, you realize that is choice property, with improvements already in place, so the price will reflect that."

"Let me look at the deeds," Jude said.

O'Brien thumbed through neatly filed stacks of ornately embossed paper. "Here they are," he said, pulling out a stack of four. "You won't find a more choice investment than this, sir. Reacquired from the original owner, and all covered under the general patent of Paradise Land Company. A first-class package ready for immediate occupancy, and your choice of four town lots to go with it."

Jude scanned the carefully penned descriptions on the deeds and compared them to the map coordinates. "That's fine," he said. "We'll take them. Sign and stamp the documents. Make them out to A and M Land and Cattle Company. The young fellow over there by the door can serve as witness."

O'Brien's eyes narrowed. For the first time he noticed the emptiness of his office, the alert stance of the youngster near the door, and the steely gazes of his customers. A shiver of apprehension went up his spine, and he hesitated.

Casually, Jubal swept back his coattail, emphasizing the big revolver at his belt.

At the front, Jonah said, "Well, they've found the notice. Quite a crowd gathering over yonder."

Like most men of his time, Thaddeus O'Brien carried a gun—a Colt "Baby Dragoon" that rested unseen below his left armpit. But O'Brien was no gunfighter. He was a salesman, and his salesman's instincts told him he was far outmatched here.

"Don't worry, Mr. O'Brien," Jubal purred. "We're not here to rob you. We don't intend to pay for the land we're claiming, of course . . . that land isn't yours to sell any more than any other land around here is. But those printed deeds are right pretty, and they ought to be worth something. We'll give a dollar apiece for them."

"Look here!" O'Brien stammered. "You can't just—"

"Yes, we can," Jubal corrected him. "We're doing it."

"Colonel DeWitt won't stand for this!"

"Do tell. Just execute those deeds, land shark."

With their deeds signed, stamped, and folded away in Jubal's inside coat pocket, the Masons escorted O'Brien politely but firmly into the sturdy little closet behind the big desk, relieved him of his gun, and bolted the door.

Thaddeus O'Brien had just finished prying his closet door open when the door of the land office crashed open and Colonel Amos DeWitt stormed in, followed by Casper Wilkerson. An angry crowd of vigilantes milled in the street outside.

The colonel waved a poster in O'Brien's face. "What the hell is this?" he demanded. "Where's Haymeadows Ranch?"

O'Brien read the poster, then read it again:

HORSES FOR SALE—PRIME SADDLE STOCK—SADDLES AND TACK—SELECT NIGHT HORSES, PREVIOUSLY OWNED BY NIGHT RIDERS—EACH ONE A STEAL—FIRST COME FIRST SERVED—SEE AT HAYMEADOWS RANCH, TEN MILES NORTHEAST. A&M LAND AND CATTLE, PROP.

"What the hell is this, O'Brien?" DeWitt repeated. "Where's Haymeadows Ranch, and who has it?"

"That's what I was coming to tell you, sir."

O'Brien gulped. "Those three drifters—name of Mason, couple of hard cases and a kid looked like a farmer—they made me issue deeds to four quarters up on Cove Creek. They said they claim that property, and anybody who wants to contest the claim is invited to try."

Out on the street a wagon had hauled up and a gray-looking little man stepped down to fasten the tie at a hitch rail. Vigilantes glanced his way, then dismissed him and concentrated on the land office. The crowd parted and Kurt Obermire stomped into the office, carrying one of the signs. "That's where our horses went!" he rasped. "Them Barlows!"

"The Barlows have friends," DeWitt said. "I want you to put a stop to this, Kurt. You and Casper, take some men out to this Haymeadows Ranch. Shoot anybody you find out there, and bring those horses back."

"The hell with that!" Casper Wilkerson said. "There ain't anybody up there, Colonel. Be a wild-goose chase, just to get us away from town. That Barlow crowd's got our horses, all right, but my bet is we'll find them right down there where those squatters are nested."

Kurt nodded. "Them an' their friends," he said. "That was more than a bunch of dirt farm squatters Jackson ran into down there. Those squatters had help, an' they knew the boys were comin'."

"So they've got some friends," DeWitt scoffed. "Bunch of drifters, likely."

"Them drifters killed Jackson, and damn near wiped out half my Vigilance Committee."

"They got lucky. And maybe some of your *vigilantes* did it themselves. Maybe Jackson isn't dead, at all. Maybe he's struck out on his own, and maybe he's thinkin' about how to come in here and take my money."

"Our money, Asa." Casper's glare was as cold as snake eyes.

"Sure, our money. That's probably it. Damn drifters want us chasin' off north to Haymeadows so they can hit the town. Well, it won't work. We know where the Barlows are. Just take the men you can trust and go down there and wipe 'em out."

"And get them horses back," Kurt said. He shot a glance at Wilkerson. "You goin' with me, Casper? Or do I do this myself?"

Wilkerson ignored the giant. In his opinion, Kurt Obermire didn't have the brains God gave a biscuit. "I don't think those are just squatters out there, Asa. I got a bad feelin'."

"You think the Barlows have an army or something?" DeWitt glared at him. "I think you're right about one thing, though. The Barlows won't stray far from their own digs. They're not going to leave their claims and go holing up somewhere else just to devil us. They held their ground against Jackson's posse. They think they've got what they want, now."

"Yeah, our horses," Kurt Obermire growled.

"I'm not worried about the Barlows," Casper said slowly. "There's somebody else, Asa . . . I mean, colonel. I'm thinkin' what happened to Folly, right here in town. I got a feelin' somebody's drawin' a bead on us."

"If not the Barlows, then who?"

"Have you ever heard of Falcon MacCallister?" a voice asked. The gray man from the wagon stood in the doorway.

DeWitt turned and squinted at him. "Sypher," he rumbled. "What are you doing here?"

"You have trouble, Asa," Sypher said. His shrewd

eyes flicked from one to another of them, and back to DeWitt. "You and your men have been identified from that job in Colorado."

"That's impossible," DeWitt growled. "We left no witnesses."

Behind the desk, O'Brien edged away, trying to fade into the shadows. At a sharp glance from DeWitt he shook his head. "I've got no part of this," he muttered. "I just sell—"

"We're all in it together," DeWitt said. "Now shut up." He turned back to Sypher. "They don't know who took that money," he insisted. "Nobody alive back there to say."

Sypher glared at him. "Do you think J. L. Horner is a fool? I told you to cover your tracks, Asa. The 'Hiram Pasco' thing was sloppy. You think they don't keep track of their security? Horner's people had you pegged within a day, and Kansas Pacific has issued a circular on you. I intercepted their message. They've called in a top gun to track you down. You and the five with you. Another thing, too. When I was at Dodge there was a wagon party taking on riders. Seems some of their men left for the Neutral Strip, looking for some outlaws that murdered a family over in Colorado. Said they raped the women, killed everybody and ran off with a prairie schooner." He gestured with a thumb. "Like that one out there across the street. Looks like you and your boys are attracting quite a crowd, Asa."

"Stop calling me Asa!" DeWitt rumbled. "Around here I'm Colonel Amos DeWitt. Keep it that way! Did you bring the right-of-way papers?"

"They're in my valise," Sypher said. "Noted and sealed. Says there'll be a main line coming right through here. So let's get to moving some acres."

"O'Brien will post the papers and mark the map." DeWitt nodded. "This will bring the big money in."

"Then we better clean out those Barlows and all the other squatters," Obermire pointed out. "Startin' with that Barlow bunch. I'll pick out the men, colonel. I've got some tough boys that'd just love to cut down the jaspers that took their saddle stock."

"We need to find out who killed Folly," Casper reminded.

Sypher glanced at each of them, his eyes hooded. "More problems, Asa?"

"Nothing we can't handle," DeWitt spat. "You said the Kansas Pacific sent for a top gun. Who is it?"

"They sent for Falcon MacCallister."

"Falcon MacCallister's dead," DeWitt said. "Billy Challis and Tuck Kelly ran across him outside Dodge. Billy killed him."

Sypher frowned. He knew about MacCallister. The man was a legend. The idea of Billy Challis putting him under . . . well, it didn't sit right. "Are you sure?"

Out in the street the noise level increased as several battered wagons rolled past from the east, led by weather-hardened riders and followed by flocks of muddy children herding livestock.

O'Brien peered out the dirty window. "Westers. They've come across the territories. They'll be looking to buy land."

Sypher stepped to the window, and sneered. "Them? They don't look like they've got a nickel among them."

"These farmers'll fool you sometimes." O'Brien shrugged. "I've seen 'em that wouldn't spare six bits to put shoes on their young'uns, but they'll come up with plenty of hard cash where land's concerned. They're all dirt crazy. Live in a pigsty and spend five, ten, thousand dollars on a barn. Never know what they got squirreled away in those wagons, either.''

Casper Wilkerson glared at the salesman. "Oh, shut up, O'Brien. You make me sick. We got squatters an' bounty hunters to worry about, and all you think about, is fleecin' farmers.''

O'Brien bristled, drawing himself up in a self-righteous pose. "You think town lots and planter plots sell themselves, Mr. Wilkerson? You think I don't work damn hard for what we bring in around here? You just look at that map there! Those little tracts turn seven hundred to a thousand dollars apiece every time I hand over a deed. Why, I've got some parcels I can get fifteen hundred for, cash money. And twice that, if they get vacated so I can sell 'em again! Don't you never look down your nose at me, Mr. Wilkerson! I'm the man that pays the bills around here!''

DeWitt growled—a deep contemptuous rumble. He wondered if anybody besides himself and Sypher really saw what was at stake here. All of this, this finagling of lands and claims, was just a sham. O'Brien's suckers were only the prime for the pump. As the claims were cleared, the town grew. And with the town came authentication of the fable that there would be a railroad.

Hell, the rails might actually *come* this way if there was market enough to support them!

The real money was out there, just watching and getting hungry—big money, maybe a million dollars or more, just waiting to be taken when eastern investors saw an established town with patents on a railhead and no way to prove that the "railroad" plans were fake.

But Wilkerson was right. There were some problems that had to be attended to before the real players began to show up. He turned. "Kurt, send somebody out to the Spring place. Get Billy and Tuck back here. Billy's had plenty of time to get well. They can help you clean out those nesters."

"I don't need Billy Challis to clean out nesters," Obermire asserted. "He's loco as a jimsoned cow. You just keep him out of my way. I'll clean out the Barlows."

DeWitt was fed up with the talk. "Then do it, Kurt! By the time Billy and Tuck get here, I want the squatters off that creek, and that mob of yours looking like an army."

Out on the street, a muddy old spring wagon with a bone-tired horse pulled up in front of the Emporium and three people climbed down. The man was a shaggy weathered old graybeard with sagging galluses, a slouch hat, and run-down boots. The old woman was tired and feeble, and it took both the man and the younger woman—a sad-eyed slip of a girl no more than twenty—to help her down.

They unstrapped a rocking chair from the shabby contents and set it on the Emporium porch, then helped the old woman into it. The old man fussed around his horse for a minute, then looked around bleakly, said something to the girl, and went inside.

The commotion had attracted the attention of some of the men prowling the street, and a crowd of hecklers gathered, preening for the girl.

"Will ye look at that, Moss?" a man said, grinning. "Grow 'em skinny where this lot's from, don't they?"

"Skinny an' dirty," another said, laughing. "But you never can tell. With a old dress like that, a man just can't see whether they's anythin' underneath worth lookin' at. Tell ye what, though, I'd wager five dollars there's some prime possum underneath there, if it was scrubbed a little."

On the porch, the girl glanced around, frightened. The other wagons, the ones they had been following, were gone now, out of sight down the bending street. The old woman seemed oblivious. As the laughing men edged closer, closing in on their prey, other people turned away, pretending not to notice. Moss and Newby and their crowd were rough men, and they wore the yellow flags of vigilantes.

The girl looked this way and that, then glared at the nearest ones in defiance. "Y'all just let us alone!" she demanded. "We ain't hurt nobody."

"My, my, Moss. You hear that? The little mudhen has a voice. Sounds like Tennessee hills, don't she?"

"Sounds just like music," a vigilante said, grinning. "I'll take the bet, though. I don't think there's nothin' but skin an' bones under them rags. Let's us have a look."

Brett Archer had just stepped out of one of Paradise's tent-flap saloons. It took only a moment to see what was happening, and he started that way, his eyes glittering. But others were there ahead of him. As Moss reached for the girl, a hand closed on his arm and swung him around. He found himself staring up into the narrowed eyes of another vigilante— a quiet slope-shouldered outlaw named Cass Jolly.

"That's enough, Moss," Cass growled. "You've had your fun. Now let her alone."

Moss blinked, and glanced around. His buddies were neatly flanked by several other night riders, all looking businesslike. Cutting his eyes back to Cass he said, "You bracin' me, Cass Jolly? What the hell do you care?"

"I was raised to mind my manners around women," Cass said quietly, "and I expect other gents to do the same."

"Don't put on airs with me!" Moss spat. "You're no better than me. They got warrants on you in Missouri, just like me in Arkansas!"

"I've had my bad turns," Cass nodded. "Same as most of us around here. But bein' outlawed don't mean a man has to act like a waller hog!"

Moss might have started the ball then, but a whang-tough drifter named Dawson crowded in, glaring at him. "I'm takin' a hand in this," the man said. "There's things I won't stand for."

The set-to lasted only a moment. Then Moss and his friends pulled loose and walked away, grumbling.

Brett Archer waited a bit, then strolled along a muddy boardwalk and sidled up to a cluster of yellow-banded hard cases. "What's going on, Cass?" he asked. "Everybody seems almighty edgy."

The man only glanced at him. "Squatters an' horse thieves," he grumbled. "First they send Jackson an' some of the boys into a shootin' gallery. Now the squatters are offerin' to sell back the horses they lost."

"Enterprising bunch, seems to me." Brett grinned.

"You think it's funny?" Cass hawked and spat. "Men get on edge, that's when the skunks show their stripes. You saw that business with the squatter girl. Some jaspers don't draw the line when they go bad. Me, I've had about all I can stand."

"But you hired on for the Vigilance Committee, didn't you?"

"Sure I did. Keep the peace and run off a few

squatters. That was all. DeWitt may pay gun wages, but I don't see him payin' war wages." He surveyed the street sardonically. "We got us some outlaws here, an' then we got some plain rotten people. The milk's separatin', Archer. Them big shots better do somethin' about this mess, or I'm fixin' to move on. Lot of the boys are gettin' fed up."

"Pretty well restricts a man when the law's after him, doesn't it?" Brett asked innocently.

"My personal problems are none of your damn business!"

"No, I guess not. But you know, if it was me I'd be thinking about settling down around here someplace. Law can't bother a man where there isn't any law . . . or where he and his good neighbors can get together and make their own."

Some of the men around Cass were listening, now. "What do you mean by that?" Bob Hudgins demanded.

Archer shrugged. "I mean, maybe some of you boys got dealt a bad hand. Happens sometimes, a man gets caught up in circumstance and next thing he knows the law is after him. And maybe being outside the law is the only choice he's got, then. I know there are men around here who can't go where they choose, even if they never started out to be outlaws. But it seems to me there isn't any better place than right here to get a fresh start, if a man wants to."

"Here? You mean the Neutral Strip?"

"Why not? This is No Man's Land. No real law here, but there's still right and wrong. Looks to me like a man could make whatever he wants out of it."

Aside, the drifter Dawson slitted his eyes. "Sounds like another feller I know," he mused. "Like somethin' Falcon MacCallister might say."

EIGHTEEN

Cassius Barlow hauled the old surrey to a stop on a ridge where scrub cedar clumps ended at a washout cliff. Tying off his reins, he set the brake and stood, looking out across rough lands. "Fur piece f'm Rocky Top," he muttered. "But I reckon it'll do."

The arid breaks and scrub hills were truly a "fur piece" from the Cumberlands of Cassius's youth and the brooding Tennessee slopes where he had set his stick so many years ago. Those hills were far away now, and in another life.

Cassius had seen little but hard times in his sixty-odd years on God's Earth. Now he was a thousand miles from the old places he remembered, and still seeing hard times. He faced each day in the Neutral Strip just as he had faced every day of his life—with the stubborn fierce determination of a man who knows he can't always win but has no mind to lose gracefully.

Down the hill from where he had stopped, a man waited for him among the canvases and cookfires of a passel of Barlows and kin. Even from up where he stood, Cassius could see the stranger—a tall thick-shouldered figure standing at ease among men who would kill him as quick as lightning if he gave them cause. The man stood taller than most around him, and Cassius could almost feel the force of his eyes looking back at him from that far away.

Even from there, the old man knew that this was a man to be reckoned with. The stranger stood tall, easy, and unconcerned, and something about him reminded Cassius of storm clouds just like those standing now above the westward hills.

Cassius looked up at the darkening thunderheads, then back at the encampment. That man—that big moon-blond man waiting down there—he was like the clouds. He went where he would, casting a long shadow. And under the solemn presence of him, lightning lurked.

Cassius was reminded of some of the old bunch back in the high-up hills. A breed apart, they were, and they strode the lands above Big Lick before the war came and thinned them out.

Nothing had ever come easily along Big Lick. Two wives and five of Cassius's children rested now in those hills back home, in the same soil that covered Cassius's sister and two brothers and other kin. There were Barlows, Smiths, Landons, and Higginses back there, and they were all cut from the same cloth, and all kin.

That had been a hard life, like the one which shaped up to be out here in the west. Cassius knew no other kind, and only two kinds of people who mattered. There were kin, and there were others. Kin might bicker and brawl, but they hung together as clans do . . . as the Barlows had, even through the war years and the worse times that followed.

Kin followed kin. When Cassius decided, three years ago now, that it was time to pick up and move, the kin moved, too. The young ones led the way, spreading westward until Leotus sent word that there was land to be had past the territories. The word spread, and family by family they had filtered into this strip called No Man's Land.

It was Leotus, Cassius's oldest still standing, who staked the first claim, and those who followed gathered to his digs. It was the Lord's work that Frank and Haden and their grown boys were there when the raiders came—the Lord's work, and a word of warning from a stranger.

Must have been some kind of a sight, Cassius mused, *when those night riders came down on Leotus's little place and met more than they'd bargained for.* Two Barlows and a Higgins cousin were buried now on the rise above Leotus's field, but they had good company. In the breaks below them, a full dozen vigilantes lay sod-planted and duly prayed over. Maybe two, three, more were put down in that squalid little town that they came from, too.

And that man down there—that towheaded big man waiting for him—had a hand in how all that went. MacCallister, his name was. Falcon MacCallister. Leotus knew him to call by name, and Leotus said he was worth meeting with. They waited down there now, for council.

When you've seen one Barlow, some said, you've seen them all. Forged in the unforgiving ranges of Appalachia, tempered by event and circumstance, they were people cut to a pattern, and that was the pattern of the hills.

At the Rabbit Creek encampment, Falcon MacCallister rested easy while he waited for the patriarch of the Barlow clan. All around him people came and went, and he observed them. There were Higginses and Taylors, Smiths and Landons, and some by other names, but they were all Barlows, and all carried the mark of the hills.

They gave him coffee so strong you could stand a spoon in it, and a bait of oats for Diablo, but few words were passed. He was a stranger, and these were not trusting people. They let him be, and he waited. The rolling hills darkened to the west, where thunderhead clouds climbed the sky. On a ridge out there, riders paused, crowding up in a wide ring around a lone figure in a surrey. Though Falcon had never met him, he knew who it was—the patriarch was here. Falcon had asked for words with Cassius Barlow, and Cassius Barlow had come.

Thunder rolled across the hills as the surrey rattled into camp, followed by its dour escort, fifteen riders in all. It wasn't until they were close that Falcon noticed three of them were women. They wore britches and rode like men, and the rifles they carried were as sure in their hands as any man's.

One of them rode directly to Falcon and looked down at him—her pretty face under a slouch hat. When she pushed the hat back to squint at him, he saw bright auburn hair. "I'm Becky Barlow," she said. "Yonder's Granddaddy Cassius. He'll see you directly."

"Obliged," Falcon said.

"Knowed your daddy," the old man said. "Only reason I come. So speak your piece."

Cassius Barlow sat on a cottonwood stump, flanked by sons and nephews, and Falcon gazed at him. Here was a man, he knew, who had met life head-on, every day of his life, and fought it to a draw. Here was one who had never asked quarter, and never surrendered.

"I want you and yours to help," Falcon said.

"Help you? Why?"

"Not me. I skin my own cougars. I want you to help yourself. You folks have come to settle here. If anybody can do it, you can. But there's a rattlers' nest that needs cleaning out, and that's your problem more than mine."

"You mean that bunch at Paradise." Cassius spat. "They done made their run at us. We laid gospel on 'em."

"That was just a few." Falcon shrugged. "When they come at you again, they'll come in force. Those men are in a game with high stakes, with money on the table. They want the land, Barlow. They want all the land, and nobody but their own on it."

The old man shook his head bleakly. "Ain't being pushed out again," he declared. "We'll fight 'em."

"You and how many? Twenty? Thirty? That head man at Paradise is running a railroad scam. Do you know what that means? He'll buy himself an army if that's what it takes."

"I got kin."

"Takes more than kin." Falcon's grin was as cold as a thaw breeze. "Believe me, I know about that."

"Make your point, MacCallister."

Falcon shrugged. "My point is, you Barlows aren't alone any more. You don't have to be. You can have allies if you're willing to team up."

"Never had nobody tote our load." Cassius glared. "Why'd anybody do that?"

"It's what neighbors do."

MacCallister pointed westward, and the old man and his flankers turned. Atop the rise to the west were silhouettes—a dozen, then a dozen more, then more than could be counted at a glance. Some of them were mounted, many were not. They came onward, plodding down the long slopes where spring grass was greening. Men, women, and children they came, with their meager stock and a few old wagons, and they carried the tools and weapons they had at hand.

"Those folks might make neighbors, if you'll let them," Falcon said. "The man in the lead there is named Iverson. He and his folks have tried their hand at mining, up by Black Mesa. But the gold around here isn't in the rocks. It's in the fertile land. They see that now. They're ready to settle in, if there's neighbors here they can tolerate."

Beyond Cassius and his sons, Becky Barlow pulled off her old hat and shook her head. Rich auburn hair cascaded to her shoulders. "Army?" she scoffed. "I don't see any army yonder. All I see's a bunch of fools with picks an' shovels."

Falcon shrugged. "It's a start."

Old Cassius shook his head. "What are we supposed to do with that bunch? Take 'em in?"

"Why not? Them and more like them. They'll need all the help they can get . . . but in return they'll give their friendship, if you're worth it. You and yours have had bad times, Barlow. Well, so have they."

"Pretty sorry lookin' bunch," Becky Barlow allowed. "We don't need strangers."

"You'd be dead now if it hadn't been for a stranger," Falcon reminded her. "Have you forgotten Jubal Mason?"

"Him? He happened along, is all."

"Well, he'll happen again. Him and his brothers. They're up at Haymeadows Ranch. Might settle in there, if they have reason to. Might even join up with good neighbors." He turned to the old man. "You ever study on the past, Mr. Barlow?"

"I read the Good Book," Cassius admitted. "An' maybe a mite more."

"Well, a long time ago there was a fellow . . . his name was like yours. Cassius. He showed how folks can take root on a land, and give a hand to their neighbors, and come fighting time it takes more than some army to put them off. You might think on that, while you say hello to your new neighbors."

The old man turned himself full around, gazing out across the greening miles. It was a tempting notion—to have neighbors beyond kin that one could count on. But hard times whispered of hard times past, and he shook his head.

" 'Tain't our concern," he said, "what t'others do. Barlows won't tolerate bein' pushed, but I don't reckon we'll push none, either. Them in that town, they'll let us alone or wish they had. But we ain't takin' no hand past that."

MacCallister sighed. "Turtles hole up in their shells, Mr. Barlow," he said. "But that doesn't keep folks that want it from eating turtle soup. You can't hide from men like that Paradise bunch, and you can't stand alone. There's people here that will help you, if you let them."

Cassius shook his head again, with finality. "Barlows quit expectin' help a long time ago," he said. "Don't ask it, don't want it. It ain't our concern."

"Then you don't want neighbors?"

The old man gazed at him thoughtfully. "There's land enough, I reckon. Not our affair if some want to settle it." He looked up at one of his sons. "Mercy Cole an' them are camped back at Rock Gulch," he said. "An' there's a plenty hauled up north of Supply, lookin' for places to light. Y'all get the word out. Land's here for takin', water for sharin'. Barlows get first claim, but anybody that'll leave us alone is welcome to the rest."

He turned again to Falcon. "Best I can do," he said. "We'll tend our own. What others do ain't our concern."

"By God," Kurt Obermire swore, "there's squatters poppin' out of the ground!"

Six miles out of Paradise, the vigilantes had crested a ridge and stopped there, in confusion. The Vigilance Committee had ridden out of Paradise in force, aiming for Rabbit Creek. They intended to clear out the last remaining squatters down there—the Barlow clan.

But even before they could see Rabbit Creek they saw settlements. In the distance was the smoke of dozens of cookfires, and closer in—spreading across the landscape all along the three little valleys that meandered down toward Rabbit Creek—were the canvas tents, wagontops, and fresh clearings of newly claimed homesteads.

Where there had been one squatter's nest—the main Barlow place—now there were dozens, spread over two or three sections of prime land. Even from this distance—a mile from the nearest claim—the vigilantes could see movement. Riders ranged across the grasslands and the saged hills, going from one claim to another.

Where there had been one occupied claim and a few burned-out ruins around it, there was now a whole settlement of squatters. Like ants to a busted den, the settlers had moved in, bag and baggage, and begun rebuilding.

And not a one of them, Kurt knew, had bought a title from the Paradise Land Company.

"By God!" the big man muttered again. "Asa's gonna go off like a bomb when he finds out about this!"

He thought of the map in O'Brien's land office, and of the marks on it that showed the railway route that weasel Sypher had brought in, and his eyes widened even more. "By God in Heaven!" he roared.

Between this sprawl of "Barlow trash" down there on Rabbit Creek and that bunch of horse thieves up at Haymeadows, the whole "right-of-way" was littered with squatters at both ends, with Paradise right in the middle.

"Lord have mercy!" Kurt said.

"We been seen," a rider said, pointing. A mile away, there were riders on a hill, bunched and looking their way. Out across the sagebrush lands beyond, other riders were appearing, coming to face the intruders.

"I thought we had this whole valley cleaned out, just a month ago," Tad Sands blustered. "All but them Barlows."

"They want to play games?" Obermire muttered. "I'll show 'em games." He waved a man forward. "Colby, take ten men and hit that nearest squat. Hit 'em hard and fast, then circle back here."

As the vigilantes galloped away, yellow bandanas flapping like signals, Kurt pointed at another of his men. "You!" he ordered. "Take the rest of these boys and swing around. You see that claim yonder, where the burned barn is? You hit that, and shoot anythin' that moves. Then head back here. Those riders out there will be followin' you or Colby . . . maybe both. I'll be waitin' under that bluff yonder. When you get back here, pile off an' take cover. We'll catch 'em in a crossfire. They won't know what hit 'em!"

NINETEEN

For a few moments, Obermire watched his gunmen making for the settlements. Sure enough, as he had figured, when the first bunch lit out the distant riders moved to intercept them. Then, when the second wave thundered south, the defenders milled in confusion, finally breaking into two groups, one after each vigilante band.

Obermire grinned in evil satisfaction. This was going to be easy. His men might make it to the claims and do some killing, or they might not. It would be a close thing. Either way, they would draw in those squatters out there and then head back here with angry settlers hot on their tails.

He had chosen his ground well. To his right was a hill eroded deep by a washout bluff. To the left were thickets of scrub cedar, crowding the crests of a dozen gullies that twisted and turned along the east side of a rising flat.

It was a fine place for an ambush. Plenty of cover for them that got here first, and a crossfire field to catch whoever followed.

He walked his horse into the cover of a cedar screen and dismounted. Up there, under that bluff, would be the best spot. From there he could direct his vigilantes' fire, and pick off anybody who tried to stray west from the pursuit.

Carrying his rifle, Kurt worked his way up the clay bank slope and climbed the hill above the bluff. Shading his eyes, he squinted out across the hazed distance. His first group hadn't made it to the exposed settlement. A gang of fifteen or twenty riders had cut them off short of the watercourse and turned them back.

Dust hid the scene out there from view, but he knew what was happening when he heard the distant ragged crackle of gunfire. The boys were throwing some lead, to get the defenders involved. They would hold there a minute or two, then feign retreat and lead their opponents right back here.

There would be plenty of time to dig in. The defenders were split and confused. They would hesitate to follow. Then they would see the pursuit of the second band off to their left, and they would join in. It was working perfectly.

For long minutes, Kurt Obermire stood on the hill and watched his plan unfold. Then he headed down to the edge of the bluff. It was time to lay his trap.

Glancing back toward the cedar brake, he saw his horse grazing contentedly on new spring grass. It was well-hidden there, except from above. Looking beyond, he caught his breath. Just beyond a scrub thicket, there was a second horse—a short-coupled paint barely discernible through the brush.

With a whispered oath, the big man crouched and raised his rifle, his eyes scanning the terrain all around. He saw nothing, and when he looked back, the paint was gone, too. It was higher up, and in thick cover, and when it moved it faded from sight as though it had never been there.

A stray, he told himself. *It's wandered into deeper cover.* Again he surveyed the area, more carefully this time, letting his eyes rest on every feature, every clump and thicket, every clay bank and patch.

Nothing.

Satisfied that he was alone, he returned his attention to the distant rolling hills, where dust feathers rose on the wind. From there he could see nothing, but he could guess what was happening. His first group was on its way back now, riding hard. But nobody was pursuing them. The squatters had broken off to go after the second bunch.

It was ideal. Colby and his ten men would arrive minutes before the rest. He would have a dozen men already in place here by the time the other twenty arrived, with squatters hard on their tails.

"Perfect," Kurt muttered. "That's just fine."

Off to the right, down below the lip of the bluff, was a washout area where the loam and clay had been scoured away by some ancient flood. A tapered, almost vertical clay bank shouldered a cut in the hillside, with scrub brush above it and a talus fall below, offering a clear view to the south. From there he would be able to see and direct the killing.

He worked his way around a shoulder and found a path to climb down to the vantage point under the bluff.

He thought again of the paint horse he had glimpsed, just a hundred yards up from his own in the brushy draw, but put it from his mind as Colby's riders appeared around a rise a quarter-mile away. They had already seen what was happening behind them, and were working their way northward, staying off the skyline.

Obermire took a hard look around him. Then he set his rifle down to wrestle a fallen cottonwood log around for cover. Powerful shoulders hunched, he half-lifted the heavy trunk and trundled it around.

A few yards away something buzzed angrily.

He dropped the tree and stepped back, but the rattlesnake slithered off into the sparse grass, heading away. He stomped and trod the length of his little fort, from downslope to clay bank, and stirred up no more snakes.

He was just reaching for his rifle when something moved. From the corner of his eye he saw the faceless clay bank shift and separate, as though one small section of it had slid slightly to the side. He looked up, and that little section was a person—a small intense presence so smeared with dry mud and dusty clay that even as it moved it was hard to see! Ten feet from Kurt Obermire, the clay-daubed figure crouched, raised a rifle, and fired.

The first shot shattered Obermire's larynx, silencing his cry in a spray of gore. The rifle's action chattered, and a second shot rode the echoes of the first. The big man's kneecap exploded, and he fell, still scrambling for his rifle. A third rapid shot punched into his shoulder, and his clawing hand went dead.

Helpless and bleeding, Obermire lay on the talus slope and watched in horror as the muddy figure methodically chambered another round in its dainty little rifle and fired again. Wave after wave of pain seared through the outlaw and convulsed in a scream that became only a gurgle through the blood pulsing from his ruined throat.

"Big *yoneg,*" the clay-smeared figure scoffed. "Big *an'da'tsi.*" Obermire squirmed, lashed out with his good hand. A rifle butt knocked it aside.

Through misted eyes, Kurt squinted up at the small figure. A kid! Just a grubby half-grown Indian kid. Even standing over him, despising him, the boy was hard to see. He was smeared head to toe with mud—stripes and swatches of dark mud, drying dust, and reddish bank clay. Even in motion, the kid seemed part of the terrain.

"You beat my father to death, *an'da'tsi,*" the figure said. "Do you remember?"

On the talus slope, the outlaw writhed and gurgled, his life pulsing from him with each spurt of dark blood.

"I am the rattlesnake," the kid said. "Remember that. When the worms ask who gave them your rot, you tell them it was a Cherokee rattler."

The final shot from the small, high-powered rifle was the last sound Kurt Obermire ever heard.

Colby's vigilantes found what was left of the big man. They had heard the shooting moments before as they came up the draw, and now they stared down at the mutilated corpse of their leader and cast wary glances at the shrubbery all around. There was no one there. Whoever had killed Kurt Obermire was gone, leaving no more trace than a spring breeze leaves in passing.

"Look at them holes," they muttered among themselves. "It's like Folly Downs was. Just shot to hell with little holes. It's devil work, is what it is."

They found Obermire's horse and hoisted the dead man across its saddle. By then the rest of the vigilantes were there. The settlers behind them had veered off, alerted by the whiplash echoes of gunfire.

Colby and some others circled around for a time, searching for sign. Then a few of them headed back toward Paradise, taking Obermire's body with them.

Most of them, though, decided to go with Colby

and Tad Sands, who were itching now to get at those squatters down along the creeks and draws. These were hired guns, most of them wanted men with nowhere else to go and little to lose. There was little loyalty among them, and less friendship, but they rode for the wages and would go on doing that until the wages ran out.

Colby had been put in charge. Now he stayed in charge, and the killing fever ran high in him. He had seen the money that came from the big overland wagon, and he knew what it meant. There were high stakes here, and a railroad coming. Obermire had failed to dominate the land, and the man who succeeded would stand to share in the profits.

Not all of the Vigilance Committee would take orders from Colby, but some would.

Off in the sloping hills, the little army of settlers that had outguessed Kurt Obermire and somehow avoided his trap began to disperse. There was work to do, and most of those squatters were farmers before they were fighters. They had families to see to, game to shoot, sheds to build, and cabins to begin.

By the time the sun was quartering in the west, there was no sign of the mounted men who had been patrolling from stead to stead. Colby and his yellow-bands made a cold meal, saddled their mounts, and headed out, but not for Paradise. Colby had read the taunting signs about horses for sale posted by an A&M Land and Cattle Company, at Haymeadows Ranch. He didn't know where that was, but if it was in No Man's Land it shouldn't be too hard to find.

Vincent Colby had been willing to ride for the colonel as long as the money was good and prospects bright. But He had seen the vigilantes thrown back twice now, and he didn't have a good feeling about that. Jackson was dead, and Obermire was dead. If the colonel had his way, Colby might wind up dead, too, for nothing but wages.

So he would do things his own way, now. First there were horses to be taken, and maybe other livestock, too. Colby knew people across the line who paid good money for critters, and no questions asked.

He was tired of working for wages. It was the leaders who got rich, not the hired gunnies. Maybe when the vigilantes were through, Colby could be calling the shots. And maybe that wagonful of money and the railroad profits it represented would be as much his as the colonel's.

Colby was no fool. He knew the odds in going up against any of Asa Parker's bunch. Each one of them—Casper Wilkerson with his shotgun, and the rest with their handguns—was sudden enough to make any man back off, if he could.

Folly Downs and Kurt Obermire were dead now, but it was from a rifle. No man had ever stood up to either of them with a revolver and lived.

Colby had wondered from time to time whether he might beat Tuck Kelly to the draw if it ever came to that. But even if he could—and somehow escape Casper Wilkerson's greener—there was still that crazy deadly Billy Challis out there somewhere.

And there was the only man Billy was afraid of—Asa Parker himself.

Still, he looked at the men around him while Tad Sands whispered ideas to him. "We're doin' things my way now," he told his vigilantes. "Obermire's gone. You take your orders from me."

Drifters and hard cases, most of them wanted somewhere, the night riders shrugged and accepted. One leader was no worse than another.

A few, though, were gone from the gang. Two yellow-rags had gone down in the aborted attack on the settlers' digs, when sharpshooters opened up on them. Some others had returned to Paradise. And there were some who decided that they had seen enough of this part of the country. Discarded yellow cloths marked where they had gone.

Billy Challis and Tuck Kelly didn't go directly to town. They started that way when Asa sent for them, but Billy veered off toward the east when they saw the smoke of cookfires. From a caprock bluff above Rabbit Creek they watched as distant bands of horsemen converged in the hazy reaches beyond a settlement of squatter camps.

They couldn't see much. Whatever was happening was miles away. But Tuck had an itchy feeling, like spiders crawling up his neck. There was somebody a whole lot closer, he felt . . . somebody who was looking at them.

He scanned the terrain all around and saw nothing. "You think maybe there's somebody followin' us, Billy?"

Billy ignored him. He didn't even glance around. He held a tight rein and studied the lower lands ahead with slow feral eyes. There were three, distinct, little valleys out there, between low crests of prairie and gentle rolling hills. The valleys all funneled down toward Rabbit Creek. And all along the valleys, spaced out at intervals of a few hundred yards to half a mile, were new claims—little squalid camps where land settlers were digging in.

"Look at that," Billy rasped.

"Like fleas on a hound dog," Tuck said. "Where in hell do they all come from?"

Tuck started to ride away, but Billy cursed and sat there, just watching.

"Let's go," Tuck grumbled. "Nothin' here worth seein'." He started to flip his reins again, then hesitated. Billy had a look on his face that he had seen before—like that of a cat hunkered on a rock, twitching its tail and watching ground squirrels play.

Tuck didn't like to rile Billy when he got that look. There was something really wrong with Billy, and it made Tuck nervous. Billy was crazy as a jimsoned cow at the best of times, but when he started grinning that way and licking his lips, it meant killing. Tuck had seen it before.

"Look at 'em," Billy muttered. "Just look at 'em. What do you 'spose they got in all those little camps?"

"Nothing." Tuck shrugged. "Those people ain't got spit. They're just squatters. Let's go see Asa."

"I bet they got women." Billy giggled. "Squatters always got women."

Tuck shook his head. Whatever was wrong with Billy had something to do with women. Billy never could seem to enjoy females the way normal men did. Tuck wondered sometimes if Billy used his knife because it was all he had that really worked, come to that.

Folly Downs had been cruel with women, too, and liked to cut them sometimes, and some of the things he had seen Folly do made Tuck sick with disgust. But Billy was something else. Billy just plain wasn't normal. "Come on, now, Billy," he urged. "Asa said come to town. We better git. You want to buck Asa?"

Billy stiffened and turned to glare at his partner, and for a moment Tuck could almost feel his fingers going for his gun. But then the crazy bastard looked past him and giggled and pointed. "Looky yonder," he crowed. "Just looky over there. That ain't any dirt farm squaw."

Tuck turned. Below the crest where they sat, Rabbit Creek ran along through its little canyon, bordered by budding cottonwoods and willows. And just where the breaks leveled out, three riders had come into view, going northward. Though they were nearly a quarter mile away, there was no mistaking the one in the lead. Flowing copper-penny hair framed her smooth dark-eyed face, enhancing and emphasizing the fine contours that shaped the linen blouse she wore. Her wide calico skirt was hitched up over small sturdy boots planted in worn stirrups at each flank of her blaze-face sorrel.

Despite the skirt she rode as steadily as any man, and the rifle across her saddle was carried expertly.

"Would you just look at what the fates done sent us," Billy Challis said, his eyes glinting.

The other two riders were young farm types—a pair of rawboned bearded beanpoles. They sat their mounts awkwardly, though the old rifles they carried seemed as comfortable to them as plow-hasps.

"My, oh my." Billy giggled, licking his lips. "We gonna have us some fun. First come, first served, but that female is mine. Whatever I leave, you can have."

Tuck sighed. "Billy, you're crazy," he said.

Billy Challis whirled, bringing his horse around with its eyes wide and teeth fighting the torturing bit against its tongue. "What did you say?" he demanded.

"Now don't go gettin' like that, Billy." Tuck shook his head. "You got Asa's message, same as me. We're s'posed to come right back into town, on the double. Asa needs us."

Billy glared at his partner as though the words

meant nothing. He had a grin on his face that held no humor, and his eyes were wide and staring—little orbs of dark fire that seemed to burn like coals.

"Come on, Billy!" Tuck shivered. "That's enough! Hell, I know you're riled up from layin' around that shack waitin' for your butt to heal, but that's no call to go off an' do somethin' stupid. Let's find out what Asa wants. Likely you'll get all the possum you want soon as we get back to work."

Billy stared at him. "I asked you what you said, Tuck."

"What?"

"Just now. What did you call me? Did you call me crazy?"

"Come on, Billy. Back off! It's just a way of talkin'. Damned if you ain't the contrariest critter I ever seen!"

Billy edged his mount a step closer, crowding in. That odd frightening look was still in his eyes. "Do you know who used to call me crazy, Tuck? My mother did. My own mother! Can you beat that? The old bitch said I was crazy as a loon, just like you've said a time or two."

"Well, I'm sorry, Billy, but I—"

"Do you know what I did when I'd heard that too much, Tuck? She said that one too many times, an' I taken a strop knife to her. I knocked her down, then I busted open her jaw an' cut out her damned tongue."

"You killed her?" Tuck stared at Billy, aghast. "You . . . you killed your own *mother*?"

"Hell, no, I didn't! I let her do that herself. I staked her out to a tree, with one hand just free enough to move a little. Then I laced my knife in her hand an' left her there. When I went back she'd slit her own throat, tryin' to reach her mouth 'cause she hurt so bad." Billy giggled. "That sure enough was a sight, Tuck. It's just amazin' how hard a body will try to keep from stranglin' on their own tongue blood."

The disgust that swept over Tuck was like sick dread. He wanted to wretch, and felt bile rise in his throat.

"Best you just mind what you say, Tuck," Billy said casually. The intense burning stare had receded from his eyes, but the look there now was cold as mountain thaw. And there was plenty of message in the way his hand hovered over his gun butt.

"I don't want to hear that kind of talk any more, Tuck," he said. "Now let's just follow along a ways. And limber up that peep-sight rifle. You're gonna pop us some squatters, an' I'll have me some fun with that little gal yonder."

Tuck's skin crawled. He remembered the way Billy had gone about having fun with a few females before, like those little girls up in Colorado. Tuck had claimed the grown woman himself, and raped her until he was satisfied, but it wasn't like what Billy did to the girls. What Billy left when he was done wasn't anything a man would want.

Tuck turned away, then felt Billy's eyes on him—like gun barrels pointing at his back. With a sigh he lifted his reins and followed along. Tuck Kelly was as tough a normal outlaw as ever lived, but he was afraid of his partner and he knew it. He'd never run across anybody quite like Billy. It just didn't pay to rile Billy Challis.

He still felt that somebody was nearby, watching, but he ignored it. Whoever it was couldn't be the problem Billy was.

TWENTY

Rufe and Elijah didn't much cotton to the notion of riding up to Haymeadows Ranch, but Becky had her mind made up so they went. From the time they were shavers back at Rocky Top, where it was generally known that Barlow women backed down to no man, the boys had understood that their baby sister was a case in point.

They'd both been there in the dooryard the day Moss Woodard came around drunk and set to cussing outside Aunt Sadie's door, and they had witnessed the gospel truth of it when little Becky, just nine years old, took a hayfork to the Swamp Creek man and drove him away.

It was the way she was—as sweet a little girl as a body might ever see, but just don't cross the line. And stubborn . . . nobody argued much with Becky Barlow. Even now, Rufe and Elijah weren't about to start. So when Becky came out dressed in skirts and linen, and mounted up and declared that she was going up to Haymeadows to get a better look at Jubal Mason, the boys just naturally strapped saddles on a pair of Leotus's horses and tagged along to keep her company.

There had been more trouble today, over in the Whiterocks. Homer Burleson had been by, looking for Cassius. He told them how gangs of vigilantes had made a run at two claims up there—the Iverson digs and Pete Muller's place. Mounted patrols of settlers had driven the yellow-rags away, but that was only hours ago, and the boys were nervous.

From Leotus's, Burleson headed north. Granddaddy Cassius had gone up to Haymeadows just the day before, to visit those boys up there and dicker for some horses. He might have already started back, unless he'd stayed over another night.

And it was thinking about Haymeadows—or maybe about Jubal Mason up there—that set Becky off.

It wasn't much more than ten miles up to Haymeadows, and most of the ride would be through lands now claimed by Barlow kin and people from Black Mesa. They could make the ten miles by dark.

As they came up through the breaks, riding at each side of Becky's sturdy sorrel, Rufe glanced over at his brother and grinned. "I wonder if it's really that feller Jubal Mason that Becky got dandied up for. Maybe she's set her cap for Falcon MacCallister, an' hopin' to find him there."

"Well, that would be a match, all right," Elijah allowed. "Even for Becky. Did you see the shoulders on him? Lordy, I wouldn't want to—"

Just ahead of them, Becky Barlow straightened her back in irritation. "Mr. MacCallister might be a devil or a saint, for all that means to me," she snapped. "You two are talkin' crazy."

Rufe shrugged. He knew they had missed the mark. "Then it's really Jubal Mason you're fixin' to visit?"

"None other, and don't go makin' anythin' out of it, either!"

Rufe rode in silence for a moment, then grinned

at Elijah again. "That Jubal, he must be some kind of dandy for Little Sis to go sweet on him like this," he drawled.

Becky turned in her saddle and shot him a withering glare. "I'm not sweet on nobody!" she said. "I just reckon a hospitality ought to be returned. He did prob'ly save my life, you know."

"Oh, sure." Rufe shrugged. "Like it's every day that you step out scrubbed and combed and wearin' a dress, and head out to meet some feller."

"Think nothin' of it, Sis," Elijah assured her, working at a deadpan expression. "It's only natural, you bein' of the gentle persuasion an' all. I mean, there was bound to come a time when some fine gentleman jumps on you an' takes your rifle away from you an'—"

"He didn't take my rifle!" Becky snapped. "I just dropped it when he lit on me. I mean, gettin' in between me and that outlaw. I swear, Jubal Mason didn't get nothin' from me but my name."

Rufe chuckled. "Well, you play your cards right, Sis, and maybe he'll give you his to replace it."

"Will you all just shut up?" she demanded. "I swear, you two come up with the dangedest notions!"

Where the breaks leveled out to rolling plains they slowed, peering northward. It was a sight to behold, all those little spatterings of new settlement spread out across three converging valleys. It seemed as though there were claims everywhere they looked— here a limestone foundation being laid by people living out of a wagon, there a pair of tents and a stack of cottonwood timbers, yonder a clearing yielding squares for a sod cabin. And there were other new claims beyond, out of view.

"That MacCallister was right," Becky said. "Give

folks a little land and fair neighbors, an' they'll spring up like weeds."

Some of the claims out that way were Barlow kin, most were not. There were people out there who had been trying to dig gold out of Black Mesa just months ago. There were some who had just drifted in from Lord knew where, and decided to stay. There were even a couple of claims—rumor had it—that were taken by men who had worn the yellow scarves of Paradise vigilantes until very recently.

The land was greening now and full spring was here, and it was a sight to behold.

They flicked their reins and headed out across the prairie, but after a minute or two Rufe turned and looked back, frowning. "You get the feelin' somebody was back there, watchin' us?" he asked.

Elijah scanned the backtrail and the rises behind. "Nobody there now," he said.

For a while they followed the scant little waterways, where the claims were, but as the sun lowered in the west Becky became impatient and cut northward, away from the settlements, up through the rolling dry hills. Within a mile they were in country as pure and pristine as though no human eyes had ever seen it—sagebrush hills, low caprock bluffs above stands of cedar, and grass so thick and rich that the pronghorns flourished on it.

"Man could raise cows on this land," Rufe allowed. "Some good shorthorn heifers and a seed bull, might come up with a right strong breed."

"They'd just scatter," Elijah scoffed. "Critters won't stand to breed without water. What you gonna do, drive 'em up from that creek every day? That's the nearest water, four, five miles away, an' that's where they'd go."

"Fences," Rufe elaborated. "Fences and wells."

He pointed at a stand of salt cedar below the crest of a sage-strewn hill. "There's water aplenty. Just have to dig to get at it."

"Hard to dig a well while folks are shootin' at you." Elijah said. "What's to keep land-grabbers like them vigilantes from just movin' in when you settle?"

It was a good question. Rufe hesitated, looking at the lonely rolling miles around them. Becky was riding out ahead, making good time as she set a course for the Haymeadows a few miles north. Up there, away from the little valleys and their brand-new settlements, the lands of No Man's Land seemed wild and remote—and lonely. Still, the valleys above Rabbit Creek had been the same, earlier in the spring, when the kin began arriving to settle around Leotus's claim.

All it took was decent people, willing to work, to make a wasteland home.

"Times will change," Rufe grinned. "Have a little faith, Brother. We're gonna see some good times out here after the bad gets swept away. It's like Falcon MacCallister told Cassius—the grabbers won't stand long against settlers that have neighbors willin' to—"

Rufe's words were cut off by the flat echoes of gunfire. His horse shied, spun, and danced and he fought to stay aboard. Then he saw Elijah's mount hightailing away, its saddle empty and its skirts flapping.

For a moment he couldn't see Elijah. Then he did. His brother lay in a heap, half-hidden among the broken stubs of a clump of scrub cedar. Even before he saw the blood Rufe knew that Elijah was dead—heart-shot with a high-powered rifle.

At a distance, he saw Becky's sorrel, just coming

around. The girl stared back at him and raised her reins.

"Run, Becky!" he shouted. "Get help!" He hauled his reins, controlling his horse, and turned desperately, trying to see where the shot had come from. Up on the lip of the east mesa, something glinted in the slanting sunlight. There was a little puff of smoke.

As the shot sounded, Rufe's horse staggered, whinnied and went down, blood pulsing from its neck. Rufe fell, dived and rolled, and another shot kicked sand in his face. Through the dust he saw Becky wheeling her sorrel, holding her rifle high in one hand. "Run, Becky!" he shouted again. "Run for—"

The bullet that hit him was like a huge invisible fist punching him in the upper chest. He tried to stand, tried to shout, but there was no sound beyond a keening moan. He almost got his feet under him. Then the world spun, and he pitched sideways. He sprawled on hard ground and bristles, and darkness fell. *Run, Little Sister!* his mind screamed. In truth he made no sound, and the silence of it shrilled in his mind, filling the void that closed around him. It was the last thing Rufe Barlow ever knew.

Becky heard the sharp reports of rifle fire and pivoted the sorrel in time to see Elijah go down. For a moment she couldn't see where the shooting came from, and in that moment Rufe was thrown from the saddle of his collapsing horse. He hit the ground hard, and sand kicked up beside him, and Becky saw the shooter—a crouching silhouette at the rim of the bluff.

He fired again and Becky returned the shot, wishing it home with deadly accuracy. At the rim, the sniper lurched backward, dropped his rifle, and doubled over. The sorrel danced around, shying at the noise, and Becky levered another round into her Henry. She tried to aim, and the sorrel shied again. With a muttered oath, Becky swung to the ground, slapped the horse away, and knelt.

Atop the rim, the shooter was bent over, swaying dizzily on widespread legs, staring down at her in shock. Even a hundred yards away, she could see his amazement. He swayed, coughing up gore to stain the limp yellow bandana attached to his shirt. Becky braced the rifle, sighted along it, and eased the trigger. At its bark, the man up there on the rim seemed to hang suspended for an instant. Then he fell backward, disappearing.

"Back-shooting varmint!" Becky stood, lowering her rifle, looking to where her brothers had fallen. "Oh, Lord have mercy," she whispered. Elijah was down, among shattered sage clumps. The gray-green foliage there was bright crimson from the spray of his blood. And in a clearing between stands of scrub cedar, Rufe—or what was left of him—lay in pooling blood like the twisted carcass of a spine-shot deer. Without looking further, Becky knew that both of her brothers were dead.

She started toward them, half-blind with rage and grief. She had run a dozen paces when thick brush exploded to her left and a mounted man surged through, directly above her. She tried to turn, to dodge, but the horse's shoulder hit her solidly and sent her tumbling. She was still scrambling for footing when the rider wheeled and kicked her rifle away from her.

A hard fist from above collided with her skull, and she fell. Then he was on her, and she felt the cuts of his knife tearing at her flesh as he cut her dress away.

With a desperate heave, Becky drew herself into a tight ball, then uncoiled. Her small booted foot collided with something solid, and the drooling grin above her became a grimace of pain. Her clawed fingers struck out, right into that face, going for the eyes.

"You damned bitch!" he yelled, and hit her again, knocking her head back against the hard ground. In a daze she fought. Her nails raked his face, her knees and fists pummeled him, but he forced her down, pulling away her bloody clothing.

Billy Challis knew about pain. With clawed fingers he mauled her, ignoring her screams. Casting aside his knife he went to work on her with both hands, his eyes alight with rage and lust.

She felt the weight of him, smelled his stench, as he bore her down. With one last desperate heave she freed a hand and its fingers closed on the butt of the gun at his belt. She pulled it, cocked it, and tried to turn it toward him. His hand was on her wrist, then, twisting, and she felt her fingers going numb.

She twisted, fought, and put all her strength into that one hand—the hand with the gun—but he was too strong. He forced the muzzle down and back, and Becky screamed. In blind rage she twisted, and turned the gun another way. When she felt the cold steel of its muzzle at her own throat, she squeezed the trigger.

At the time all this was going on, Falcon MacCallister was a few miles north, stripped to the waist and sitting on a plank table in front of Doc Linsecum's little sod cabin just across the Kansas line.

"I never seen the like," Doc said, leaning close for another look at the healing scars on the big man's back and belly. "I've planted corpses with less damage than you got here, Mr. MacCallister. You must be about the luckiest jasper this side of the flint hills. No more bleeding?"

"Some," Falcon said. "Sore as hell, too."

"Skin's a tough material," Linsecum said. "That's why arrows have arrowheads—just to get through the skin. The shaft is what kills. Best I can figure, that bullet entered your back at an angle and was deflected. It kind of skidded on your ribs. You got a couple that are at least cracked, maybe more. Compound fracture, possibly, because there's something inside you that isn't holding plumb. If you were a horse I'd either put you out of your misery or lace you up in a buckskin truss."

"That's all? Just loose ribs?"

"Let's hope it is. No way I can tell. But that bullet did some damage. Like an auger goin' through. It ricochcted . . . along here." Raising MacCallister's arm, he drew a callused finger along the livid bruise that still darkened his side.

"It sort of like dug itself a tunnel through the subdermal tissue," he explained. "That means it just burrowed along under the skin, but couldn't get through it until it got to your belly. The skin's thinner there. 'Course, when it did get out . . ."—he indicated the ragged scabbed-over wound just left of Falcon's midriff—"it tore hell out of the epidermal tissue. That's why you bled so much."

He stood back, scratching at his scruffy beard, while Falcon pulled on a shirt. "Some would call it an act of God that you're still alive," the horse doctor mused. "First time they brought you in here, I never thought you'd make it. All depended on how much you wanted to live, I figured."

Falcon glanced at him ironically. "I guess I wanted it enough."

Linsecum shook his head. "I've done some readin' on that," he said. "Fellow named Packard, wrote a whole book on the 'will to live.' He allows it's a natural thing in young critters, but a matter of choice when a man's grown up. He says a fellow has to have a 'strong abiding reason' to hold onto life the way you did. And he says generally that comes to a man who's been ready to die, then found a reason not to. Like unfinished business that won't let him just turn loose. Somethin' he just can't let go of. Did you find a reason like that, Mr. MacCallister?"

Falcon thought about it, grimly, and nodded. "Guess I did. You know what happened in Colorado . . . what I found up there. I guess I didn't care about much anymore, 'til I saw that. But I couldn't put that out of my mind. It reminded me of other senseless tragedies. It was . . . just one straw too many. The men who did that . . . they have to answer for it. I can't let it go."

"You fixin' to kill somebody? That won't make things right."

"It's retribution, Doc. As close to justice as I can see."

"Retribution." Linsecum shrugged. "That's like hangin' the thief after the stock's been stole. Don't bring the stock back."

Falcon stood, finished dressing, and put on his hat. "You're a philosopher, Doc," he said. "Not to mention a pretty fair medic. But I can't say much for your philosophy. Anyhow, I'm obliged."

"Generally I doctor horses, and now and then a cow." Linsecum shrugged. "They got no use for philosophy."

"How many humans have you treated?"

"Damn few. But skin's skin an' bone's bone, and people's blood runs red just like any other critter's. I'll tell you this, though—you got bone damage, and some muscle tissue and tendons just hangin' by a hair inside you. You stress those too much, I don't know what it'll do. You ought to lay up for a spell."

"Pigs ought to fly, too. What's a truss?"

"Kind of like a leather corset, laced so tight nothing inside can move. Things either fix or mortify. I've tried it twice, on horses. Killed one, cured the other. Best thing you can do is bed rest."

As MacCallister dropped a pair of eagles on the table, Linsecum shook his head, resigned. "Like talkin' to a post," he said. "Well, at least take it easy and be careful. I hear things from No Man's Land. Hear tell there's a war makin' up yonder. Just try not to get shot any more, will you?"

"I'll do my best," Falcon said.

"While you're up here, there's somebody been askin' around about you. Railroad dude by the name of Wylie. He's prob'ly over at the Franklin place by now."

"Where's that?"

"Three miles west, on the road to Hardwoodville."

"Thanks."

TWENTY-ONE

Pap Higgins found Becky Barlow's blaze sorrel. He brought it up to Haymeadows because Cassius was there.

They went backtracking while evening light was still in the sky. Jubal went with them because he knew Becky's horse. It was a wide land, with few clear trails. It was near midnight when they found the breaks below the bluff. They gathered there, with brush torches for light, and it was a time before they sorted it all out.

They found the boys, and they found the owlhoot who ambushed them, Tuck Kelly. They were all dead. Then they found Becky . . . or all that was left of her. Her head was blownhalf away, and the rest of her horribly mutilated. No animal had done that. Not even the coyotes or the prowling lions of this wild land were so brutish.

Her pretty dress was scattered all around, torn shreds among the scrub brush.

"May God have mercy on this child's sweet soul," Cassius Barlow whispered over and over again. Mostly they stayed back after one look, not wanting to get too close. All except Jubal. He just hunkered there on his knees on the bloody soil, holding his hat in his hands, and never made a sound.

One of the Higgins boys found two more strayed horses and spread the word, and Homer Smith came with his dray cart. A few others drifted in, drawn by the fires they set.

"Billy Challis," some whispered to others. "Nobody I know is crazy enough to do a thing like this except Billy Challis."

Come dawn they scouted a little more, then loaded up what they could. With Cassius Barlow's rig and Homer's cart they loaded up the bodies of the Barlow boys, and tenderly laid out the mutilated corpse of the girl. Tuck Kelly was slung across the saddle of his own horse. The nearest place with decent shelter was Haymeadows Ranch, so they took them there and laid them out beside the barn.

They might have taken the Barlows south to bury them on Rabbit Creek, but Jubal faced them down. On a rise above the hay fields some of the men set about digging graves—good, six-foot plots for Becky and her brothers, and a shallow hole for the outlaw.

Nobody particularly noticed when Falcon MacCallister rode in with another man—a wiry thin little man with a derby hat and eyeglasses. The stranger held back, but Falcon rode right up to the barn, and after a time some of them noticed him there. He sat atop Diablo, just looking, like he wanted to fix it all in his mind. A big blond man on a big black horse, he looked like death fixing to happen, and those who approached him were startled at the look in his narrowed eyes.

"It was the same man," Falcon told Cassius Barlow. "The same one that did that slaughter in Colorado."

"Billy Challis," a tough squatter said. "It was him. He's been hidin' out at the Spring place, gettin' over a sore butt. Him and Tuck Kelly. That's Kelly, layin' yonder. Looks like he done the two boys—ambushed 'em from a bluff—while Billy laid in wait for this girl."

"You know those men?" Falcon asked.

"Sorry to say, I do." The squatter nodded. "I'm Dawson. I wore a yellow flag for a time, but I lit out on my own."

"Why?"

"Didn't like the company I was keepin'," the man said simply.

Jubal Mason squatted by the blanket-covered remains, holding a torn piece of dress in his hand. Now he looked up at Falcon, moisture on his streaked face. "Did we wait long enough now, Mr. MacCallister?" he demanded. "Is this what we were waiting for, for it to all happen again?"

The funeral they held, out there above the hay fields, was simple but profound. Falcon MacCallister stood apart from the crowd, hearing Cassius Barlow say words for his granddaughter that Falcon wished he had known how to say for those little girls he'd found months ago, up on the high plains of Colorado.

"Maybe there's a reason why the Lord tolerates the kind of man that could do a thing like this," the old man said. "Maybe He's testing our patience . . . testing our souls that the Good Book says should be full of forgiveness. Or maybe He has another reason for letting such things happen."

Cassius raised his face to heaven for a moment, his eyes tight shut. Then he gazed around at them one by one. There was no sting in the gaze that singled out MacCallister, nor any hint of blame, but Falcon felt a pang of guilt. This didn't have to happen. He had known for weeks who the woman-butcher was, and where to find him.

Yet he had held back. At first it was his wounds that delayed him, then that stubborn will to not settle for just one or two of the gang. He had to get them all.

"Maybe," old Cassius continued, "maybe the Good Lord just wants to see how much pure meanness we—who are made in His image—will tolerate before we let loose our god-given outrage and put an end to it. Killin' is killin', but what was done to the dear young soul we have to bury now just never should have happened. Not to her. Not to her, Lord, and not to anybody."

Falcon lowered his head, and the spring winds blew haloes of sunlight in his loose blond hair. *I've been selfish,* he told himself. *I came upon an atrocity and set out to make amends, because it gave me a thing to hang on to . . . a purpose where there was no purpose.*

Then, when the killers were in plain sight, I hesitated. I lingered. Get them all, I told myself. Don't take a chance, and don't settle for less. And that was selfishness. I didn't want to put an end to this, because then I wouldn't have had a purpose any more.

Was I really out to avenge those people up in Colorado? I never even met the Blanchards. But it reminded me of what happened to Marie, and it gave me a purpose. I didn't set out to avenge Dorothy Blanchard and her family. I was trying to make it right about Marie.

Selfishness. And because I was selfish, this is what happened.

"Mr. MacCallister?" The voice beside him cut through his dark thoughts, bringing him back to awareness. It was Jubal Mason, and Falcon realized that the memoriams were done and most of the men present had wandered away. Only a few neighbors remained, wielding spades and miners' shovels to fill in the graves. Jubal stood facing him, an arm's length away, and his two brothers were right behind him. It was hard to tell which they were feeling most, grief or anger.

MacCallister unclenched his fists and put on his hat. "I'm sorry," he said.

Jubal nodded. "We're all sorry," he said. "But it wasn't your fault, for waiting. If we'd gone after that bunch like we wanted to, we'd have missed the one who did this."

"You were right, Mr. MacCallister," Jude added, "We need to wipe out that whole rotten bunch, like you said. This wasn't your fault for waiting, any more than wanting her to come here was Jubal's fault. We know whose fault it is, though, don't we?"

"Billy Challis," Falcon muttered.

"Billy Challis." Jubal nodded. "And that Colonel DeWitt, and whoever put them up to this land swindle in the first place."

"They all killed Becky and her brothers," Jude added. "Like you said, it was all of them. Just like they killed our kin up in Colorado. We're going after that bunch, and we aim to get them all, just like you said."

"Parker." Another voice spoke up, and they all looked around. The little dude who had come in with MacCallister was there, holding his derby hat in both hands. "I guess you already know it, but the name isn't Colonel DeWitt. It's Asa Parker. He uses a lot of names, and he's fooled a lot of people. But he's Asa Parker."

"This is Mr. Wylie." Falcon gestured. "He's with the Kansas Pacific Railroad. Tell them what you told me, Wylie."

"Yes, of course," Wylie said. "Asa Parker, who calls

himself Colonel DeWitt now, is running a scheme to sell a big piece of the Neutral Strip to an investment syndicate back east. He's working with a land shark named O'Brien, and they're capitalizing their operation with little swindles—selling plots and sites to settlers, then chasing them out and selling again."

"Eastern investors?" Jubal frowned. "How do they aim to swing that? Everybody knows the Neutral Strip is No Man's Land. Those big buyers wouldn't touch a thing like that."

"You're right," Wylie nodded. "They're not fools. But Parker's gang will offer a plausible title, even though there's no patent on the land. They'll offer quitclaim deeds to property described as eminent domain, sealed and sanctioned by an agency of the U.S. government. Who's going to argue? Especially when they sweeten the pot with a documented railroad route, for profit."

"How can they do that? They got somebody in the government?"

Wylie sighed. "Exactly," he said. "A gentleman named Sypher. Technically, Sypher's a clerk for Jonathan Boles Stratton—head of the agency that designates rail routes. But Stratton's a lame duck, going out with the present administration. Sypher is running things to suit himself. He has secured forged maps and letters of approval with Stratton's signature on them, indicating railway intent, with the right-of-way right through here. There are even detailed railroad plans, and Stratton's office will verify them. And authenticated trackage means government sanction."

"There really *will* be a railroad through here?" Jude shook his head. "I never believed that."

"Probably not." Wylie shrugged. "The whole scheme will unravel when it goes before the senate committee overseeing Stratton's department. But the new investors will have purchased the land by then. Sypher and Asa Parker and the rest will be gone with the money, and only the people swindled will suffer."

"Damn!" Jubal breathed. "This Sypher . . . is he the one heading up all this?"

"He is," Wylie nodded.

"Where is he?"

"Probably with Asa Parker and O'Brien, over at their town. Paradise, I believe they call it. It was already there when they came. It was called Prosperity, but it wasn't a legal town or anything, just a little settlement where squatters exchanged their goods."

"Well, it's more than that now."

"Of course it is. Parker's Vigilance Committee has been at work. Paradise is a stage—a money trap, being set up to snare the big investors when they arrive. Parker plans to show them a booming town, a settled community, and a fine site for railroad business. That's where the deal will be made, and the money will be cash transfers to Kansas City and St. Louis banks, not recoverable. It's a real sweet swindle, if you look at it that way."

"When are those investors coming?"

"They're probably on their way now," Wylie said. "There was a private conference in St. Louis a month ago that we wondered about. Big money, very quiet. Boston money, mostly. We heard about it from our bankers, but not much. I think it was about Sypher's plan."

"Damn!" Jubal said again. "Lordy, where's the law when you need 'em?"

"That's what makes it work," Wylie said. "There is no law. Not any kind, at any level. This is No Man's Land. According to the U.S. Justice Department and the Department of the Interior, there's nothing here. Just a hole in the orderly world of bureaucracy that goes away if you don't recognize it. There's no law here because this strip doesn't exist officially."

"Then we'll be our own law." Jubal frowned. "Somebody's got to be. Where's Brett? He knows about things like this."

"He's over at that town," Joshua said. "Nobody knows him there, so he comes and goes . . . listenin'. He's heard about this by now, I expect— about Becky and all. Prob'ly everybody yonder has. And you know Brett. He's gonna be layin' for Billy Challis now—for Dorothy, and for all the rest."

"Brett won't stand a chance against Billy Challis," Falcon said. "Brett's good with a gun, but not that good. And he's a gentleman. He'll hesitate to kill. Billy Challis won't."

"Then we'd better be there with him," Jubal said. "Now."

"Do you boys know what you're up against?" Wylie demanded. "Do you have any idea who those people are?" He looked at Falcon, who shrugged.

"Tell them, Mr. Wylie," Falcon said.

Wylie took a deep breath. "Billy Challis is a lunatic, with posters on him as far away as Illinois. Crazy as a bedbug. But he's also the slickest gunhand this side of Fort Smith, barring maybe Asa Parker himself."

"Then we'll have to get at him another way," Jubal rasped. "I don't care whether the son of a bitch is shot or hanged. I just want him on his way to hell, the sooner the better."

"If Brett can't take him down, then who can?" Joshua glanced aside. "You, Mr. MacCallister? You're still hurting, I see it every time you move sudden.

You think you can outdraw a gunslick like that, with those cracked ribs still slowin' you down?"

"Maybe not," Falcon admitted. "But maybe I've got more chance than Brett does."

Cassius Barlow hadn't said a word through it all. The old man just listened, his head bowed in thought. Then he squared his shoulders. "Mr. Mac-Callister," he rasped, "I reckon now this whole business is Barlow concern."

TWENTY-TWO

Utsonati had squatted in a cedar clump, as unnoticed as the gray-green fronds around him, and watched Tuck Kelly die. He had been so close that the second bullet through the outlaw sprayed him with crimson drops.

The man had perched himself up there to ambush three riders below. Utsonati knew that two of them were dead. But the third one, the woman, had been luckier. Twice her rifle had found its target, and then the one called Tuck had lain sprawled on grassy caprock a dozen feet from where Utsonati squatted.

The outlaw had gasped, and bloody froth billowed at his lips. He'd turned his head, gaping in disbelief, and Utsonati shifted a little, letting himself be seen. A look of amazement had shadowed Tuck's dimming eyes.

"Dirt!" Utsonati said, his boy's voice cracking like a whip. "Earthworm dung, I see you dying. I will still see you when you are dead."

A sound like gurgling sobs had escaped the bubbles at Tuck's lips, and new blood gushed there. Then the man was gone.

Utsonati had crept to the edge of the caprock and peered over as screams came from below, followed by a single gunshot. The boy had watched for a moment and then drawn back, feeling sick. At that distance he could not see exactly what the man was doing down there, but what he was doing it to was no longer alive. With a frown, Utsonati had raised his rifle, but his hands were unsteady. He'd turned away, taking deep breaths, willing the sick feeling to pass.

When he returned to the edge of the bluff, the man had been gone. Only sprawled pale limbs and death lay where he had been.

Utsonati had almost quit, then. He had seen too much of blood and horrible death. But deep in his mind a spirit had stirred. *Didanawa-i* didn't quit. The legendary warriors of the Cherokee were tenacious beyond belief. It was one of the things that had made *Didanawa-i* the most feared of men. All across a continent in a time long ago, the *Tsalagi* were known and respected . . . and their *Didanawa-i* were feared. Among all the true people—the Shawnee and Iroquois of the east, the Cheyenne of the west, the Huron of the north . . . even the haughty Lakota and all their kin—the Cherokee were revered and feared.

Even the horse people of the southern plains, the snake people whose name among their neighbors was Comanche and meant enemy, there was one man to always be feared—any man who was *Didanawa-i*.

Didanawa-i never quit. Utsonati would not quit. With grim determination, the boy had set out afoot toward a canyon a mile away where his horse waited. Then, mounted and ready, he had taken the trail of the white man who butchered women.

* * *

Within three miles, Billy Challis had known that there was someone behind him. The bloodlust that consumed him for a time—that wild thrill that always came from hearing the screams of a female, dominating and hurting her—had been denied him, and he was wild with anger. The bitch had killed herself! There had been no thrill in what followed. Only rage.

Over darkening terrain he had pushed his frightened horse, careless of its caution, until the hot rage died a little, wearing away as lust does and leaving the same dissatisfied anger that it always left. The frenzy in his head had died to a feeble trill. And with his senses cleared, he had known that he was being followed.

He'd doubled back a couple of times, ridden into a draw, and then whipped his horse until it climbed frantically to the top, giving him a sudden unexpected view of his backtrack. There had been no movement back there in the dusk, not even a hint. But he had known that someone was there.

With animal cunning he'd spurred his horse, breaking into a run, and pummeled its ribs for a fast quarter-mile. Then he'd swung down, slapped its rump and watched it skitter off into the darkness. It wouldn't go far. It was hurt and exhausted.

Then he had cut to the right, scrambled to the top of a rise, and had lain down to wait. It was dark then, and he thought that whoever was back there had probably stopped. But the darkness would pass. The pursuer would come, sooner or later. And Billy Challis would be waiting.

As stars came out overhead, Utsonati had slowed his horse to a walk, sniffing the evening breeze.

There had been water near. He could smell the sweet odor of damp earth, a hint of mud, and the faint stench of tadpoles. *Not a creek, then,* he had thought. Probably just a little pond, where rainwater still stood trapped waiting for hot sun to reduce it to mud flats.

He'd stopped, standing in his stirrups to listen to the night birds, turning his head this way and that. The rider ahead had no longer been moving. The birds had sung of quiet all around.

Thoughtfully, the boy who was a rattlesnake had squinted at the starlight prairies around him, then stepped down and led his horse. He'd chosen a low place—a little swale between hills—and unsaddled the animal to graze. He'd made no fire, but eaten a little pemmican and drunk water from his canteen, then given water to the horse. Then he had gone on, on foot.

The pond nearby was just as he had thought—a natural tank in a low spot between overhanging caprock ledges. Not a good place to be at night. Every wild thing within miles would come there to drink . . . everything with fangs or claws, fur or scales. It was their place, not his, and he'd respected that.

Skirting around, he'd heard faint sounds coming from the shadows. Some creatures were already there, defending their territory against intruders.

Beyond the ledges he had squatted to smell a sage clump, then another, and found the trail of the man he was following. Sudden buzzing almost at his feet had startled him, but he stood still, and the rattler slithered off into darkness. *"Utsonati,"* the boy had breathed, "You know me. You are my brother now."

The low prairie, between the hills, was alive with creatures of the night, but Utsonati had walked among them secure. He was *Didanawa-i,* and they knew him.

Without realizing it, Utsonati had passed within a hundred yards of the crest where Billy Challis lay waiting. Only when he found the man's half-crippled horse, still saddle-bound and standing in a field of fresh grass, had he realized that the man was behind him. The murderer was on that caprock ridge that he had gone around. He was waiting there, in ambush.

And it was then, as he worked his way back toward the hilltop, that the prairie had betrayed him. Just where caprock began, Utsonati had edged around a cedar thicket, and soft limestone crumbled. His feet had gone out from under him and he tumbled, rolling down the incline into moonlight. Shards and fragments clattered around him.

He'd heard a shout, and a bullet sang off stone just inches from his head. The boy rolled, dodged, and scrambled to his feet as another shot rang and something tugged at his jacket. He had run, out of the moonlight into dark shadows.

Chalk fragments whistled around him. A bullet whisked past his ear, and dark talus exploded before him, blinding him. And then there had been no footing. He fell, rolling and bouncing, into deep darkness.

Darkness and sudden silence. Carefully, painfully, he had wiped the dust out of his eyes. He was in a black place, with no light at all except the faint glow of moonlight through a jagged crevice in the stone. *A cave,* he had thought. He'd stirred, squinting, trying to see. He'd felt around for his rifle and couldn't find it.

Just darkness and silence . . . and something else. Something like a low-pitched rasping growl that was very close, and he had sensed the presence of another creature, so close he could feel its body warmth. He'd reached out a tentative hand, and frozen as his fingers touched thick fur.

The growl became a threatening rasp, and in the patch of moonlight there was a silhouette. It had wide alert ears and a wide furry face, and even in the darkness he had seen the glint of feral eyes and bared fangs.

"Wa-hya'," the boy whispered. In Cherokee, the word meant wolf.

"Got the son of a bitch!" Billy Challis had giggled as the dodging shadow below him disappeared over the edge of the caprock slant. He could barely see in the faint light of stars and quarter moon, but there was no mistaking that last glimpse. The shadowy figure down there hadn't jumped or dived from the ledge. It had fallen.

Thrusting fresh loads into his .45, Billy had started down the slope, angling toward the ledge. At its edge he'd peered downward but seen nothing—just the jumbled shadows of broken eroded limestone and the brushy slope below, angling down toward a pool of water. Whoever was down there had been invisible, hidden by darkness and the night.

Scuttling to the right, Billy had worked down the taper of the caprock, where the ledge disappeared into hillside slope. Twenty feet, then another twenty, and the brushy slope was only a few feet below—a weedy darkness beneath the wedge of pale stone. He'd gauged the distance, started to jump, then stopped as high-pitched buzzing came from directly beneath him.

Rattlesnake!

Billy had backed away, shivering. He hated snakes, and it had sounded like a whole den of them, right there at the base of the rocks. It was full spring. The days were turning hot, and the nights belonged to the rattlers. He'd angled farther to the right, stepping carefully, then stepped gingerly to the lower slope and eased down toward the water, going wide around the snakes but still keeping his eye on the place where the pursuer had fallen.

When he figured he was clear of the snakes, he had started up the slope again, heading for that spot. Scours and crevices made the limestone bluff a puzzle of dim shapes and darknesses.

Billy had been almost at the bluff when he heard the growl, and as he jerked upright it had become louder, more ominous. Somewhere just ahead something big lurked, and its growl was so near that he could almost smell its hot breath. Plain animal fear had washed over Billy. He dodged back, and rattlesnakes sang and buzzed all around, echoing one another's warnings.

"To hell with this!" he muttered.

Thoroughly spooked, Billy Challis had turned and run. Something solid hit his boot and he'd felt its writhing tug as he tore free. With a shriek, he'd sprinted, gained the top of the bluff, and didn't stop there.

First rattlesnakes, then prairie wolves! Whoever was down there in that hole, he wasn't worth it. Billy ran, looking to find his horse, to get the hell away from there.

Nobody in Paradise knew that the stages were coming until riders came in from the northeast and reported three fast coaches crossing Wolf Creek at the downstream bend. By the time Asa Parker, Sypher, and O'Brien gathered at the land office, the three stagecoaches were close enough to see.

"It's them!" Sypher said. "The syndicate people! My investors! They're here!"

Parker exploded. "How did they get here without you knowing about it? You said they'd meet up with that idiot Stratton at Emporia, and we'd have plenty of word!"

"I don't know." Sypher returned his glare. "Maybe they came straight from Wichita. Anyway, they're here. And don't try to blame me, Asa! You've had all spring to nail down this territory. Why aren't you ready?"

"Jesus Christ!" O'Brien muttered, scribbling furiously at papers littering his desk while he squinted at the elaborate tract map hung on the wall. "Asa . . . I mean, colonel . . . I don't have titles ready for all the tracts we marked out. Hell, I don't even know for sure which ones have squatters on them."

"Shut up!" Asa Parker roared. "So we got a few squatters down on Rabbit Creek. Fine! Let's just make the best of it. Now get ready to receive payin' guests, and make it good, O'Brien! This is the one that counts."

The parade into town was by far the most elegant sight ever seen in Paradise: three ornate Concord stages, each pulled by a six-up hitch and sporting laquered panels and brass trim, all flanked by riders of a different cut from the rabble that roamed the Neutral Strip.

They pulled up and stopped in the rutted street between the hotel and the land office, and dignitaries stepped down, gazing around at the ramshackle little settlement that they had come to judge.

Wearing his best St. Louis attire, quickly donned in the covered overland wagon which still served as his headquarters, Asa Parker came out to meet the men whose opinions would decide the investment of several million dollars.

The man who stepped forward to study him with shrewd calculating eyes was almost as tall as Parker himself, though far more trim and manicured.

"Colonel DeWitt, I presume," the newcomer said. "I'm John Wigginton, chief investment officer for the Morley syndicate. We've come to discuss purchase of this . . . well, of whatever it is here that you are offering for sale. Let me introduce the rest of my party, and then perhaps we can rest a bit. I assume you have accommodations for our party?"

"We'll have the hotel cleared for you very shortly, Mr. Wigginton," Sypher assured him. "We're a bit remiss . . . we didn't know you were coming just now."

"Of course you didn't." Wigginton's unctuous smile was as warm as pond ice. "The wires are down west of Emporia, and there are no mail routes past Hardwoodville."

"But I suppose you met with Mr. Stratton? That he vouched for me?"

Some of the elegantly dressed men standing behind Wigginton chuckled and whispered among themselves. "He didn't vouch for anyone," Wigginton said. "The honorable Mr. Stratton had barricaded himself in a whorehouse at Emporia, in a drunken stupor. We decided to proceed, and see for ourselves what this Paradise Railhead plan might offer."

"Yes, sir." Sypher recovered quickly. "Well, fortunately, I have all of the necessary documents with me, and Mr. O'Brien is prepared to show you the holdings involved. He has a map, and charts. I assume you and your party are empowered to take title?"

"If there is title to be had." Wigginton shrugged. "This is, of course, undefined territory. We're not interested in buying blue sky, sir. Our investors will require uncontested deeds."

Sypher looked offended. "Mr. O'Brien can issue deeds, of course. Deeds of clear title based upon grant of lands for railway development. What could be more secure?"

Wigginton shrugged off the rebuff. "We want to see the actual real estate, of course. And by the way, Mr. Sypher, we passed through some of those unoccupied steads Mr. O'Brien's literature proclaims. A fair number of them seem quite occupied. There are people on the land, sir. We saw structures being built, fields being plowed, fences raised. Not precisely what we expected." He looked up at the big man standing beside Sypher. "Do you have any comment, Colonel DeWitt?"

Asa Parker scowled. "Squatters!" he rumbled. "Nothin' but trash, squattin' on land that isn't theirs. A minor problem. The Paradise Vigilance Committee will tend to them. I guarantee it."

"I hope so," Wigginton frowned. "We're prepared to invest here, sir. Don't take us for fools, though. We're aware that without a court of jurisdiction we're only looking at a railroad site patent and quit-claims. We can live with that. But at final transaction, we'll require some assurance of possession."

"Colonel DeWitt" nodded. "You'll have it."

Wigginton pursed his lips, took another slow look around at the "town" sprawling around them, and turned to his lead coachman. "Samuel, see to the coaches and the stock, please. I'm sure these gentlemen will direct you to accommodations."

While Sypher escorted the visitors to the hotel, Asa Parker signaled to Casper Wilkerson. "How many men do we have that we can still trust?"

"Maybe a dozen here in town," Casper said thoughtfully. "Few more ridin' patrol. Maybe twenty altogether. Vince Colby's took off with the rest. The boys figure he went to stake out that Haymeadows Ranch, maybe get some horses back. Ain't heard from him since."

Asa swore. The drawback to hiring drifters and owlhoots was that they were as changeable and unpredictable as the wind. "Damn bunch of fiddlefoots," he growled. "Have somebody find Colby, and get word to everybody else. I want every man that's drawin' vigilante wages right here in town. Spread them out where they can watch every direction, but keep them clear of the stagecoach people yonder. And tell 'em to keep their eyes open an' their mouths shut. Where's Billy?"

"He's holed up in one of them whore shacks down at the hogpens. Nobody wants to get near him. You heard the story goin' around, didn't you . . . what Billy did to that squatter girl that killed Tuck?"

"I heard. So what? Everybody knows Billy's crazy. But right now I need him. So you round him up. Make sure he's sober and tell him to stand by. If any of them squatters try to come in, you all know what to do."

"Billy won't listen to me." Casper shrugged.

"Well, he'll listen to me!" Asa snapped. "And he'll listen to money. You tell him it's comin' on payday. If that doesn't work, tell him he'll either take orders or he'll answer to me, face-to-face."

"What are we gonna do, Asa?"

"Well, we sure aren't goin' raidin' again. That takes too long. O'Brien's got land titles here in Paradise, and Sypher's got the buyers here. We'll get our deal, all right. And once it's signed, those squatters won't own a thing."

"They'll know what's goin' on here," Casper said, glancing around at the shabby little town. "They got plenty of spies right here to tell 'em."

"Do you know who the spies are?"

"Not rightly," Casper admitted. His hooded eyes roved the crowds nearby, pausing momentarily at a well-dressed, dark-haired young man standing alone, pretending not to watch what was going on. "I got some ideas, though. We got one jasper around here that makes me right itchy."

"Why?"

"Hell, he's always around, listenin' and pryin'. Puttin' ideas into folks' heads."

"What kind of ideas?"

"Ideas like goin' out an' settlin' claims of their own. Like joinin' up with the squatters."

Parker nodded. "Tend to him, then. Just don't make a fuss."

"I'll do that," Casper muttered. Through hooded eyes, he watched as the young slicker wandered off toward the stable, carrying a leather valise. "Word's still gonna get out, though."

"Good!" Parker said. "Let 'em try to come in and stop us. We're on our own ground here. We'll bury them in it. Spread the word—there's a bonus of fifty dollars per man if no more squatters get into town alive."

TWENTY-THREE

Brett Archer was one of a dozen or so tenants evicted from the ramshackle Paradise Hotel to make room for O'Brien's visiting dignitaries. Because the Virginian had become known around town, and because most of the vigilantes were more than a little timid about the quiet quick-eyed young dandy with the low-slung gun, they were polite about it. But it was an eviction. Two yellow-flagged hard cases met him at the hotel door, handed him his valise, and told him he didn't live there any more.

Brett wasn't surprised. He had seen the stages coming in, and been close enough to hear some of what passed when the passengers landed.

He had known for some time who had robbed and killed the Blanchard family, way out there in Colorado. He knew all but two of them by sight. For days at a time, in the past few weeks, he had watched them. First there was Asa Parker, the deadly giant who headed up the gang and now went by the name of Colonel Amos DeWitt. Parker was big and mean, and smart. He held himself a cut above the outlaws around him, in his carriage and his manner of dress, but he didn't hesitate to use his big fists and boots on any man who got in his way.

He led by cunning and by fear. They were all

afraid of him, and it showed. Beyond being a bully, Parker was as treacherous as a big spider, with that hidden .44 up his sleeve. But all of that, Brett knew, was just the style of the man. When it came down to it, Parker was lightning quick with the big iron at his hip. Some around there, who knew of him from the past, said that Asa Parker was the fastest man with a .45 that anybody had ever seen.

Then there was that scowling scarecrow, Casper Wilkerson. Wilkerson always reminded Brett of a hunch-shouldered buzzard. He always wore a long filthy coat that covered him from scrawny neck to below the knees and fit him like a tent would fit a turtle. The coat looked way too big for his spare frame, but it bulged oddly around the chest.

And Wilkerson always carried that big sawed-off shotgun. Like a part of him, it was never out of his hand. Of them all he was the quietest, and in some ways the most ominous.

There had been another big hulking man in the gang—Kurt Obermire. But Obermire was gone now, like the ugly flap-eared Folly Downs was gone—riddled to painful death with placed shots from a small rifle.

A small rifle like the one carried by that Indian kid Falcon MacCallister had found.

And there were Tuck Kelly and Billy Challis. Brett had never seen them, but he had heard the whispers. Womanizers and hell-raisers, both of them. Of the pair, Billy Challis was worst, they said. Kelly was known as a rapist, but they said Billy Challis just went crazy at the sight of a good-looking female.

What he liked to do to women . . . Brett's eyes went flat and cold each time he heard the rumors. It was what had been done to Dorothy. And now Billy Challis had been at it again. Even the outlaws of Paradise—the lowest dregs of mankind—shied away from Challis now.

The stories that filtered in from the settler camps were explicit. And there was hardly a man in this land who wasn't disgusted. Only a crazy man would do things like that . . . to a dead woman.

Tuck Kelly was dead now, they said. That made three of the six who had slaughtered Owen Blanchard's family. Owen's big overland wagon stood tall in the center of the dirty little town, like a monument to evil, and Asa Parker guarded it like gold. Casper Wilkerson was always around, dark and ominous, always watching.

Billy Challis had been just a name passed around. But now he was here, and Brett knew where he was.

He strolled to the dismal pole barn that served as a livery. The place was bustling now with the activity of preparing space for three big Concord stages, and feed for their teams. He left his valise there in the same roped-off corner with his saddle and gear. Then he went back out on the street and looked southward. Out on the flats, just at the edge of town, was a squalid little settlement of dugouts, sod-roof sheds and stained tents—the hogpens, some called it. Others referred to it as Boys' Town.

Once, in times past, when the great southern herd was being systematically wiped out, it might have been a buffalo camp. Then some squatter had tried to raise hogs there, giving the place its name. Now it was something else—a squalid little nest of gambling, drinking, and whoring that not even Colonel DeWitt's crude Paradise would claim.

Like a separate settlement it lay out there, less than a mile away. The men who kept it going weren't Parker men, and the only law was primeval law— He who is meanest prevails. Still, it thrived. In the months since Paradise had grown, and with it customers, more enterprisers had drifted in from the Territories, bringing their whores and their whiskey. There wasn't a thing out at the hogpens that wasn't for sale.

Billy Challis was out there.

In the alleyway behind the stables, Brett brushed back his coattail, crouched and drew his gun—drawing, cocking, and pointing in a single fluid motion. Fast and sure. But was he good enough?

Several more times he drew the pistol, each time imagining that Dorothy's killer was standing there, facing him. The gun whispered from its leather and aligned, and each time its point was dead-steady.

With a sigh, Brett checked the loads in the revolver, then dropped it back into its holster and let his coat fall over it. "For you, Dorothy," he whispered. "I'll see that maniac in hell, or I'll see you in heaven, pretty soon now."

Easing back into the pole barn, he gentled his horse and tossed a saddle on him. He waited until the livery teams were being unhitched, then led the animal out and rode away, trying to attract no attention.

Even in the noise and confusion, though, there were eyes on him as he left.

From a crude porch across the street, Casper Wilkerson watched thoughtfully. He didn't care one way or another about the quiet young dude from Virginia. He was only watching him because it kept him in town. Asa had pretty well cleared the streets of vigilantes since the spenders arrived. A few were holed up here and there, but most were out on the roads, to keep the Barlows at bay. Casper didn't want to leave. Of the six who knew of the railroad money in the big wagon, only three were left, and Casper had a notion that Asa Parker didn't intend to share.

But now, watching the dude head for the hogpens, a quick intuition told Casper what he was up to. Brett Archer was looking for Billy Challis.

If there had been any humor in Casper Wilkerson, it would have struck him funny. Casper had seen Billy Challis in action. Crazy he might be, but Billy was hell on wheels with a handgun. Asa Parker might be his equal, but no one else ever would.

The idea that some squirt dude from back east was out to get Billy . . . Casper's eyes narrowed as the intuition became an idea. Maybe no gunslick could kill Billy, but Billy could be killed.

He looked around, slowly. The town looked almost deserted. Parker and O'Brien were over at the hotel, with the land buyers. Here and there a few drifters moseyed around, and there were men tending stock at the livery. But for once the main street stood empty, with the big overland wagon standing out there unattended.

Besides himself, only Asa and Billy remained of the six. Making up his mind, Casper strode across to the livery. "Saddle that big dun for me," he told a swamper. Then he went on through, to the little locked shed beyond—his private quarters by right of possession.

He was back in a minute or two, still covered from neck to boots by that long dark coat of his, now looking more bulky than before. Without a word to anyone he climbed aboard the big horse and headed south at a slow trot, following the distant figure of the Virginian.

In the back of the barn a shaggy sweating man was raking fouled hay. He saw Brett ride away and saw Wilkerson follow. It might have been simple curiosity that prompted Cass Jolly to follow along, or it might have been something more.

Cass had wandered away from Paradise for a while, after getting crossways with a few of Obermire's vigilantes. He had even thought about staking a claim of his own and trying his hand at the plow.

Hunger had brought him back—that and a natural aversion to the lonely hard work of farming.

But he was off the payroll now. Just a little too old to bluster his way back into Asa Parker's crowd, and just a little too slow to think seriously about robbing them, he had settled for what he could get—a crap-wage job in town. Like a lot of men these days, Cass Jolly was in No Man's Land because he had no other place to go. It was just as Iverson said—if a man had a rope waiting for him in Texas and federal marshals in Kansas, the only choices left were hell and No Man's Land.

In its own way, Paradise was booming. There was work to be had, if a man didn't care what he did. Through the cold days of this peculiar spring, several corpses had accumulated over by the bluff, and now there were holes to dig and remains to plant. Men with skills were working on some of the buildings, men without were carrying slops and swamping out the few places that had floors.

Cass had signed on to work with the remuda, which meant in his case cleaning out the stables every few days.

Just lately, Cass had been giving some more serious thought to what Brett Archer said about starting fresh there in a place where the rules hadn't been made yet.

Rules, he reasoned, ought to start with a simple

judgment of what's right. What he saw now—the dark-eyed young Virginian heading out toward the hogpens with his pistol fresh-slicked in its leather, and Casper Wilkerson watching him leave like that—well, that wasn't just right.

Cass set the hay rake aside, doused his face and hands from the water bucket, and dug out his possibles from the dingy loft. Then he slapped his old saddle onto a peaceable little roan that had outlived at least two owners and slipped off southward. Out ahead of him, Brett Archer was still in sight. And behind Archer—like a buzzard on a big horse keeping to the cuts and washes—rode Casper Wilkerson.

Like a spread out little parade, they all headed for the hogpens south of Paradise. Slanting sunlight cast long shadows as they passed, and none looked back.

If they had, they might have seen—from the rising prairie beyond the creek—something that no one in Paradise saw. Up on the higher flats, behind the bluff just north of the creek and beyond the chalky caprock that stood over fresh graves there, men moved toward the little town. Here a head and shoulders were skylined against the northern hills, there a glimpse of hats and rifle barrels. Elsewhere for a brief moment a rider was silhouetted in passing, with other riders behind.

Asa Parker had the town sealed. Dozens of yellow-bands were out on the eastbound road and in the breaks southeast of Paradise. There was even a sniper post, and several riders were out on the west trail where Wolf Creek curled down from the table lands. But from the little settlement called Paradise, there was one blind direction—north, past the caliche bluff. And there, out of sight, dozens and more dozens of riders made their way toward the town.

* * *

Vince Colby might have gone straight for the horse herd at Haymeadows if it hadn't been for Tad Sands finding that calf in the gully.

It was a wobbly legged calf, barely weaned and no more than coyote bait out there in the breaks north of Rabbit Creek. It had become separated from its mother and wandered into a gully too narrow to follow and too deep to climb. Tad found the critter there, and he shot it.

Colby and the rest didn't mind. It was late in the day, and they had traveled hard to make barely four miles since morning, skirting around first one squatter camp and then another to keep out of sight.

Colby had in mind to come up on the capstone flats northeast of Paradise, then scout out that outfit that called itself A&M Land and Cattle Company. That was where some joker claimed all the lost horses had gone, and Vince wanted them. They were all broke from the last visit to the hogpens, and needed a grubstake.

So when Tad killed the calf they were out in the breaks with evening coming on, and all of them were tired and hungry.

They made a fire and butchered the calf, and settled in to rest a while. And it was then that they found the cow tracks, heading north.

"I make it maybe fifty head," Jimmy Stone reckoned. "Three, four, riders pushin' 'em. They've come a piece, from the way the cows keep to a herd, but this ain't no trail crew. You can tell these boys ain't drove cows afore."

"Rustlers," Vince decided. "The Supply trail's fifty miles southeast of here. I guess these fellers cut a herd down there and helped themselves to what they could get." He turned north, peering at where little herd had gone. "What's up there that a man would drive cows to?"

"Kansas," John Moline offered. "If it was me, I'd be takin' 'em up toward Hardwoodville."

"That's across the line, ain't it?"

"Yeah. But not far. Me and Cabot know our way around up there, Vince. Not much law 'til Dodge. Some rawhiders got a place up there most everybody knows about. They'll buy cows, then sell the beef at Dodge. They don't ask questions."

"Fifty head of beef make a nice grubstake," Stone suggested. "Them rustlers ain't all that far ahead of us, Vince."

Print Olive had been labeled "the meanest man alive" in Texas, for his treatment of rustlers. Olive and his whole family hated rustlers, and Print found ways to express that hatred. When he moved to Nebraska he took his methods with him, and expanded his attentions to homestead farmers and rawhiders.

One of the trademarks of Olive's style of justice was the "horizontal hanging"—involving a stump, a noose, and a team of horses. There was a story in Texas of a rustler caught by Print himself and several of his black cowboys. Having no trees handy, Print used a stump as anchor, and a wagon.

Unfortunately, the wagon's team spooked and ran.

After being strung out, they said, the rustler was solemnly buried in two counties.

The Olives were also noted for the burning of corpses, and for shallow burials with an arm or leg sticking up out of the ground to mark the grave.

Print Olive left Nebraska the same way he left

Texas—ushered out because of public outrage at his excessive methods. He had settled finally at Dodge City, Kansas.

In Kansas, the Olive bunch modified its behavior. Old Print was tired of being run out of places by his neighbors. But his attitude toward rustlers and herd-cutters didn't change. He didn't tolerate them, and used whatever means he had to put an end to their activities.

The difference was that by the early eighties Print had begun to work with the law—if there was any—instead of around it.

Print Olive was well on his way to becoming respectable when Joe Sparrow shot him down over a ten-dollar debt.

Print had been dead for a couple of years now, but the Sawlog and Smokey Hill ranches he founded near Dodge City still maintained his philosophies. So it was that, as the cattle drives began showing up this season, Marshal Sam Stroud was involved in the investigation of rawhiding operations over west of the sand hills, around Hardwoodville.

The dressed beef that came in from there almost weekly, in the form of butchered carcasses hanging from the slats of high-rack wagons, was stolen beef. Everybody knew it, but everybody bought it anyway, and the commerce cut deep into the profits of Sawlog and Smokey Hill.

The big ranches swung some weight with the merchants of Dodge, and merchants ran the city. They brought so much pressure to bear on Stroud that he sent Ben Wheaton over to Hardwoodville to see if he could dig up some evidence. And because Sawlog held a seat on the Western Kansas Stockman's Association board of directors, orders came out of Topeka to provide the deputy with a military escort.

Wheaton and the soldiers had been digging—literally—for most of a day before they found what they were looking for. Behind Wendell Murray's place, they uncovered dozens of buried cowhides still fresh enough to read the trail brands. Most of them were Texas stock.

Murray and the half-dozen men he employed on his place sat in glum silence as the stink of unearthed evidence increased.

"I guess we got enough evidence here," Wheaton told the Kansas-State Militia Lieutenant John Colgrave. "We'll haul a few of these back to Dodge and let Sam decide what to do about it."

"You're not going to arrest anybody?" the lieutenant asked.

"For what? Butcherin' beef? The only charge I've got here is receipt of stolen property. If I was to start arrestin' people for things like that, I'd have to jail damn near everybody in Dodge City."

"How about rustling?" Sergeant Jack Lyles suggested. "Maybe these here boys rustled some of those critters they dressed out."

"Can't prove it." Wheaton shrugged. "And tell you the truth, I doubt it. These fellers haven't got the makin's of cow rustlers. They just buy 'em from whoever does." He thought it over, then cocked his head, looking off to the south. "Now, if we could catch us some actual rustlers coming up from the strip, that would be a different story."

"Are we in a hurry?" Lyles looked around at the ugly chutes and slaughter pens of the butchering camp. "Those wagons over yonder have fresh rope on their meat hooks, but I don't see any beef wai-

tin' to be loaded . . . or any cows ready for cuttin'.
Looks to me like they're expectin' a new crop."

"I guess we could wait around a little while."
Wheaton nodded. "Just in case. Might take the pressure off Sam if we could bring in a few rustlers with
fresh Texas beef. I expect that Sawlog outfit would
enjoy seein' a real lawful trial of malefactors at
Dodge City."

"Molly . . . facters?" a soldier muttered. "Is that
the same as outlaws?"

"Don't remember that happenin' very often,"
Lyles commented.

"Been a while," the deputy agreed. "Lot of folks
get planted at Dodge City. Happens all the time. But
it's usually just social occasions. Been a while since
anybody was hanged proper."

With Murray and his rawhiders under guard, the
Kansas State Militia—or that part of it consisting of
Lieutenant John Colegrave and a patrol from Com-
pany B, Second Kansas—waited.

In the clear light of high plains evening they saw
the cattle coming up from No Man's Land when
the little stolen herd was still eight miles away. Fifty
head or so, and at least a dozen riders pushing
them.

It wasn't in the young lieutenant's nature to wait
much longer. It was clear that the cattle were stolen,
and it was obvious they were crossing into Kansas,
heading for the slaughter camp.

"You know they'll run when they see us coming,"
Wheaton commented, saddling his mount.

"Of course they will," Colegrave said. "And that
gives us a hot pursuit situation, to cross the line. A
fine opportunity to exercise the troops."

Sergeant Lyles hid his smile. Colegrave wouldn't

be a lieutenant much longer, he decided. The youngster had *cojones,* if not common sense.

"Give that shavetail a few more years," he told Wheaton, "he'll be wearin' birds. Maybe even commandin' a regiment."

TWENTY-FOUR

The weird spring of that year had run its course and wrung itself out. Dry hot winds blew now from the south, and the fresh green grass of weeks before had begun to parch as probing roots sucked the last of the winter's moisture from arid sandy soil.

On a rise west of Paradise, four riders and fourteen riderless horses—several of them saddled—filed down from caprock just as the full sun of evening touched the distant hills. Falcon MacCallister and the Mason brothers had been on the move since morning. Moving at a steady pace, they had pushed the little cayuse herd from Haymeadows Ranch westward, circling finally to approach from the west while a far different kind of force gathered three miles above the north rim of Wolf Creek, ready to move at the setting of the sun.

Falcon and the Masons paused now to watch the deployment of distant riders moving down toward Paradise—tiny specks on the deceptive plainsland, but none the less ominous for their distance. There were only twenty or so riders out there, but somehow their coordinated implacable thrust toward the north bluff above the outlaw town seemed like the tide of doom descending.

Twenty or so motley riders, and behind them a

plodding line of men on foot, were dotted here and there by ramshackle wagons, drab carts and barrows, and ambling draft animals. The riders at the point all carried long guns of various types, and some of the walkers had firearms. Most, though, carried spades and scythes, axes and sledges—implements of all kinds.

The entire assemblage moved toward Paradise, angling toward the east slopes of the chalk bluff that stood above the north verge of Wolf Creek.

"Our pa faced folks like that in the war," Jude drawled. "Just like those Barlows out yonder. Folks from Tennessee, Kentucky, Virginia . . . hill people."

"Pa had bad dreams all the time," Joshua added. "I guess I see why, now. When he used to talk about 'Johnny Reb' I 'magined regular troop soldiers in gray uniforms. But he didn't mean ordinary soldiers. He meant Barlows."

In the distance below, the jumbled little sprawl of Paradise lay like thrown refuse along the south bank of Wolf Creek. Lingering breezes from the south blew across the hogpens and carried their smoke and stench toward the main town, then died against the high bluff on the north. Paradise lay misted with eddying smokes, like dying smoking embers on a trash heap.

"I'd hate to be the one those dirt farmers go after," Jude allowed.

Falcon nodded. "Plain people," he said. "Just pushed one push too far."

Jubal eased out ahead, getting a better look at the panorama. He moved carefully, even though the lowering sun behind them would hide them from view of the town. Joshua sat off to one side, checking the loads in his rifle and his handgun while he kept the little horse herd tight.

MacCallister stepped down from Diablo and took off his coat. He stripped off his linen shirt, baring his torso. Despite the ugly scars that had formed there, back and front, he looked as smooth and muscled as a draft horse.

Like an oak tree, Jude thought. *Big and tall, and rock-hard solid. Just looking at the big moon-haired man, a body wouldn't guess at the damage inside him, where the bullet ripped across bone and through muscle.*

The wounds were healing, but it would be a time yet before the big man was truly sound.

"You want to give me a hand, Jude?" Falcon asked. From a saddle pouch he drew out his old buckskin hunting shirt and slipped it over his head. Then with his knife he began making little holes in it—a string of little holes two inches apart running from breast to waist down the right side, and another string of holes on the left.

"What are you doing?" Jude asked, puzzled.

The holes completed, Falcon reached into his saddle pouch again and brought out a roll of cut thong. "Binding," he said. He began threading thong through the holes in the buckskin, left to right to left, starting at the bottom and working upward. With two holes on each side laced, he lapped the shirt close over his belly and drew the laces tight. They left a four-inch gap.

His cheeks paled slightly, and his breathing went ragged. "You do the rest," he told Jude. Spreading his arms like wings, he stood firmly as Jude took the strings. "Tight as you can pull them, all the way up."

At the third lace, Jude hesitated as a groan escaped from MacCallister's clenched teeth. The big man only glared at him. "Tighter," he rasped. "Put your shoulders into it."

Jude continued the lacing, putting all his strength into the pull of the thongs. Once or twice he thought MacCallister's knees would buckle, but the big man steadied himself, bracing against the pull.

When all the crisscrosses were tight, Jude tied off the ends in a hard knot.

"This ain't ever gonna be untied, Mr. MacCallister," he apologized. "Only way to get it loose will be to cut the cords."

MacCallister took a deep breath, his heavy muscles swelling against the confining buckskin. "It'll do." He nodded.

He strapped on his gunbelt, tested the smooth draw of the holstered .44, and slipped the other .44 into his waistband. "It'll do," he said again.

Jubal was back, holding hard rein on a skittish horse. "Well, are we goin' in?" he demanded.

MacCallister took Diablo's reins, stroked the big black's powerful neck and shoulder, then stepped into the stirrup and swung aboard. It was the first time Jude had seen him mount a horse without gritting his teeth.

In the saddle, Falcon looked down at the corset-laced buckskin wrapped around his belly. "It'll do just fine," he said. He turned to glance at the evening sun, which sat like a big intense ball on the horizon. "Good a time as any," he said. "Let's get these remounts strung out and moving, boys. It's time to go to town."

Evening sun sat a smoky haze over the twisted warrens of sheds and lean-tos of the hogpens when a stifled scream cut the air—just an instant of blood-chilling animal sound, abruptly silenced.

Such sounds were not uncommon around the hogpens, and hardly anybody even looked around when a filthy flap was pushed aside and Billy Challis stepped out into the evening. If anyone noticed the fresh scratches on his cheek or the blood on his hands and his stained shirt, they thought better about mentioning it.

"Damn Injun whore," Billy muttered. "Not even worth the trouble." He paused, looking around, then picked up a fallen jug, pulled the cork, and tipped it up for a long swig.

Two swallows, and it was empty. With an oath he cast it aside and headed for the shallow cistern that served as a water well. Men stepped aside as he passed, giving him a wide berth. By now everybody in the settlement knew about Billy Challis, and not a man among them—not even the hawkers and vendors who prowled these alleys, was interested in catching his eye.

A butcher of women, the rumors said. Crazy as a loon, and just plain mean.

Billy had never been much to look at, but in the past few days he had become a filthy strutting scarecrow, bearded and unkempt, his dark-stained clothing hanging around him in tatters. It was as though, without Tuck Kelly to rile him and ride herd on him, he had just gone to pieces.

But the unkempt sloppy appearance of him was only surface. Like a snake shedding its winter skin, Billy was more dangerous than ever.

Tuck had been, in some odd way, a rudder to him—an influence checking and balancing his wild impulses. Tuck was gone, and Billy didn't miss him. Now nothing held him in check.

At the cistern he dropped a bucket, hauled up water and leaned over to douse his head. The cold water made the scratches on his face burn, and he growled. The squaw had marked him, and now a barely contained rage burned in his eyes. Wiping his hands on his stained shirt, Billy fingered the gun at his hip and turned slowly, full around, daring anybody to so much as look at him.

But there was nobody near. Folks tended to get scarce when any gunman's mood turned ugly, and when it was Billy Challis they scattered fast.

Muttering, Billy turned back to the cistern and drew up another pail of water. Cupping his hands, he dipped and drank. Then he froze as a crisp voice said, "Turn around, you killer of women. Turn and face me!"

Billy straightened slowly, and his frown became a grin of anticipation. "Now who the hell is that?" he drawled, not turning. "You sure you want me lookin' at you, Mr.? You sure you hadn't better just shoot me in the back?"

"I said turn around, you son of a bitch!"

Billy glanced around, and his grin widened. The man behind him was fairly tall, slim, and somehow elegant—dark hair neatly cut, clean-shaven, clothing of foppish Eastern cut . . . and though he stood slightly crouched, his coattail pushed back to clear his holster, he had no gun in his hand. A slicker! A duded-up young gentleman playing by some kind of sporting rules!

"Well, well," Billy purred. "Looky what we got here."

Slowly, arrogantly, he turned and faced the dude. "That how you want it, Beau?" he smirked. "I'm lookin' at you now. Make your play."

The dude glared at him with eyes as hard as flint.

"Billy Challis," he said, "You are a woman killer, and a beast. Draw your gun when you're ready, because I intend to shoot you—"

The talk ended there. Brett Archer was skilled with a gun, and had the nerve to duel, but he was no match for Billy Challis. Brett didn't even see the blur of Billy's hand as the outlaw's hogleg sprouted there and belched fire. Something hot and vicious smacked him in the upper right chest and spun him halfway around, carrying him backward to sprawl on the littered sand.

He coughed and tried to move, to reach his gun, and a disinterested voice said, "Damn! I must be drunk! You ain't dead yet!"

Standing over the fallen slicker, Billy Challis shook his head and giggled. He hesitated, trying to decide whether to finish the dude off or let him bleed a while. Then, on impulse, he put his gun away and drew his knife. The man on the ground was still moving, struggling.

Suddenly Billy realized what the stranger was doing. He was trying to roll over, to reach his gun with his left hand.

Billy kicked him. Then he stepped over him, turned, and kicked again.

"A goddam hero!" He chuckled. "Of all things! Well, go ahead an' roll over. I never castrated a real, honest to God dude before. Might just gut you, too . . . see how you holler."

Once more Billy kicked the dude, rolling him over onto his back. Pain-filled eyes stared up at him, hating him. Then the man's left hand darted across, reaching for his weapon, and Billy dropped to one knee beside him.

In that instant a roar like thunder filled the air. Billy's hat flew off and talons of fire raked his scalp.

Throwing himself to one side, the outlaw twisted and rolled. His gun came out blazing, but the shot was off.

Just behind where he had been, Casper Wilkerson stood, his dark hat, black coat, and shadowed beak making him look for all the world like a tall somber buzzard rearing upright in the evening's haze. Casper's big shotgun smoked from both barrels, and he was breaking the action to shuck the loads.

"You wormy bastard!" Billy shrieked. Half-sitting on the ground, he raised his .45, thumbed its hammer, and fired point-blank.

Almost drowned in the Colt's roar was the sound of ringing metal, like a muffled iron bell. Wilkerson staggered back a step, then straightened and pushed fresh loads into his greener.

The twin muzzles came up and Billy rolled frantically, firing again as he turned. The shot was dead center, but this time Casper didn't even stagger. He just stood there, raising the shotgun to his shoulder.

Billy bumped up against the cistern, grabbed the loose pail from its hook, and flung it as hard as he could. As Casper dodged it, he got his feet under him and ran.

Last rays of evening sun lit the smoke haze as Billy crawled under a broken wagon, out the other side, and dodged among the ramshackle sheds and sties of the hogpens. "Bastard tried to kill me," he muttered. "What the hell's the matter with—"

He cut through a stinking alley and ducked behind a shack, and then the answer came to him.

"He's going for the money!" Billy hissed. "That bastard Wilkerson! He's after the money in the wagon!"

A hundred yards away, Casper Wilkerson gave up his search. He had missed, and Billy was moving.

Beside a collapsing soddy, Casper paused to unbutton his coat. He had bruises on his chest and under his arms, but the iron plate had held. A two-foot square piece of tank plate, hammered into a curve and slung on harness, the thing had stopped Billy's slugs. Deep dents pocked the rusty surface now, but the bullets had not gone through.

Fastening his coat, Casper hurried toward the alley where he had left his horse. He had to get back to Paradise now. It wouldn't take Billy long to figure out what he was after, and then Billy would come.

The sound of distant gunfire, drifting in on the evening wind, was scarcely noticed in Paradise. In upstairs rooms at the hotel, though, a few of the day's newcomers paused for a moment to listen. John Wigginton, who led the Morley Syndicate delegation, stepped to a dusty window and looked out. The sun was almost down, and though there was still daylight he could also see the fires and lanterns of a cluster of structures in the distance.

"It's from out there," he pointed. "That little camp or whatever it is, out on the prairie."

"It's nothing." Colonel DeWitt shrugged. "That's the hogpens out there. Slaughter pens, and a whiskey camp. There's always somebody shooting."

"Think nothing of it, gentlemen," O'Brien added. "This is a rough country now, but let's consider how it will be when the railroad comes through with its new commerce."

"We don't need drummer speeches, sir." Wigginton frowned. "Just facts. When can we look at the maps and domain instruments?"

"It's getting late," DeWitt interrupted. "First

thing in the morning, we'll show you gentlemen around and then go to the land office. Plenty of time then to talk business. In the meantime, we have cooks preparing your evening meal, and a few bottles of fine wine that should be sampled."

He picked up his hat and motioned for Sypher and O'Brien to follow. "We'll leave you to your rest now, gentlemen. All of your questions will be answered tomorrow, I'm sure."

Downstairs he grabbed O'Brien by the lapel and hauled him outside. "You heard me, O'Brien," he growled. "I don't care how you do it, you just have all those documents in order by sunup."

He pushed the salesman away, and O'Brien brushed himself off, recovering his dignity.

"I'll have it all ready, colonel," he said. "But you'd better keep a lid on this town until everything is signed and sealed. And make them quit shooting those guns! I can't deal with nervous buyers."

O'Brien headed for the land office, and Asa Parker prowled the street until he found a vigilante he trusted.

"Get out there to the hogpens, Smith," he ordered. "See what's going on and put a stop to it. Take some men with you."

"We ain't got but six or eight in town right now," Smith said. "Ever'body's out on the roads, lookin' for squatters."

"Well, take what you can get! And bring Billy Challis back with you. That crazy possum's been lazing around long enough. I need him here!"

"Yes, sir."

"And see if you can find Casper Wilkerson, too. He's supposed to be here on the street."

"Maybe he's takin' a crap, Colonel."

"Find him!"

"Yes, sir."

Smith hurried away, and Parker headed for his overland wagon. From the high perch of its box, he scanned the roads out of town, east and west. There wasn't much to see. The day was ending, and long shadows trailed away to the east, where sunlight's trailing edge crept up the long sloping prairie away from Wolf Creek.

To the west, the glare of red sunset hid everything but itself. He had men out there, too, guarding the town, but against the sundown nothing could be seen.

Just one more day, Asa Parker told himself. *One more miserable day, and I'll see the last of this hellhole.* Ducking into the wagon he lit a lantern, drew the flaps closed, and opened the hatch on the strongbox in the floor.

Of the nine thousand dollars he had taken from the Kansas Pacific Railway, more than seven remained. Seven thousand dollars. A lot of money in some respects, but only a drop in the bucket compared to what he would have once those eastern buyers signed over their collateral accounts tomorrow.

He would leave the wagon, leave the locked strongbox, and leave Paradise far behind. Oh, there would be those expecting a share, all right. Sypher would want half of it. O'Brien was in for a tenth. And the rest—he realized that now it was down to Billy Challis and Casper Wilkerson—they would want shares of the remainder.

But Asa Parker didn't mean to share with anybody. The collateral accounts would go straight into his own account in St. Louis, and he would be far from Paradise before anybody realized he was gone. Sypher would be on his own, holding worthless paper that would trace only to him when the transaction was investigated. O'Brien might rant and rave, but what could he do? He was only a land drummer.

Casper and Billy? Well, they were another story. He would have to deal with them eventually. But that might be a while.

Out of habit, Asa Parker cleaned and oiled the .45 he always carried and returned it to its holster with fresh loads. Then he retrieved the little .44 hideout gun from his sleeve and cleaned it, too.

When the time came, Casper Wilkerson would be no serious problem. The man was a killer, but not a gunfighter. When the day came that it was necessary, Parker would simply ventilate him before he could even begin to raise that ugly shotgun he carried.

As to Billy Challis, Parker had little doubt that he could beat the beat the loon in any stand-up match. It would be close, but slick as Billy was, he still was only a fast hand.

Asa Parker had made a study of shooting. Back in St. Louis he had learned from the best—a professional duelist named Clay who had once instructed at the Military Academy at West Point. Asa's craft with a revolver was honed to perfection, and tested to his satisfaction twenty-three times.

He could take Billy Challis if it came to that. But why take chances? Billy knew about the .44 hideout gun. They all knew about it. Funny thing, though, even though everybody knew Asa carried a sleeve derringer, nobody ever seemed to expect it.

He put the gun away and doused his lantern. Again he heard gunfire in the distance, and he frowned. Those damned fools couldn't do anything right!

Oddly, though, the sounds didn't seem to come from the south this time. If he hadn't known better, Asa Parker would have sworn they came from the west.

TWENTY-FIVE

As the sun lowered from quarter-high to horizon, Ram Sullivan and five other drifter vigilantes prowled the westward road out of Paradise and shaded their eyes against the lowering glare. By the time the sun touched the horizon their eyes burned, their tempers were short, and all but Sullivan were snugged into a little gully a hundred yards off the trail, playing cards.

"There's nobody comm' in from out here," they generally agreed. "Hell, there's nobody out here but us. DeWitt's just tryin' to keep ever'body out of town while he flimflams them easterners."

Ram Sullivan was about to give up and join them when he heard muffled hoofbeats on the road and shaded his aching eyes one more time against the sunset.

There was movement in the glare. Reining his mount to a halt, he tensed, trying to see. A riderless horse ambled past, then three more, two of them carrying empty saddles. There were others just behind them, strung out the way riding stock will when being moved from place to place.

"What the hell," Ram tensed as a lineback mare that he knew very well came into view. It was his own horse—one he had stolen back in the territories and then lost the night Jackson led the raid on those Rabbit Creek settlers.

He stared at it, then at the man riding the big, black, stud horse just beyond. The man was a stranger—a big wide-shouldered hombre with hair the color of moon-straw blowing wild beneath a flat-brimmed hat.

The man reined toward him and approached, waving casually. "How do," he said. "Does that yellow neck-wrap mean you're one of Asa's boys?"

Ram squinted. "It means I'm Paradise Vigilance Committee," he said. "Who are you? And who's Asa . . . ? and where did you get my horse?"

The big black ambled up alongside him. "I meant DeWitt," the stranger said. "Colonel DeWitt. I guess you work for him, all right. I got horses here from Haymeadows that I heard some of you boys lost."

"Damn right we did!" Ram spat. "How'd you get hold of 'em?"

"Oh, I was there," the stranger drawled. "I took a few of them myself. So you boys are still hangin' on with Asa Parker and that crowd, huh? Don't you have anything better to do?"

It was then that Ram realized that the man had edged in right beside him, way too close. With a snarl, Ram went for his gun, and suddenly an arm the size of a corner post shot out and a steel-hard hand closed over Ram's gunhand. "Don't do that," the stranger said. "You'll just wish you hadn't."

"Like hell!" Ram twisted, and found his arm was imprisoned in a hold he couldn't break. Just beyond the stranger, a dozen or more horses were plodding past, and the sunset glare made silhouettes of the men driving and guiding them.

Ram felt sudden panic. His horse skittered and he was dragged half out of his saddle by the unyielding hand that held him. "Boys!" he yelled. "Fellers, help me! Shoot him!"

A hundred yards away, surprised heads popped up from a gully's rim, and a wild gunshot rang out.

"Now that was really dumb," the big stranger told Ram. A fist like a mule's kick lashed out, and Ram Sullivan toppled from his horse.

Falcon MacCallister loosened his grip and let the cowboy fall, then reined toward the gully and dug in his heels. Diablo bunched his powerful quarters and sprinted, straight toward the gully. There were shouts there, and two more gunshots. A bullet whipped past Falcon's ear, and then his .45 was out and thundering.

It was all over in an instant. Jude Mason watched his brothers wheel away to gather their startled herd, then cut northward across the trail. At the edge of a wash—a runoff gully that had been a creek not long ago—Falcon MacCallister sat easy in the saddle of his black stallion, with his gun in hand. Below him on the sloping bank, two terrified-looking outlaws stood with their empty hands in the air. Three more lay scattered on the slope, none of them moving.

"Better gather up those guns," Falcon told Jude. "Then swing around yonder and pick up these boys' horses. They won't be needing them."

Jude gawked, then grinned. "Hot damn," he said.

When all the fallen guns were gathered up, Jude took Ram Sullivan's mount on lead and swung northward to bring in the picketed animals of the other five.

"You boys are out of the vigilante business," Falcon told the two still standing. "Pick up your pard over there." He gestured over his shoulder at the sleeping Ram Sullivan. "And get moving. Either that, or die right here."

"Get . . . get movin'?" one of them managed. "Where?"

"Go someplace else," Falcon shrugged. "Kansas is that way, Texas is that way, and there's a whole lot of No Man's Land out that way. Just start walking, and don't stop."

"It's gonna be dark soon, Mr.," the owlhoot whined. "You ain't gonna set us afoot out in those breaks . . . at night?"

"You afraid of snakes, bub?" Falcon's deep voice was hard as steel. "Your choice. Out there, the rattlers might not find you. You come back this way, though, and I will."

There was no room for argument, and the yellow-bands knew it. They just weren't welcome in hell any more.

Falcon watched them get their buddy on his feet, and watched idly as they plodded away, going more or less southwest. They wouldn't be back.

Joshua Mason rode up beside Falcon. "Ain't this somethin?" The kid grinned. "Seems like a land with no law just plain sprouts horses. That makes twenty right here an' twenty more back at the place." He chuckled. "Found horses! This horse-takin' business could be habit-formin'. How you holdin' up, Mr. MacCallister?"

Falcon paused thoughtfully, and nodded. The buckskin corset under his coat was makeshift, but the chronic pain in his midsection was only an ache now. The horse doctor, Linsecum, had been right. Whatever had still not healed inside Falcon, the lacing seemed to be holding everything in place. "I believe I'm hanging together just fine, Joshua," he said.

Jude came back from the point, glancing at the setting sun. "This was all they had between here and the town," he reported. "The main bunch is out east, along the trail. You were right—they expected company from that direction."

"Fine." MacCallister nodded. "Let's go to town."

The first Asa Parker knew of the invasion was when the street filled up with horses. He had just come out of the big prairie schooner and was on his way to the cookshed, where a couple of hired cooks were pit-roasting a beef while swampers set up plank tables for the visiting investors.

Sypher and O'Brien were already there, supervising, and Asa started to call to them. . . . Then he sidestepped as a wandering mount, still wearing its saddle, pranced from an alleyway and cut him off. Several others followed, and suddenly there were horses everywhere.

Skittish and wild-eyed, the animals milled around, finding nowhere to go as dusk-shadowed riders cut them off east and west.

Parker cursed and sidestepped again as a nervous roan switched ends and tried to kick him. Somewhere in the dusk a deep commanding voice said, "Lay down your weapons, Asa Parker. You're through here."

For an instant, Parker couldn't see where the voice came from. Then he spotted him—a big shadowy man with pale hair, tall on a midnight horse.

The horses milled, and Parker took advantage of that to slip between turning animals, hidden by the shadows. "Who are you?" he yelled, moving as he did, taking cover among the horses.

"My name's Falcon MacCallister. I'm here to deliver you to the Kansas and Pacific Railroad Company. They want to talk to you about a robbery and murder in Colorado."

Parker straightened, squinting over the backs of horses. Dust and descending darkness made it hard to see, but the man wasn't where he had been. He turned, saw the tall figure again, and drew his gun. "The hell you say!" he rasped. He raised the weapon to fire, but a raised horse head blocked his view.

"I need help here!" he shouted. "Intruders!" He scurried aside again, working toward the cookshed pits, and had a glimpse of the pale-haired man dismounting, over toward the hotel. Shoving and kicking at the nearest horses around him, he turned in that direction.

Now where did he go? he thought. *He's playing a game here, hide-and-seek.* "Stand still, damn your soul!" he demanded. "What's the matter, bounty hunter? You afraid to face me?"

There was no answer. On impulse, Parker straightened up to stand tall, turning this way and that, squinting and searching. "You're lying!" he prodded. "Falcon MacCallister is dead! Billy Challis killed him up north of here!"

Now the voice answered again, from somewhere behind him. "Billy Challis has done a lot of things, Parker, but he didn't kill me. This is the last warning, Parker. You surrender now, or this is where you'll die. Your choice."

There was no taunting in the voice, nor even a hint of a threat. It was just a proclamation, said as a statement of fact, and abruptly Asa Parker's blood ran cold. Desperately he wheeled around, saw no one in the choking dust, and ducked again, pushing at horseflesh and dodging hooves as he changed position.

Over the din of the milling horses he heard shouts and curses. There was a gunshot, answered by three more, then a thunder of gunfire that seemed to come from all around. It seemed to Parker that the dust hanging in the dark air had begun to glow. And there was a distinct smell of smoke.

"Wilkerson!" Asa shouted. Then, "O'Brien? Sypher? Where the hell is everybody? Where's the vigilantes?"

Like echoes in the distance, a rattle of gunfire drifted on the wind, sounding as though it came from a long way off. Standing upright, Parker sensed the direction of it. It was east, out on the main road. Somewhere out there, people were shooting.

Barlows! he thought. *The damned squatters are trying to get to town!*

From overhead he heard a shout and glanced up. In lighted windows of the hotel, men were crowding to look outside.

"Colonel?" Wigginton's voice called. "Colonel DeWitt, is that you down there? What's happening, sir? Where did all those animals—"

A shot rang, window glass shattered, and the clamor from above went still. The windows were empty.

And now the glow was brighter in the dust aura. From two points beyond the herd, flames leapt upward. The land office was ablaze, and across from it the old barn that had served as a tackle shop for the building of Paradise.

For an instant, Parker made out the figure of a rider circling the milling herd, bunching them inward. He snapped a shot and knew he had missed, but was encouraged when nobody shot back. The horses. They didn't want to shoot into the horses!

But then there were shots—a thunder of them from the west, just beyond the herd, and the horses wheeled as one and bolted.

Asa Parker dived out of the path of a rearing, neighing saddle horse and skidded on his belly in the dust and filth, his arms up to cover his head as the animals stampeded over and around him.

The vigilantes standing guard on the east road sort of let their guard down at sunset. They hadn't seen a thing all day, not so much as a single squatter trying to make his way toward Paradise. They were tired and hungry.

By twos and threes, they clustered at a point where scrub cedars blocked the wind, and most of them dismounted. It was time for a stretch, and nothing was going to happen before morning now that the light was failing.

Tired and angry at the detail they had pulled, they didn't notice the stillness of the evening or see even a glimpse of what was coming.

When Horace Barlow's mounted unit swept down on them, the vigilantes didn't know what hit them. These were hard men, outcasts and drifters who had survived by their reactions. A few cut and ran when the first riders appeared, but some put up a fight.

The engagement lasted no more than three minutes. At the end of it, eight vigilantes were dead, four more down hard, and an uncounted number heading for other places.

Two Barlow men—a farmer named Hewitt and a sometime preacher turned miner by the name of Poley—were dead.

Hewitt had left a wife and three shirttail urchins at his little digs on Rabbit Creek. Poley had been considered a stranger among the Barlow clan, but his death there and then made him kin.

Three of the yellow-scarf vigilantes—one with a bullet burn on his neck—were caught in the cleanup.

It was full dark when they got it all sorted out, but Horace Barlow was of no mind to wait for morning. In the distance, to the west, firelight grew above the town of Paradise, and in the eddies of breezes they could hear gunfire from there.

They found only one tree big enough to hang men from, but it had a sturdy branch big enough for three ropes neckties.

In the west, a glowing cloud of dust swept leisurely over Paradise, flickering with the light of dancing flames below. "I 'spect we're wanted yonder," Horace decided. "Looks like the party done started."

For a big man, Asa Parker was quick. Elusive and cunning, he moved among the milling horses, and it was all Falcon could do to keep track of where he was.

But when Jude and Jubal got the horses bunched in the middle of town, then set them off with some shots in the air, only dust remained to hide a man.

Holding Diablo on tight lead, Falcon had backed off around the corner of the hotel. But when the thunder of the stampede had passed he dropped the reins and stepped out into the street. There was no need to shout orders, and no one to shout them to. The Mason boys knew what to do, and they were doing it.

While Jude headed off to knock down the fences

at the livery and corrals, Jubal prowled the edges of the town, looking for snipers. He had already found one, and the man lay sprawled under the rickety water tank. Now Jubal was hunting for more of them, keeping pace with his little brother Joshua as the kid moved from building to building, setting fire to everything that would burn.

Fading babble, punctuated by shouts, dimmed as the various noncombatant residents of Paradise fled for their lives.

Falcon strode the fire-lit street, his hunter's eyes cutting this way and that. The street was a littered shadowy clearing where dust still swirled on the breezes like mist on a pond. From knee-level down, it was hard to see anything.

Down the street Jubal yelled a warning and Falcon ducked and turned, feeling a jab of lingering pain as his .44 came up. It bucked once, licking at the gloom with a fiery tongue, and a man with a yellow sash pitched headfirst from the roof of the old trading post.

Falcon was past the big wagon when some impulse made him turn and duck. A bullet sang past his ear.

There in the street, rising out of the settling dust, was a man as big as Falcon himself—a man with a spitting gun in his hand.

Falcon dodged, tumbled and rolled, and the pain in his middle was a living thing. But there was no give there, no feeling of things tearing loose. It was only pain. Two more bullets kicked up dirt beside him as he rolled again, coming up on his elbows to return fire.

The specter in the dust dodged wildly, and ran. In an instant he was out of sight beyond the wagon.

Falcon came to his feet, advancing. A broken-down trough hid the underside of the wagon, and he started around it, then doubled back and went the other way.

Asa Parker was waiting for him, crouched in shadows behind a tall wheel. He held a ready .45 and leaned outward, ready to shoot the instant Falcon cleared the water trough.

Falcon circled around the lashed-up tongue and stepped past the iron tire of the off fore wheel.

"Time's up, Parker," he said levelly. "Colorado, or die?"

If he expected Asa Parker to react suddenly, he was disappointed. The big outlaw didn't even move for a moment. Then he raised himself slowly. His hands went up, and his .45 dropped to the ground.

He turned slowly. "I guess you got me, MacCallister," he said. "I'll come along peaceably."

And pigs can fly, Falcon thought. He stared at the outlaw for a moment, then lowered his gun as though accepting his surrender.

Parker's eyes glittered in the gloom. Slowly he lowered his hands, and extended his right hand as though to shake it. The flicker of motion at his sleeve was almost undetectable.

Falcon's .45 roared once, then again. Both shots took Asa Parker front and center, forming two dark little holes that could have hidden behind a playing card.

The outlaw stood for a second, weaving on braced feet, then fell facedown in the dust. In his outflung right hand was a nasty looking little .44 derringer, exposed as his dead fingers uncurled from it.

The man some considered the fastest draw of all died like that on a No Man's Land street, without demonstrating his fast draw. Asa Parker, who went by many names, had decided to rely on deception one more time.

It was one time too many.

Sighing and aching from old wounds, Falcon Mac-Callister stepped out from behind the big wagon. Joshua's fires were blazing brightly now, lighting up the whole stinking town as building after building smoldered, flared, and went up in flame.

The hotel still stood, and Jubal was there, herding people out into the street, peering at them one by one as they lined up staring into the muzzle of Jude's rifle.

In the crowd a man fussed and hollered. "I want to know what this is all about!" he demanded. "See here, you can't treat us this way! I'm Wigginton, of the firm of—"

"Shut up, Mr. Wigginton," Jubal Mason told him. "I'm lookin' for somebody, and any of you that isn't him is free to leave."

"Leave?" the man blustered. "See here!"

"Yes, sir. You can leave. Matter of fact, I'd recommend it. Your coaches are over there in the south pasture, and all the draft stock's around here someplace. You all just light yourselves some torches and you can—"

From somewhere, Wiley the railroad man appeared beside him. "Not him," he said, pointing at a small gray-looking man hanging back in the crowd. "That's Sypher. There'll be charges against him." He turned, looking along the line. "And him, too!" He pointed again. "Hello, O'Brien, you swindler." He smiled. "Looks as if the land shark business has finally turned to bite you."

Jubal ignored them. "He's not here," he muttered. He glanced around at Falcon, tears of anger on his cheeks. "Damn it, Billy Challis isn't here!"

At that instant, a wild-haired figure appeared at the far corner of the hotel building. Billy Challis had just arrived from the hogpens. He was behind Jubal and out of the line of sight of Jude. Only Falcon saw him.

Quick as a snake, Billy's hand darted to his gun and the gun that seemed to simply appear in Falcon't hand thundered.

He had almost no target. His shot whipped past Jubal close enough to burn his sleeve, and seared across the flesh of Billy's right shoulder. The outlaw didn't complete his draw. Instead he turned, dived, and disappeared into darkness.

TWENTY-SIX

It was a day of arrivals and departures, and a day of change.

Morning sun fell on the smoking embers and scorched remains of what had seemed, just yesterday, the town of golden opportunity. Paradise wasn't a town any more. It wasn't much of anything, just smoldering ruins with a big prairie schooner standing at one end and some elegant coaches loading passengers at the other.

The vigilantes were gone, as were the men who had hired them. Here and there, one-time residents of the town stood around in little clusters, wondering what to do now.

Joshua and Jude helped the easterners hitch up their teams, then curtly ordered them aboard their coaches and watched them leave—eastward, toward Wichita.

The land shark and the pirate, O'Brien and Sypher, were chained to a stump to keep them out of trouble, and Wiley stood guard over them while Falcon MacCallister and various Barlows did an inventory of the town.

They found a few things of value, including enough evidence to convict both Sypher and Wiley three times over once they were returned to the realms of law and courts.

But there was no sign of the money stolen from the Kansas Pacific Railway. Obviously, some of it had been spent. The rest was just gone.

Soon after sunup a man named Cass Jolly came in from the hogpens with two locals carrying Brett Archer on a makeshift stretcher. Archer's wound was bad, and would cost him his right arm, but he was still alive. They put him into the bed of the prairie schooner, and Jude Mason went to round up the big wagon's draft horses.

"We're taking back Tom Blanchard's wagon," he told MacCallister. "Joshua wants to take Brett up to see that doctor that fixed you. I expect Brett'll want to head out for Colorado when he's able."

Some of the Barlow riders helped them hitch up the team, and they rolled out, with Cass Jolly driving and Joshua riding along. Past the chalk bluff, they turned the big rig north.

Joshua's brothers watched them go, and Falcon approached them. "What about you two?" he asked Jude.

"We aim to stick around for a while," Jude said. He wasn't grinning now, but there was a sparkle in his eyes. "Jubal, he's gonna stay on with Becky's kin for a time, while them and me get all these loose horses moved up to Haymeadows. We decided they're ours, since they don't rightly belong to anybody else. Mighty good horse country around Haymeadows."

It was high noon when a squad of the Kansas-State Militia rode in from the north, led by Lieutenant Colgrave.

"Chasing some rustlers," the lieutenant told Falcon. "We were in hot pursuit, but we only got four of them. Passed a big covered wagon up the way, though. They told us what happened down here. Anything we can do to help?"

"Not that I know of—" Falcon began.

"Yes, there is," Wiley interrupted. "I have two prisoners here, and I need an escort to Kansas. Those men over there." He pointed at Sypher and O'Brien, chained to their stump. "They are charged with various state and federal crimes ranging from murder and robbery to falsifying government documents."

With plenty of men to help him, Jubal Mason led a search of the town and surrounding areas, looking for any sign of Billy Challis. They found no trace of the gunman, but they did find something else.

"This one's name was Wilkerson," Jubal explained when a drenched and bloating corpse was laid out on a plank in front of what remained of the land office. "Casper Wilkerson. He was one of them . . . one of the six who killed the Blanchards and stole the railroad money. With him dead, that's five out of the six."

Men gathered around to look at the dead outlaw, amazed and baffled. "What happened to him?" someone asked. "Where did you find him?"

"We found him in Wolf Creek, a mile or so upstream," Jubal said. "Looks like maybe he fell off his horse and drowned."

"How can any man drown in Wolf Creek?" a settler demanded. "Water ain't hardly more'n three, four, feet deep, anywhere."

"I guess you could if you were strapped into an iron keg." Jubal shrugged. He pulled back the dead outlaw's coat. Beneath it was a curved surface of heavy iron, tied on with leather straps. From the dents in it, it might have been worn as body armor.

* * *

Falcon MacCallister avoided the trails as he headed northwest, preferring the clean landscape of the grassy high plains around him.

His mind spoke in the silence of the winds: *I've done all I can do here, Marie. It doesn't bring you back. Doc Linsecum was right about that. No amount of retribution can bring you back to me. But it seems right, anyway. Right or wrong, though, I had to do what I could.*

Do what you can, the winds seemed to echo. *Did what you could.*

With the place that had been Paradise behind him, Falcon did not look back. There was nothing there to see.

The work that Joshua Mason had begun—burning all the buildings—the Rabbit Creek settlers had completed. When they were through, not a structure remained standing.

Then they came with their picks and their plows, their spades and shovels and rakes, and leveled the ashes. When that was done they put plows to it and turned it under. Nothing remained on the bank of Wolf Creek now, but a quarter section of dark tilled earth that—given a season's sun and rain—would go back to the grass it had been.

There was nothing to look back on, so Falcon kept his eyes ahead. The wide lands rose ahead of him, hypnotic in their vastness, and beyond would be the mountains and the trail home. It was time to go back, at least to look in for a time. And it would be all right. Marie's memory was not out there in those mountains. Her memory lived inside him, and it would go where he went.

Diablo set a long pace, and Falcon gazed out across the rising distances ahead. Twenty miles could seem but one out there, and the trick was that it didn't make any difference. Yonder was still yonder, no matter how far.

Ahead . . . ahead was something rising above the endless prairies. Buzzards were circling in the high sky, and not far from their circle was a tendril of smoke that was whisked away almost before it was glimpsed. It was almost straight ahead.

In an hour he could see where it came from, and an hour after that he found the source.

"Get down, *yoneg*," the boy invited as Falcon rode into his camp. "Got good beef here. Texas trail brand on its hide, but nobody around to claim it. Get down an' come in."

"I waited for you," Utsonati explained, serving up hot beef from a willow-pole stove. "Knew you'd come this way. Been watchin' you since sunup, too. Got somethin' to show you, but eat first." The Cherokee boy waved a casual hand toward where the buzzards were circling above a gully. "Kinda stinks over there today," he added.

The corpse had begun to bloat and ripen, but it was still recognizable. It was the same man who had put a bullet through Falcon's chest, back in the cold of spring.

"Same man, sure," Utsonati said, as though reading his mind. "Same man as did a lot of bad things. Won't do that anymore. Name he had was Billy Challis. He isn't anybody now."

"How'd you find him out here?" Falcon asked.

"Didn't find him, *Towo'di*. I put him here. Followed him all the way from that town you burned. Finally caught him here."

Falcon nodded. That part was obvious—just as ob-

vious as what had killed Billy Challis. His body was
riddled with bullet holes—one in each knee, one in
each arm, one through the neck and one through
the belly.

They were small holes, about the size of the bullets in the Cherokee boy's .32-20 rifle.

"Utsonati killed him," the boy said matter-of-
factly. "Took half a mile and half a day to get it
done. Bullets through his arms so he couldn't shoot,
through his knees so he couldn't run, in the throat
so he couldn't holler. Crazy *an'da'tsi* just kept on
tryin' to get away."

"To get away from you?" Falcon asked.

"Prob'ly from the wolf," the boy said. He paused
and pointed. On a rise a hundred yards away, something sat watching them—inquisitive wolf ears atop
a feral head silhouetted against the sky.

"Not really a wolf at all," the boy said. "Big dog
some *yoneg* tried to hang. I call him *Wa-hya'*. He likes
me all right, but don' like *yonegs.*"

Falcon smiled faintly. "You're going to be something when you grow up, Utsonati," he allowed.

"Not Utsonati any more, *yoneg.*" For the first time
since they had met, Falcon saw a real grin on the young
Indian's face. It made him look even younger than his
twelve years. "Utsonati was a war name. I'm just
Woha'li now. *Utsonati . . .* uh, *rattlesnake . . .* he bites,
but don't fly. Eagle is better. Remember, 'bout eagle
and falcon? Woha'li flies higher than Towo'di."